Sweet Little Lies

Sweet Little Lies

Ted Darling Crime Series

'Someone's lying. Who? And why?

L M Krier

LIVRES
LEMAS

Published by LIVRES LEMAS
www.teddarlingcrimeseries.uk

Cover photo
Neil Smith

This is a work of fiction. Names, characters, places
and incidents are the product of the author's
imagination or are used fictitiously. Any resemblance
to actual persons, living or dead, events or locales is
entirely coincidental.

Contents

To eagle-eyed Maggie.

Thank you for all the errors pounced on to save my bacon!

Chapter One

'I'll save you all the bother of saying it or thinking it. Yes, we've all heard it all before. More than once. The stark truth is that we've all but lost the public's confidence.

'The reason you're hearing it again today is quite simply that if we don't do something – something radical, and soon – to restore at least some shred of trust in the police service, then we're in far worse trouble than even the pessimists amongst us could have predicted.'

Detective Chief Inspector Ted Darling, from Serious Crime, based in Stockport, was listening to the words of Greater Manchester Police's Chief Constable, Jon Woodrow, at HQ Central Park. He was surrounded by senior officers from all over the GMP area.

It was the first time that Ted had seen his Chief since he'd suffered a bad accident in a squash tournament which had resulted in a serious fracture/dislocation of his shoulder. One of the Chief's arms was still in a sling and he looked pale and drawn. Rumours were rife that he could be forced to retire early if there was no improvement soon.

Given the current climate surrounding the police service, Ted had a sneaking suspicion he might be relieved to have a valid reason to go. Possibly even to jump before he was pushed.

'Today's meeting is not in any way a blame game. I'm not looking for scapegoats. What I want, as I'm sure most of you do, is a blueprint going forward of what we can do to improve things. Some concrete proposals to show the public we're listening and trying to put our house in order, at least.

'I'm now going to hand over to ACC Evans as I have somewhere else to be. Not by choice but of necessity. I look forward to hearing what suggestions you come up with. Thank you, everyone.'

Every single officer present had at least half risen from their seat as the Chief had entered the room at the start of the meeting. Several made the same gesture as he headed for the door. There was a lot of respect for him. A proper copper's copper, not just a political appointee, who'd served on the front line of policing and had the facial scarring to prove it.

Almost before Assistant Chief Constable (Crime) Russell Evans had opened his mouth to carry on where the Chief had left off, Ted was on his feet and starting to speak. Quietly, as always. It was his way, usually resulting in others telling him to speak up, but he always found it a useful method of getting people to listen to him.

'Sir, can I make a point which might be controversial, but I feel it needs saying?'

'Controversial, Ted? You? Surely not,' Evans told him with a smile.

His comment raised a ripple of amusement which ran through the room. Ted was universally known as a bolshie little sod, never shy of speaking his mind in front of anyone, including the top brass. Even Ted grinned in acknowledgement, despite the seriousness of the subject matter.

'Sir, as a lot of those here will know, I'm currently trying to fill a vacancy on my team left by DC Gina Shaw leaving the service. I've seen some candidates already, but I have to say I've been disappointed by attitudes I've encountered. So should we be starting from the beginning? Looking harder at the recruitment process? At candidates who are being allowed into the service? And that does seem to be a countrywide issue, from what we all see too often in the press and media.'

'Ted, you're right, of course, as you often are. But this isn't the forum for that discussion. This is about cleaning up our act – now – in a big way. Improving our conviction rate radically, and rebuilding the trust of the public.

'We will speak about your suggestions though, as soon as possible. Before you leave here today, make an appointment with Vanessa when you and I are both next free and let's sit down and see what we can come up with. But meanwhile back to the subject in hand ...'

Before he could go any further, a Chief Inspector from Uniform stood up and started to speak.

'Sir, at the same time we surely need to address the big elephant in the room. The percentage of totally false accusations from members of the public with an axe to grind who, to put it mildly, lie through their teeth about an alleged incident. We then have to waste time investigating a complaint that most of us know is a load of old b...,' he checked himself in time and finished, 'nonsense, sir.'

Russell Evans was gearing up to respond but the officer, Dave Watson, clearly had his own agenda and was not about to stop until ordered to.

'That's what happened recently to one of my men, sir. This was a good officer. Never anything dodgy about him. Long Service and Good Conduct Medal, plus a Chief's commendation. A serious sexual assault allegation. Of course, he had to be suspended while it was investigated, which all took time. He was cleared, completely, as we all knew he would be. None of us had any doubt. But it all but finished him. He's been off sick ever since.

'Worse, CPS decided there was insufficient evidence to proceed against the so-called victim for their false claims, so he won't even have the satisfaction of seeing the record officially and publicly put straight. And that's what's broken him. That nobody seemed to have his back in all of this.'

Several heads were nodding from those in the audience. It wasn't the first such story they'd heard of. They all knew there were rogue coppers within the ranks of many police services, but most of them were decent enough officers, trying to do their best, and ensure those under their command did the same.

But dealing with those falsely accused always depended on the Crown Prosecution Service feeling there was sufficient evidence for any prosecution of the accuser to be in the public interest. Always difficult with any allegations where there were unlikely to be independent witnesses, which was often the case with sexual assault.

'I hear what you say, Dave, and I know of that particular case. I'm sorry it turned out as badly as it did, but there's nothing more to be done. So can we all now please come up with some suggestions as to how to deal effectively with any bad apples we do have in our respective barrels, to at least start restoring public trust.'

* * *

'So what amazing things did you learn in tonight's

lesson? Can you manage a whole sentence of English yet?'

It could have been an innocent enough question. Apart from the sneering tone he used. And the fact that he was speaking in rapid English when he knew how much she struggled unless he spoke slowly. That's why he'd agreed to let her go to the evening classes for English as a Foreign Language, when he normally kept a close eye on her all the time.

She was surprised that he had. He was so controlling of every other aspect of her life. The classes had turned out to be the highlight of each week for her. The only time she felt free to be herself, not constantly minding her words and actions, always ready for the next slap – or worse.

She wasn't going to give him the satisfaction of trying to reply in English. He'd only laugh at her efforts. So she switched to her native Polish, which he also spoke fluently. He was second generation Polish but had long since anglicised his name and everything about him.

She told him, 'I am trying very hard to learn. The teacher, Yulia, is very kind, very encouraging.'

She tried never to lie to him. He always seemed to know when she wasn't telling the truth. But she hadn't wanted to tell him their teacher was actually a young man, and a good-looking one. That was why she always left the class before anyone else, either to walk home, to get the bus, or to intercept him if he was coming to pick her up, so he'd never seen the teacher. So far.

She'd made the mistake of using the Polish pronunciation, 'Yulia', with a Y. Realised too late that he would pounce on that. She should have said the name, at least, the English way, because the teacher was English, but it was too late to go back on that.

'Juuuuulia, with a Juu, you daft bitch. Juuuuu. You need to purse your lips and move your tongue to say it. Like this.'

He reached out a powerful hand and clamped his thumb and forefinger round her lips, pulling and compressing them into a shape to form the sound.

He kept the vice-like grip as he told her, 'You try it. Keep your lips like I've shown you.'

Fear had turned her mouth as dry as parchment but incredibly, he did seem to be trying to help her, for once. She struggled for a moment to find her voice at all, but then managed a quiet and hesitant 'Juuuulia.'

'Good. That's better. At least you can say your teacher's name properly now. That's a start, considering how thick you can be.

'So what are we eating tonight? It better be something good and sustaining. I've been checking the calendar and tonight's the night. Your favourite. Baby-making! And this time we're going to succeed, finally. About bloody time too. We've been trying for long enough. Who knows, we might have a little girl and call her Juuuulia.'

He got hold of her lips again as he said that but gently this time. Almost playfully. He pulled her against him, kissed her neck, ran his hands over her, which sent a shiver through her, but it was as close to an affectionate gesture as he ever came.

She could smell the beer on his breath. He must have been for a drink with his work colleagues before coming home. She tried not to flinch away from him.

There would be no baby. Not a little girl, nor a boy either. He had no idea she was taking the pill. He would never have believed her capable of going to a doctor or anywhere else to get it prescribed for her. But she had managed.

Desperation had forced her to find the means.

She had to keep her precious pills somewhere he would never find them. She dreaded to think what the consequences would be if he knew how hard she was trying to avoid falling pregnant to him. Once she did, she would be tied to him forever more.

He kept telling her that as his legal wife she had the right to remain in the country. Even more so when she became the mother of his children. But if ever she left him she'd become an illegal immigrant who could be deported immediately, if she was found.

She wouldn't mind going back to Poland. She'd thought her life there was difficult, and that it could all change if she married him. He'd been charming then, when he was playing for her heart and her mind. But now he had her, and had convinced her that she had no choice but to stay with him, he made no attempt to hide his bullying, controlling personality.

He'd never seriously assaulted her. Yet. Not enough for her to have needed medical attention. But he was a complete control freak, in charge of everything she said and did. Starting with their finances. He grudgingly doled out her weekly housekeeping allowance which was barely enough for the essentials, with nothing left over for any form of luxury.

She did her best to manage but he complained constantly about the poor quality of the meals she made, particularly towards the end of the week when she was running out of money and didn't dare ask him for an advance.

He was careful never to leave a visible mark on her that might be seen by someone. Especially now she was going to these classes to try to improve her English. His favourite trick was to grab her by the wrist and bend it right back on itself. That and seizing one of her thin arms in two powerful hands and wringing it, hard, like getting water out of a wet towel. That hurt. A lot. And it always left marks, so she wore long sleeves whenever she went out.

Her precious pills were hidden in a small plastic box, buried under a large stone in the garden. He had little interest in gardening. She was the one who kept it looking as tidy as she could manage. Hopefully, he wouldn't discover her secret hiding place.

For now she somehow had to keep stringing him along until she could find someone who could help her to know what her rights actually were. Because he'd told her in no uncertain terms that if she went off by herself and was found, being sent back to Poland was not the only option open to the Home Office. They could send her to some unknown third country, he'd said, where she knew no one, had no grasp of the language, and which she might never be allowed to leave.

* * *

Ted had travelled up to Central Park with his senior officer, Superintendent Debra Caldwell. They were in an official car, being driven by former Roads officer Hector, known to all as 'Eck.

'Are things really that bad, in terms of replacing DC Shaw?' she asked Ted as soon as they were free of snarled traffic and heading back south to Stockport. 'Because that's clearly a vacancy you need to fill as soon as possible. There must surely be a candidate who could be trained up to your standards?'

'I was surprised by some of the things candidates were saying in interview. But listening to what the ACC was telling us, I shouldn't be.

'I'd really hoped to find a candidate who could hit the ground running without needing someone keeping a watching brief on them. We're busy enough with the latest murder case, but that has so many potential red flags I'd need to be very careful who I entrusted with any part of that. A race element, religion, possibly immigration status, three female victims, and already the hint of some superstitions about the birth of twins. I'd want to be a hundred per cent sure of not having anyone judgemental working on it. It's not just the victims and their immediate family, it's their wider community we need to consider. The last thing we want to do is to spark anything like race riots.'

'Would it help if I put out a few feelers?' she asked him.

'Anything would help. I really need the extra officer, but I don't want an appointment that's going to come back to bite us in the future.'

* * *

The sight of youngest cat Adam, sitting gazing adoringly up at him as soon as he opened the front door, was exactly what Ted needed after a hard day. That and the tantalising smells wafting from the kitchen.

He scooped Adam up to cradle him in his arms as he walked into the kitchen, where Trev was sitting at the table in front of what looked like the aftermath of an explosion in a stationery shop.

'At least someone loves me,' Ted said with an ironic smile, indicating the purring bundle in his arms as he leaned over to kiss his partner on the cheek.

Trev immediately got to his feet, scattering papers, and smothered Ted and Adam in a bone-crushing hug.

'Well, I do too, of course. That goes without saying. Which is why there's a disgustingly sweet and sticky pudding in the oven, because I thought you might have had a difficult day up at HQ. Was it as bad as that?'

'Worse,' Ted told him, putting Adam down, greeting the rest of the feline family then taking his jacket off, which Adam had stopped him from doing as soon as he got in. His tie had been relegated to his pocket as soon as he'd got into his own car to drive home.

'Complaints against the police are going up, conviction rates are going down, and I still haven't found a suitable replacement for Gina.'

He picked up a random paper from the table to glance at.

'English lessons? How are your latest students getting on?'

Trev was starting to clear things away to make room for them to eat at the table. Which in his case consisted of scooping up papers and moving them from one place to another.

'One or two of the newer ones are still a bit quiet. You know I like to keep an eye on them, in case there's something going on in their background. Some cultural issue that makes them reticent about speaking to a strange man.'

Ted was systematically tidying up the dumped papers into neat piles, well away from any culinary spillages. He could never understand how someone as brilliant as Trev could surround himself with such chaos.

His tone was serious as he told him, 'Do be careful with your students, won't you? Not to get too involved, nor do or say something which could possibly be misinterpreted. I've spent some time today hearing of good, decent coppers whose careers, and sometimes their mental health, have been wrecked by fabricated claims of sexual misconduct against them.

'I know you like to help people, but always remember your boundaries. I wouldn't want anything like a false allegation of some sort ever to happen to you.'

Chapter Two

Ted began the morning briefing with his own team by giving them the broad highlights of the meeting he'd attended the previous day.

So far there'd never been a complaint against any of them, in no small part because Ted would always jump on the slightest hint of any inappropriate language or behaviour from them, including within the office when there were no members of the public present.

DC Maurice Brown was always the one most likely to put his foot in it by saying the wrong thing, but never maliciously. Everyone knew there was no one kinder or more compassionate than the team's 'Daddy Hen'.

'I know all of you are meticulous about the language you use, which is why we've escaped any of the complaints I was hearing about yesterday. Please keep on doing what you do. Meanwhile, I'm still trying to find the right person to take Gina's place ... and yes, Mike, I know that's now a matter of urgency,' he cut across his sergeant, DS Mike Hallam when he saw him about to speak.

'I've simply not yet been impressed enough by any of those I've interviewed to invite them to join us. And I'm particularly conscious of the many potential pitfalls of our current murder case if any team member made a comment which could be taken in the wrong way.

'So, Mike, update, please. Where are we at on this one?

Any progress?'

'Honestly not making excuses, boss, but it is frustratingly slow. We knew we'd have to rely on interpreters for the main suspect and most of the witnesses to this. What I hadn't factored in was things like how many different languages and dialects we're actually dealing with. That's been throwing up more problems than I thought it might in finding enough interpreters.'

DC Jezza Vine cut in at that. Even in the most serious circumstances she could never resist the urge to tease her best friend, DC Maurice Brown.

'You should have factored that in, sarge. Look how often we struggle to understand the Geordie in our midst.'

Ted gave her one of his looks and a quiet, 'DC Vine,' to remind her of the seriousness of the case they were dealing with.

For once even Maurice ignored her attempt at humour as he said, 'Boss, I can't understand this one at all. I'm struggling with it, to be honest. If the killer really was the bloke we have in custody, it's bad enough for him to kill his wife. But those two tiny babies? Newborns? What kind of a man could do that? And seemingly all for some superstitious nonsense, claiming to believe they couldn't be his because he didn't know of any twins in his family.'

Ted slid off the desk he'd been perching on and moved to stand in front of the team. This case was affecting all of them, especially the parents. It wasn't helping being a team member down. Ted was, as usual, doing a juggling act to make up numbers. Pulling in spare officers from wherever he could find them to ease the pressure. They needed a result on this triple murder as soon as possible, as much for the morale of the team as anything else.

'All right, everyone, I know this is a hard one. But you're professional officers. You need to remember that and stay detached. That doesn't mean you can't have emotions about the case. But you share those between yourselves round at The Grapes. In the back room too, please. Well out of the way of being overheard by members of the public.

'There are so many aspects of this case which could come back to bite us if anyone makes an unguarded comment anywhere they might be overheard. We've got all sorts of elephant traps in the form of ethnicity, religion, superstition, gender issues and everything else. So please, keep a lid on your feelings.'

He looked again to Mike as he went on, 'Just a reminder, Mike, I have to go over to Nexus House shortly. We're on final checks of the case file on the delightful Whittakers and their sweatshop and we want to make it as tight as we can. With the modern slavery and people trafficking charges, not to mention the murder of one of their workers, we're quietly optimistic they'll both be going away for a long stretch.

'I'll also drop in on Jo at Ashton while I'm out and about. He's deputising for me on Saturday as there's somewhere I need to be, come what may.'

Ted wasn't about to tell the team that he was committed to being best man at the wedding of someone he'd first met when they'd been a suspect, albeit briefly, in an earlier murder case.

Oliver Burdon – 'with a D' as he always added – was a porter at the local hospital. A man with moderate learning difficulties, he could so easily have become a scapegoat, potentially fitted up to face charges by anyone with lower ethics than Ted and his team.

Instead, Ted had seen him cleared of all suspicion and

won his undying gratitude. So when Burdon had met and fallen in love with the diminutive Mary at the soup kitchen where they both volunteered, he had immediately asked Mr Darling, as he always insisted on calling him, to be his best man.

The wedding had been long delayed by various unforeseen outside influences, but Ted had promised to be there and he was determined that he would be.

'And don't forget, everyone, we need another officer for the team, urgently. One good enough to fill Gina's shoes, and certainly one with the sensitivities to avoid the pitfalls of this murder case in terms of all the things I've already mentioned and possibly ones we've not even considered yet. So ask around, and I'll ask Jo, once more, if he's heard of anyone looking for a move, for the right reasons.

'We'll have a catch-up end of play when I should be back, so let's hope for some news of progress by then.'

* * *

It was raining heavily and not showing any sign of stopping before she would need to set off for her English class.

Raining cats and dogs as they'd been taught, she reminded herself. She'd thought that was funny, in a charming way. She'd repeated it a few times to herself, smiling as she did so, while she was walking home the evening it had come up. Her grandmother in Poland had always said 'throwing frogs', which at least had more logic to it for wet weather. Others where she was from would say 'pouring like from a bucket', which also made sense. But she couldn't imagine any cat wanting to be out getting wet.

He'd said he would be home late tonight. So no chance

of a lift to the class, even if she'd dared let him drive her there. She was always so scared of him seeing that the teacher was a man, not a woman called Yulia.

She mentally chided herself and tried the name again, in the English way. Julia. Juuulia. She used her own fingers, but gently, to put her lips and tongue into the right shape to make the unfamiliar J sound. At least she could get better at saying the made-up name next time he asked her.

It was a name she'd heard from someone in the class. Someone with English children or grandchildren – she couldn't remember which – and one of them was called Julia.

One of the early lessons had been about introducing themselves and saying something about their home, their family. She hadn't felt ready to share her own details yet, even if she'd had the right vocabulary. She had successfully learned to say, 'I am from Poland. I am married. I have no children.'

It was a start.

Their teacher was always so kind, and so careful to avoid any subjects which might be uncomfortable, as some of them in the class would possibly have lost family members in terrible circumstances.

Her teacher really helped her because when she struggled to find the right word he'd sometimes speak some Russian to her until she found the word she needed. He spoke good Russian and she had learned it at school. Done well at it, too, so she couldn't have been quite as stupid as her husband kept saying that she was, although she always felt that way in his presence.

She really wanted to go to the class. It felt like a blessed relief to get out of the house and away from the controlling presence. But even the reasonably low fare she'd have to pay to get the bus would make a hole in her already meagre housekeeping. And that would lead to more trouble from her husband when the standard of the meals she produced dropped even further towards the end of the week.

She'd have to put on her most waterproof coat and run between the raindrops. Again she smiled to herself at the image of that saying which had come up in the same lesson. Because of course, everyone knew that you couldn't. Run between raindrops. It was simply impossible.

Some things you couldn't avoid, if they were heading your way. Like a blow. Because unless you were very fast on your feet – fast enough to really run between raindrops – a blow was always going to get you. It was always going to find its target.

* * *

DC Jezza Vine was sitting at the wheel of a service vehicle, parked up in a quiet spot. She had her arms round Maurice Brown, who was sobbing unashamedly on her shoulder.

DS Mike Hallam had sent the two of them to interview first responders and witnesses to their triple murder investigation – the mother and her newborn twin babies.

He'd hesitated about sending Maurice, knowing how deeply the death of any small child was bound to affect him, but even more so that of twins, as he was the father of two sets.

Mike was simply in the unenviable position of not having enough officers to go round for the cases they currently had on their books. And at least he knew that no matter how upset he got, Maurice was unlikely to lose it completely and thump someone who said the wrong thing. Some tactless throwaway comment which might be nothing more than an individual's personal way of dealing with such a horrendous tragedy.

Some of the first responders had been put straight on leave to recover from what they'd had to deal with and would need follow-up counselling before they could return to work. But it was essential to get their witness testimony as soon as possible, hence sending hopefully sympathetic officers to see them in their homes.

'Sorry, pet. Sorry,' Maurice told Jezza, making a visible effort to pull himself together. 'I know it was worse for them, having to see that first hand when I only had to listen to them telling us about it.

'I know some sick bastards get rid of unwanted puppies like that. Swinging them against the wall. But how can anyone do it to a newborn baby? Never mind two of them.

'And for what? All for some superstitious nonsense about overpopulation someone had been spouting, and him believing they couldn't even be his because he hadn't heard of any twins in his family!

'Why did no one stop him? It sounds like there were enough of them in the room, what with the supposed midwife person, no end of relatives and goodness knows who else. So why didn't they do something? Even if they were too shocked to react to the first killing, why did no one grab the second baby to protect her from the same fate, for god's sake?'

Jezza fished a handful of tissues out of her bag and handed them to him as he at least started to get his feelings under control.

Maurice wiped his eyes dry, blew his nose noisily, then

gave her a watery grin with more than a touch of sheepishness behind it.

'Sorry, bonny lass. Sorry. You know I'm too soft for this sort of case. Anything to do with bairns. Promise me you won't say anything to the rest of the team. And especially not to the boss.'

'You should know me better than that by now, Maurice, you big soft lump. What happens in the car stays in the car.

'Right, come on, we've got more harrowing detail to sit through so we'd better get it over with.'

* * *

Ted was just getting into his own car to head for home, not quite as late as he'd feared, when his phone rang. An unknown number, so he answered in a neutral tone.

'DCI Darling.'

'Eddie! Darling!'

He recognised the voice straight away and smiled his pleasure, even at the end of a totally crap day.

'Gina! This is a nice surprise. I imagine your ears have been burning. I've mentioned you a few times already this week because I've not yet found the right person to fill your shoes. How are things with you now?'

He was tiptoeing as softly as he could around the delicate subject of the suicide of Gina's sister, Jenny, after years of her having been posted as a missing person.

'Hopefully on the up. I told you I was going back into marketing and design. I pitched to quite a big and prestigious company, more in hope than anticipation, I have to confess. But I've at least made it to the face-to-face interviews, which is unexpected and exciting, and for that I'm going to need references.'

'I'll certainly give you a glowing character reference, Gina, with great pleasure.'

'I need a bit more than that, though, boss. I need references to do with my design work, and I've not done any for ages. I did do some for you when we first met if you remember, as our cover story. And I've done some more, based on a company you're supposedly setting up. Even though you don't know you are.

'By any chance, would you have half an hour any time tomorrow to give me? I know it's short notice but so is my interview. Please?'

'Can you meet me in The Grapes at dinnertime?' he asked her then, remembering she was posher than he was, he quickly revised it to, 'Lunchtime, that is. I'd promised myself a hotpot and a quick catch-up with Dave.'

'Perfect, boss, thanks so much. See you then.'

Ted was smiling to himself as he drove back to the house. He'd been sad to lose Gina, although he understood her reasons, so he would be pleased if he could help her to get the new start she deserved.

Trev looked up in surprise from packing up his paperwork for his evening class when Ted walked into the kitchen, his hair wet from just the short walk from the car to the front door.

'You're back early, so this is a nice surprise.'

'I thought you might like to take the car tonight rather than the bike, with as much rain as this. But please promise me that no matter how wet it is later, you won't do the gallant thing and want to drive any of the females in your class home afterwards. Nor the males either, come to that.'

'Ted, surely you know me well enough not to get any

jealous thoughts about me, with women especially!'

Trev was making light of it but Ted continued, his tone earnest.

'Of course I do, but I'm getting paranoid about false allegations. I've been hearing of more of them in the service. I heard one today, well outside our area, but the officer ended up taking his own life because he couldn't prove his innocence.

'That's often the problem with sexual assault cases. They're not always reported early enough for DNA to be of any use. There's seldom any CCTV or other corroborative evidence, so it generally comes down to one person's word against another's. And if it ever does get as far as court, on who a court believes.

'And that's not even considering a jealous other half who's been spun a line for some reason and comes looking for revenge.

'So please, promise me. Be careful.'

Chapter Three

Ted avoided the press and media pack like the plague whenever he could. He would only face the cameras or speak to any of the reporters when ordered to do so by a senior officer.

Some of the more tenacious, including the seemingly timid local reporter, Penny Hunter, knew his car by sight and would picket the station car park, looking out for it, when there was a big local story.

Ted preferred to do the commute to and from his home in his own vehicle when he could. The garage at his house was a designated safe space for Trev's precious motorbike and there was barely the room for both that and a car, even one as small as Ted's. Certainly not for an official vehicle.

Ted reckoned the way things were going in his once quiet and relatively law-abiding neighbourhood, if he left his service vehicle outside these days it risked being keyed at the least, or jacked up on bricks and the wheels stolen. If it was still there at all by the following day.

This morning, there was a mob of media lying in wait at the station. As soon as Ted's modest Renault appeared in the car park entrance, the members were after it like greyhounds following a hare.

Ted had done advanced driving courses, and was a reasonable runner, though middle distance rather than sprint. He knew he could have shaken them off. He considered it, but dismissed the thought. He could imagine the comments which would head his way if he was caught on camera doing wheelies on screeching tyres round the car park, then racing away to escape the mob.

He wasn't surprised that it was Penny Hunter's recording device which was the first to be shoved into his face as he got out and locked his car. She, like him, was small and quiet, so was often overlooked by the others. She used her advantages to slither under their outstretched arms and somehow often managed to pop up in front of them.

'Chief Inspector, is it true that there's a suspected witchcraft connection to this current triple murder case? That there was actually some sort of a shaman in the room when the mother and her babies were killed?'

For someone who didn't play cards, Ted had mastery of the perfect poker face when he needed it. Externally, he stayed serene and polite as he replied, 'Thank you for your question, Penny. At this point, no comment.'

Internally, he was cursing whoever had leaked that piece of information. And it could have been anyone. He doubted it was any member of his regular team, or someone drafted in to work on it. They would surely all know better.

It might conceivably have been one of the first responders, or even a neighbour from where the incident had happened. Whoever it was, Ted was determined he would find them and seriously mark their card for them. Any such ill-informed story in the local media was bound to stoke racial hatred and the last thing which was needed on an already sensitive case was any chance of race riots.

As he spoke, he was trying to find a way through the jostling throng, now effectively blocking his escape, without resorting to karate kicking the crap out of them, as he was coming close to wanting to do.

In the end he stopped abruptly, so they piled into one another and had to juggle precious phones and cameras before they were dropped, smashed and rendered useless.

When he spoke to them it was so quietly that they were obliged to stop jabbering all at once to be sure of hearing what he was saying. Politely, as ever.

'No comment at all, at this stage, ladies and gentlemen. A press conference will be arranged as soon as we have anything of value to share with you, and you'll be kept informed of when that will take place. Thank you for your patience until then.'

Ted was in a murderous mood by the time he reached the sanctuary of the nick. He pounded up the stairs to his office, two at a time, already thinking the day merited the murder of another wastepaper basket, although he'd promised himself he'd given up doing that.

He headed straight for his kettle. This was definitely a green tea moment. He was the first of the team in, which was not unusual. He was not surprised when, after the briefest of taps on his door, the Ice Queen strode in. She led by example, always. As did Ted.

'Good morning, chief inspector.'

She began, as so often, with the formalities, but surprised Ted by adding, 'If by any chance you have some green tea going spare, I wouldn't say no.'

Even using his rank rather than his name, it was still a surprisingly informal beginning, by her standards.

She'd already taken the spare seat and was waiting for Ted to put the drink in front of her before continuing, 'I saw the press scrum from my window. Did you manage to avoid compromising questions?'

'I did, but there was a concerning development,' Ted told her as he sat down with his own drink. 'There's clearly been a leak from somewhere as they were asking about some sort of witchcraft connection and the presence of a shaman. That can surely only have come from someone close to the case, so do we have an informer somewhere? And do we need to find them and put a stop to it before we can concentrate on anything else?'

She paused to try her tea, which was too hot for more than a sip.

'In an ideal world, yes, that would be the starting point. In reality? When we're working with other agencies over whom we have no control, only cooperation? I don't see how. If it would help, I am happy to send round a memo to all those other agencies asking them to please remind everyone about how essential it is to avoid leaks. Perhaps you can do the same, not just for your team but for anyone else working on this case.'

She took another sip of her tea then asked, 'And is there? A witchcraft connection with this terrible case? Real or imaginary? Or am I being too cynical in wondering if that's some foreshadowing? The beginnings of setting up some form of defence or mitigation for a heinous crime?'

'Now that would certainly be devious. At the moment, I don't know enough about the case to form any judgement on that. I might know more after briefing shortly. Oh, and I told our friends from the press there'd be a conference at some point to update them on the case. I hope that was all right?'

She gave a small sigh at that.

'Inevitably there will at some point. Preferably when we have something newsworthy to tell them. Please update me after your briefing.

'Incidentally, who will be attending the post-mortem? Is Professor Nelson thinking of doing all three victims at the same time? It would certainly seem to be logical to do the babies together, at least. But whoever does attend, we need to be aware of their welfare in what is going to be a very harrowing ordeal. Especially for anyone who is a parent.'

'It's for that reason that I've already ruled out Maurice Brown. Especially with the twins element, as he's father to two sets. I'm not sure he could hold it together. It might be one it would be wise for me to take myself.'

'As ever, with the caveat of avoiding spreading yourself too thinly. But perhaps that might give you a valid excuse not to do the next press conference, should the timings coincide. Please keep me informed at all times.'

Ted smiled to himself as she left the office. That had almost sounded like her handing him on a plate a valid excuse to avoid the press, something he always tried to do.

All the expanded team members, including officers drafted in from other divisions, were in on time for briefing, being held downstairs in one of the larger rooms to allow for increased numbers. Nobody was ever late twice for DCI Darling. His methods might be quiet and calm but he could certainly make his point if he felt anyone was falling below his exacting standards.

He began by asking Mike Hallam for an update on when the post-mortem was going to take place.

'Tomorrow, early doors, boss,' Mike told him. 'So who do you want me to put on it? Bearing in mind how harrowing it's likely to be.'

'I'll go. As SIO, I should be there in person, I think, and this is one occasion where I think the fewer of us who have to sit through it, the better.'

'I don't think you'll get any argument from any of us on that one, boss. Thank you.'

'So where are we up to generally? What's our main suspect, the husband and father, saying so far?'

Their suspect was still in custody. Unusually, in anything like domestic abuse cases, even extreme ones, concerned neighbours had been sufficiently worried by screams and shouting from the house where the horrific killings had taken place to call the police. Too late to save any of the three victims, but it had at least led to several arrests, starting with the husband of the dead woman and presumed father of the murdered twins.

Everyone found present at the property had been arrested initially on suspicion and brought to the station for questioning. So far, no one was saying very much. However the case panned out, it was clearly going to rely in no small part on forensic evidence from the scene and on the bodies. It was unlikely that anyone who was there was going to say much at all.

* * *

Ted was punctual, as ever, for his meeting with Gina at The Grapes, but found her already there, waiting for him.

'Hello, boss. Thanks for agreeing to this. I know how busy you are. I've been following details of your latest case on the news. It sounds horrific. I can't say I envy you that one.

'I took the liberty of ordering you a Gunner and a hotpot.'

'Ted, Gina. Ted is fine, now you're not serving. And I know, Dave told me when I went to order, but I told him I'd pay. You know I'd have to declare a gratuity otherwise.'

He grinned at her as he said that but Gina suspected he meant it. He was perhaps the most by-the-book senior officer she'd ever worked closely with.

Dave appeared with their order, quietly and efficiently, then melted away to leave them to whatever they needed to discuss. He was used to Ted's team using the back room when they wanted a quiet place to relax, away from the public gaze.

'So how are you, Gina? And your parents? Losing Jenny must have been awful for all of you. I can't begin to imagine how much so. Especially after having lost your brother as you did.'

Gina knew the boss never drank. Never anything stronger than a Gunner. The way she was looking at him now suggested that in the absence of any other explanation, she was doubting his sanity.

'My brother? I don't have a brother. I've never had a brother. There was only me and Jenny.'

It was Ted's turn to look surprised.

'Your older brother, Andy. Died of a drugs overdose at university. I understood that's what made you choose to go into Drugs.'

'Honestly, Ted, I've never had a brother. I don't even know an Andy that I can think of, alive or dead. Certainly not within the family, at any rate. And I would surely have known. Whatever gave you that idea? Did somebody say something? I can't imagine who would make up something like that, or why. Who told you?'

But suddenly Ted could imagine. The why, certainly. And he could definitely remember the who.

His team had been working with Drugs on a complex murder case. Then as now there were leaks which could only have come from within the team. From someone who had first-hand knowledge of what was going on.

The finger of suspicion was pointing everywhere, especially towards Gina, as she was the newest member of the Drugs team. Ted had met her sergeant, a man called Ian Bradley, working in deep cover. Bradley had been the one who had told Ted about Gina's supposed brother.

No doubt he'd done it for the best of intentions. Trying to deflect suspicion away from Gina, clearly convinced she was not the mole and wanting to provide her with a valid reason why she'd be the last person to be passing on information to a drugs gang.

Now he thought about it, Ted could also remember a chief superintendent mentioning the seemingly imaginary brother, although Ted vaguely remembered him referring to 'Andy' as a kid brother, whereas Bradley had said he was older.

Ted wasn't about to tell Gina his source. But he now knew that Bradley had lied to him. To a senior officer. Whatever his motives behind it, as far as Ted was concerned, that was a serious matter, which needed dealing with.

To Gina, he laughed it off.

'So sorry about that, Gina. I must be going more senile that I thought and got the wrong end of the stick somehow. I'm sorry, my clumsiness must have given you a jolt.

'Now, tell me about this business I'm starting up and show me your designs for it so I can write you a glowing reference.'

* * *

'Wendy, I'm home.'

He called out one of his usual quotes as he opened the

front door, laughing to himself, as he usually did, at how much he knew that greeting frightened her.

She wasn't called Wendy. But he often made her sit down and watch a scary old film with him where the female lead was called that. The Shining, it was called. One which he seemed to really like. Probably because of its violence by a man to his wife. He enjoyed that. It never failed to arouse him. Another reason she both feared and hated it.

He made her watch it in English. There were chunks of it she didn't understand at all. But that scene, to which the quote was reference, terrified her. She'd try to grab a cushion to hide her face, every time, but he'd rip it from her hands and the ensuing struggle never ended well for her.

She hoped he was just using the phrase out of habit and it was no indication of how he planned the evening to go. He was bound to insist on sex. Probably several times. He always did, when he knew she should theoretically be at her most fertile. He was determined to make her pregnant. It seemed to be almost like a badge of honour to him. To be able to boast to all his mates that he'd impregnated her.

At first she'd wondered why he hadn't dragged her off to the doctor before now, when she hadn't fallen pregnant, despite all his efforts. She'd finally realised why he didn't want to do that.

She knew, because she'd researched it, that where infertility issues were suspected, both of them would be routinely tested. And she knew that with his over-inflated ego, and loving to play the big macho man, he would never accept that he might be the one with the problem.

He wasn't, of course, but he didn't know that.

If he were ever to find that out what was actually going on, he would automatically lash out at her, verbally and physically, and she dreaded to think where that might end.

Chapter Four

There would usually have been more people in attendance at a post-mortem. Home Office pathologist Professor Bizzie Nelson allowed some of her hand-picked students to attend for training purposes. A regular slot on a Monday morning, and sometimes a select few could be present for something out of the ordinary. But not this one.

Ted would often have more than one of his team present, as well as being there himself for an overview. Given the sensitivities of the current case, attendance was minimal.

Family members of any deceased person were not allowed to be present at the PM. They could request their doctor to be there to represent them but in this case they clearly hadn't opted to do so, although their rights should theoretically have been explained to them.

On this cold and damp Thursday morning, it was just Ted and the coroner in the viewing gallery, plus the professor and her assistant pathologist, James, working on the three bodies. That of the mother, a young woman in her twenties, and the tiny forms of her newborn twin babies. Both girls.

Ted and the coroner exchanged their usual reserved, formal greetings.

'Sir.'

'Chief Inspector.'

There had been a subtle, slight thaw in their relationship recently when the coroner had made a somewhat out of character favourable remark to Ted, but he couldn't ever visualise a time when the two of them might so much as have coffee together after a post-mortem.

As ever, there was little by way of social chit-chat from the professor. Simply the factual basics.

'Good morning, gentlemen. You'll see I haven't allowed my students to attend, although this has the makings of an interesting case. I will, however, share notes and footage with them, as this type of thing comes along so seldom. Mercifully.

'I imagine the burning issue for you both is the order in which these deaths occurred. Could it have been possible for the mother, for whatever reason, to kill her newborn babies before she was herself killed by someone else present in the room, for example.'

'If it's helpful at this stage, professor, sir,' Ted addressed them both, to give what background details he could, 'we don't seem to be short of other potential suspects in this case. I'm not sure whether it was for cultural reasons or something specific to that family, but there were quite a few people present in the room during the birth and seemingly during what happened immediately afterwards, as far as we can tell at this early stage of our enquiries.

'We're trying to get all those who were present interviewed individually, but they apparently all need interpreters and there seem to be a few difficulties with various languages and dialects being used. We'll then, of course, need certified translations of everything said in interview by all of them. Which all means that it's likely to take longer than usual to present a full file on this to CPS, unless we get a breakthrough.

'We don't think there's a specific race element because

there were different nationalities present, although it could be a cultural or religious thing, perhaps.'

'And, I believe, there was some mention of the presence of what I've seen referred to as a shaman, or a holy man of some sort, during the birth,' the coroner put in. 'Do please ensure I am kept informed of any sort of religious, ethnic, cultural or any other such issues concerning this case as soon as they arise, chief inspector.'

'You both know by now that I never prejudge anything. I base my findings solely on what the science tells me,' the professor went on. 'From the initial tests which James and I carried out on the bodies, I can tell you that the mother suffered significant blood loss in childbirth which would in all likelihood have left her too weak to do what was done to the babies, although that is still somewhat speculative.

'The indications so far are that someone present in that room killed all three of them, and certainly that the babies were killed very soon after they were born. I hope to be able to tell you more once we have finished here. But with the caveat that this promises to be a complex case, with no easy answers for any of us.'

* * *

Ted was usually ravenous for a bacon barm or two after a post-mortem, for reasons he could never really understand. After what he'd sat through that morning, even he didn't have much of an appetite. The best he could manage was a cinnamon Danish and a cup of hot chocolate, hoping the sugar rush would lift flagging spirits.

He was psyching himself up to go and feed back to the team everything he knew so far, to help to advance the case as much as they could. And he was dreading it.

They needed to know the full details and they were shocking. He'd sat through all sorts in his career to date. He'd even thought he'd heard it all. But it seemed there was no limit to human depravity.

He couldn't begin to understand what would drive anyone to swing vulnerable newborns against a wall, shattering delicate, fragile skulls in an instant.

The mother had died by strangulation. Manual strangulation. By someone with powerful hands. Even with the strength used, it was not a quick way to die.

Above all else, Ted couldn't get his head round the fact that all of this happened in a room apparently full of onlookers, with no evidence to date from the post-mortem nor from the crime scene that anyone had even attempted to intervene. There had been some shouts and screams, which was what had alerted the neighbours, but no signs of any physical intervention.

He'd told Mike Hallam in advance to go ahead with a team briefing on the basics but that he would update on what he'd learned whenever he got back and the team members could be assembled from whatever they were doing.

Ted's day was already shaping up to be a full one once more. At dinner time he had yet another possible candidate to fill Gina's post coming in for interview. Surely, on the law of averages, he was due one who at least showed some promise and not too many strikes against them from the start. She certainly looked a good candidate, on paper. But then so had most of the others, which is why they had been invited for interview.

'What about straight after dinner, boss, for a full team briefing?' Mike suggested. 'Give you time to do your interview and grab a bite, and a logical time for me to pull people in. Most of them are on interviewing anyone local, but who wasn't at the scene itself, who's not yet been spoken to. At least they're finding people willing to talk to them on this. Even with the few details which have inevitably leaked out, people know how bad it is and that seems to be breaking down barriers.'

'I don't know the specific area where this happened all that well, so can you fill me in on a few points. Is this somewhere where most people tend to be of the same ethnicity, or religion, or anything like that? What I'm getting at is are people likely to band together and go into denial mode? We've had that before from different communities which may be resistant to us coming in to investigate.'

'Quite the opposite, in fact, boss. That's why we had so many calls about it initially. It's a multi-ethnic area, with different religions, age groups, profiles and so on. Whatever happened in that house, all of the nearby residents who've been spoken to so far are beyond appalled by what they've heard, and probably as keen as we are to see people brought to trial for what they've done.

'I'd go as far as to say that if we didn't already have the main suspects in custody, we'd be in the position of having to consider police protection for them as they might be likely to be strung up before they got to trial.'

* * *

DC Alison O'Malley was surprised when DCI Darling came down to reception himself to show her to where she was to be interviewed for a possible place on his team. She'd expected him to send a minion to show her the way. Perhaps all the tales of him being one for equality were true. It was a hopeful beginning.

She was even more surprised when he held out a hand in greeting as he said, 'DC O'Malley? I'm DCI Darling. Thank you for coming. If you'd like to come with me, we'll go up to my office to talk.'

By now she was half anticipating him standing aside to allow her to go upstairs first, which he did. And for once she felt with a certainty he wasn't doing it just for a chance to check out her legs and backside.

Once upstairs he led the way through a main office to his own small one, where he opened the door then again stood aside to allow her to go in first, inviting her to take a seat. She'd heard on the grapevine that he was always polite, and he was certainly living up to his reputation.

'Tell me first of all why you're looking to move on from where you're currently working, please.'

She hesitated for a moment, then told him frankly, 'Sir, I had all my answers carefully prepared and off pat. But now I've met you, I think you probably want honesty, no matter how blunt.'

Ted smiled at that.

'That would be my preference, yes.'

'In that case, I want to broaden my experience on a team where I'll really be treated as an equal. I don't want to be given the soft jobs because I'm female. I don't want to be treated like a babysitter for all the vulnerable victims and witnesses. I want to do the same role as anyone else on the team, whatever their gender.'

Ted smiled to himself. That was more like it. He wanted honesty, candour and she was starting to show it. He decided to test her a little more.

'My team are currently investigating a particularly nasty suspected triple murder. It has a number of aspects – sensitivity issues – about it that makes it an extremely tricky case to handle. If I give you the basic details, tell me, please, what things you consider would make it so.'

He gave her the broad outline of everything they had to date and watched while she considered a moment before replying.

'Ethnicity and cultural issues are the most obvious ones, of course. But there's the possibility of misogyny too. You said both babies were girls. Would that indicate the father wanted sons instead? Might he have killed them because they weren't boys, and killed his wife for presenting him with the wrong gender?

'And you say that of the other people present for the birth, no one seems to have intervened or even tried to, to prevent the killings. So does that perhaps indicate that such thinking is not untypical with a certain race, religion, or cult of some sort?'

She stopped abruptly at that point, looked at him and smiled as she said, 'Sorry, sir, I'm probably going off in totally the wrong direction and making you think I'm a racist, or anti-religion or something.'

Ted smiled back at her as he said, 'On the contrary, DC O'Malley, I'm thinking you're very astute in going to the heart of the questions we're already asking ourselves. So my next question to you is how soon are you available to join us?'

There was one quick phone call Ted wanted to make after Alison left his office and before he went to brief the team on the post-mortem. He wanted to get in touch with DS Ian Bradley, the officer who he now knew had lied to him about

Gina's so-called brother.

He may have done it for the best of intentions, but he had still lied to at least two senior officers. Now Ted wanted to meet the man face to face and have him explain his actions. Ted didn't remotely have the time to spare for such a mission but he knew he'd be distracted until he could establish whether Bradley had been mistaken – possibly repeating something someone else had told him – or whether he'd told a bare-faced lie, for whatever reason.

* * *

As Ted had suspected, Maurice was the first to break down in tears on hearing the report from the post-mortem, even though he watered down the details as much as he could.

Jezza had moved her chair closer to Maurice in anticipation. She took hold of his hand in both of hers as he wiped his eyes on his handkerchief then blew his nose while he tried to get a grip.

'Sorry, boss. Sorry. I know I should keep it together and stay professional and I honestly am trying. It just gets to me. I keep remembering when my first two were born. My girls. Holding them in my arms for the first time. I'll try and keep it together. Sorry.'

'I know this is a particularly hard one for some of you, but we all need to stay professional, please. Maurice, I think it's best if we keep you off any face-to-face interviewing of anyone present at the scene so Mike, Maurice on collating statements, please, and chasing up any translations needed, at least for now.

'How are we getting on with witness statements from around the area? Anything known about any of those present at the time of the killings?'

'Nothing so far, boss. We have a small problem in that there seem to be a few fathers and sons with identical names within the family circle concerned, so we're trying to get accurate dates of birth to sort out who's who. Another ethnic or cultural thing, perhaps.'

'Have we got someone who can advise us on such things for this particular community, Mike? We really do need someone so we don't put a foot in it. Liaise with CPS. They're bound to know of someone. Let's not get close to charging then find someone somewhere has said or done the wrong thing so some vital piece of evidence is disallowed. Let's be absolutely certain of getting this all the way to court and getting a conviction.'

* * *

'Where's my little wifey? I've brought you a present.'

He sounded in good spirits as he came through the front door and called out to her. That was a hopeful sign. He also sounded as if he'd been drinking, which was less so. He was later than he'd said, too, which probably meant he'd been for a drink with his mates once more and stayed on a bit longer.

She went out into the hall to meet him, trying to look pleased. If she at least acted that way, he might be happy enough not to find fault with everything she did or said.

'We're going out for a meal tomorrow with my workmates and their partners, so I want you to look your best.'

He thrust a carrier bag at her, swaying slightly on his feet and beaming proudly at her with a ridiculous drunken grin.

She recognised the bag as coming from a charity shop,

but she didn't mind that. If he'd bought something expensive it would have meant even less money for housekeeping than he already gave her.

More than a little apprehensive, she reached a hand inside to withdraw whatever it was he'd bought her. Sometimes he showed good taste on the rare occasions he bought her anything. Sometimes he was so wide of the mark that she hid a garment away in the back of her wardrobe until he'd forgotten its very existence.

Her fingers encountered soft-touch, stretch fabric, and not much of it. She slipped the garment out of the bag and held it up by the shoulders. Charity shop or not, it was stunning. So sexy. The classic little black dress. Almost indecently short, with ruching at the side to reveal most of a thigh. One long sleeve, one provocatively bare shoulder.

She could never imagine herself being brave enough to wear something so revealing.

'Take your clothes off and put it on,' he ordered her, his voice husky.

'I'll need to go upstairs ...' she started to say, but he grabbed her arm, gripping until she winced as he said, 'Do it now. Here. Everything off, then put it on.

She was crying already, silently, as she did as he ordered, trying not to look as he ripped off his own clothes. Then he flung her backwards to the tiled floor so violently she banged her head, hard.

She hoped it would be hard enough to make her lose consciousness.

Unfortunately, it wasn't.

* * *

Ted heard Trev from the kitchen, talking in German, when he stepped into the house, to be greeted by cats. His partner switched to English when he heard him arrive.

'Ted's home now, Oscar, so I'll put it to him and see what he says, then I'll let you know. Tschüss.'

Ted walked in to kiss him as Trev was ending his call and putting his phone down.

'You and Oscar seem to be getting disconcertingly pally. And what is it you're going to put to me and let him know about?'

Trev laughed as he returned the kiss.

'Always the suspicious policeman's mind. You know I like Oscar. I'm forever grateful to him for finding you and bringing you safely home to me. And you know he wants us to go to Germany to meet his Oma whilst she's still alive, which I would love to do.

'Then I had an idea, when I was talking to your mother. Do you know she's never been abroad? Ever? And she sounded so wistful about it that I asked Oscar if Annie could come with us when we visit. He was delighted! He said we could all stay in his Oma's house, which is apparently huge, with plenty of rooms. Think what fun that would be!'

Ted was thinking about it. But fun was not the first word which was springing to his mind.

Then he looked at his partner's face, positively shining with excited anticipation and he thought of all the times he'd had to let him down at the last minute. Cancelled dinner dates, being called back into work when they'd tried to go somewhere together, and he made a decision he hoped wouldn't come back to bite him.

'If that's what you want to do, go ahead and make the arrangements with Oscar and mam. Just give me plenty of notice to book leave with a definite Do Not Disturb label on it.

'Oh, and speaking of such things, I will definitely be free on Saturday. Jo has sworn on the head of every one of his children that he will deputise for me come what may. So Oliver will have his chosen best man at his side for his wedding.'

Chapter Five

She'd spent most of the night crying as quietly to herself as she could, desperately trying to control the violent trembling of her body.

He hadn't just raped her once, in the hallway, where she'd felt incredibly vulnerable. Nobody could see into the house – not that they had many uninvited callers. But lying there, bruised, battered and bloodied, so close to the entrance, made her feel she was on display, in all her painful vulnerability.

As soon as he'd finished, he'd fallen asleep, breathing fumes of beer and whisky on fetid breath, straight into her face. She was pinned there, his dead weight making all attempt at movement impossible.

All she could think about at the moment was the dress. He'd been so rough, tugging it out of his way, that she was afraid he might have torn it. And it was a beautiful dress. The nicest gift he'd ever given her. He would be bound to insist she wore it the following evening to go out with his colleagues. She could do basic, simple sewing and repairs, but nothing like invisible mending, if that was what was required.

It would also need very careful washing and ironing before it would be fit to wear. It would almost certainly be marked as Dry Clean Only, although she tended to ignore such labels. A careful hand wash in lukewarm water seldom did any harm.

More than anything, she wanted to rip the dress to shreds. With her bare hands, with a knife, with her teeth, for what it now represented to her. To jump up and down on the remnants, then set fire to them. A glorious, blazing bonfire, cleansing the dark memories. Then to bury the ashes, deep in the garden, and with them, the knowledge of what had happened.

She knew she could never do any of that, though. With the same certainty as she knew that some memories would never fade. Ever.

He slept deeply, but not long enough. The smile he gave her when he woke up was almost fond, affectionate. Almost. His eyes always betrayed him, though. They stayed cold, scornful, as he pulled her up off the floor, dragged her up the stairs, and started all over again.

This time he pinned her arms above her head, squeezing her wrists so hard she had to bite her lip not to cry out. She'd learned the hard way that it didn't do to show how terrified she was. It only excited him more.

Once he fell asleep a second time, having mercifully rolled his weight off her first, she knew he would stay out for the count now until his alarm woke him in time for work.

All she could do, knowing sleep would totally evade her now, was to lie there thinking through, as so often, what she could possibly do to get help for her situation.

Someone must know where she could go for help. To find someone who could explain to her if she really did have no rights at all in this country, unless she stayed with him. The trouble was she had no idea where to start. Who to ask to help her.

The only person she could think of, who she somehow

instinctively trusted, was the young man who taught her English. He was always so kind and polite, with all of them in the class. Always trying to help any of them who needed it.

Best of all, with his good Russian, she could talk to him. To explain, without risking making too many mistakes in her poor English. She instinctively felt she could trust him. But how and where could she talk to him without others around them? She only saw him once a week, for the class. He was always on time but never early, as she sometimes was. And she couldn't risk staying on once the class was finished. If she was late home it would be bad for her. Very bad. And she risked her husband coming looking for her if she was very late. Then he would find out there was no teacher called Julia. Only this very good-looking young man with the incredible blue eyes.

Perhaps she could write him a note. Find a way to slip it to him during the next class. She could perhaps write it in Russian. He spoke it well, but her husband didn't speak any, although he would know what it looked like. He'd have seen it before. But at least if he should find it, he wouldn't know what it was about. He could try running it through a translator online, but if it came to it, she could always say it was some homework. They had to write an imaginary dramatic scene about something, and she'd done it first in Russian then was going to try to translate it into English.

It might work.

And what was her alternative?

She'd start straight away, once she'd washed and repaired the dress. She could write it as a letter and start it Дорогая Юлия – 'Dear Yulia'. So if he found it at all, that might just work.

It might.

* * *

Ted had just pulled up in the station car park when his phone rang, the screen showing an unknown number.

'DCI Darling.'

'Ian Bradley, Ted. You were trying to get in touch with me. What can I do you for?'

The DS's tone was informal; jokey almost. Whatever he thought Ted had been trying to contact him for, he clearly didn't expect it was anything to be bothered about.

'I need to talk to you, DS Bradley,' Ted told him, hoping his formality might set the tone. 'Sooner rather than later. When and where are you available?'

'Sounds ominous, if intriguing,' Bradley was still sounding totally unconcerned. 'As it happens, I'm currently not that far off your patch, and I do still need to eat and drink. We could meet at a roadside burger van I use sometimes, if you can manage to arrive looking not too much like a copper and risk blowing my cover. Assuming this really isn't something we can do by phone. On visual, if necessary.'

'It isn't,' Ted told him curtly. 'I have a change of clothes in the car. Tell me when and where and I'll meet you there.'

Once they'd fixed the place and time, Ian Bradley spent a moment looking at his mobile phone screen after the call was ended, as if it could somehow give him a clue as to what was going on.

'Well, Ted Darling,' he told the blank screen, 'I'd heard you were a dangerous one to cross. You got cuffs on me once, out of the blue, but you'll not do it again, whatever the reason. No chance.'

* * *

Ted began the morning team briefing with news of the appointment of DC Alison O'Malley.

'Some of you might already know her, possibly. She certainly stood out as the outstanding candidate of those I interviewed, plus her reasons for wanting a move sound genuine, and in keeping with the ethos we try for here.

'An experienced officer, too, so she should be able to hit the ground running and be an asset to us.'

'I've met her on a course, boss,' DC Tibbs told him. 'She was happy to sit next to me, even though I is black.'

Virgil, self-deprecating as usual, making fun of the racism he still encountered, far too often, from some members of the service whose bosses clearly didn't jump as hard on them as Ted would at the slightest hint of any kind of discrimination.

'Seriously though, she stood out. Very good, knows her stuff and very open to learning anything new they threw our way.'

'Good to know. Right, where are we up to with witness statements on our murder. Mike?'

'Nothing known about any of those present at the scene, and the neighbours are all saying they were a tight-knit and rather closed community. Didn't mix with anyone locally. Barely spoke to anyone, in fact. There's certainly been no hint of any such thing previously. No shouting, no sounds of violent disagreements. Because it was so unusual it rather worked in our favour. It meant we had several calls when it all kicked off. Sadly too late for any of our victims, but at least it was reported, which doesn't always happen with anything which sounds like a domestic.'

'Do we know more about this supposed shaman? The

coroner was certainly very interested in that at the PM. He seemed to think it might not be the right word at all. Where did it come from, initially? Do we know? And have we checked its accuracy, in case it's relevant?'

DS Rob O'Connell answered that one.

'Boss, I had shaman said to me from early on, by one of the neighbours who'd seen a procession of people going into the house before the birth. Unless there's been any update, I've no idea what religion or sect or whatever we're dealing with here. I've passed a message along to the interpreters to see if they can come up with something more accurate for now, but it's another thing which is proving tricky at the moment. They seem equally as uncertain about whatever sect this might be, so they're not sure of the correct term.'

'Fair enough, but can we please avoid using that word for the time being, everyone. It might be so inaccurate as to confuse the issue. Can we use their name, perhaps, for now?'

'We could, boss,' Mike told him, 'except it's another confusing thing. The only name we've heard for him, a surname, is the same as some of the others present. And he was one of those present who made himself scarce before anyone got there, we think. Shall we go with Person A or something for the time being?'

'It will do until we know better, at least. Can we start to put together a graph of all such information, please? Names, who's related to who. You know the sort of thing, Mike. Up on the board, so we can easily see who we're talking about.

'And what about the religion or sect or whatever it is? Have we identified it, or tried to? Checked out if they have a church or temple or whatever locally, and has anyone spoken to people there who might know this group in particular? Who's on that?'

'Me, boss,' Jezza told him, 'but that might possibly have to change if I find out it's something where women asking questions would be unlikely to get answers, if they were even granted an audience.

'I'm not trying to trivialise it in any way, but from what I've found out so far – which amounts to pitifully little – I am starting to wonder if it's some small extended family type of thing, not recognised by the wider world. A bit like some of the sub-cults in the States.'

She noticed the boss's expression change and went on hurriedly, 'Not that I'm prejudging anything, that's just the initial impression I formed, but I will carry on digging until I get to the facts.'

'Good. Keep me posted, please. Meanwhile I'll be in my office for now, but I have to go out at lunchtime. I may be some time. And just a reminder, Mike. Jo is deputising for me tomorrow and I am not available. For anything.'

* * *

DS Ian Bradley was leaning nonchalantly against the catering van, a cup of coffee in one hand, the other lifting a well-filled beefburger to his mouth. His appearance had changed since Ted had last seen him, but he still looked nothing at all like a police officer. Not even anything many people might expect a deep cover officer to look like.

He barely reacted as Ted, wearing his walking gear and boots, went up to the van's counter to order tea and a bacon barm. Once served, Ted turned to walk away, Bradley falling into step next to him. There was no one else around. It was on the early side for most of the lunchtime customers. Both men had the seasoned police officer's trick of eating what and when they could, never knowing when the next opportunity might present itself.

'We can sit in my car while we talk'

'No chance, Ted,' Bradley told him quickly. 'Last time I got in your car you cuffed me, and I'm not having that happen again, whatever the reason.'

'Despite appearances, DS Bradley, this isn't an informal chat, so first name terms do not apply.'

Bradley merely arched an eyebrow and asked, his tone ironic, 'So do I need my Federation rep to be present?'

Ted decided to ignore his tone and stick to the facts, the two of them walking away to stand well out of earshot of anyone coming to buy food from the van.

'You'll have heard, I'm sure, that Gina left the service after losing her sister as she did.

'She's going back into graphic design and she came to ask me for a reference. I thought I'd better say something, about the shock of losing her sister after the earlier death of her brother.'

Bradley said nothing, merely drank more coffee.

'Which was apparently news to her, as she has never had a brother.'

Bradley shrugged, looking totally unconcerned, then said, 'So? I knew there was no way on earth Gina was the informer on the team, so I came up with a plausible story for why she'd be the last person to be passing info to a drugs gang, to turn suspicion away from her.'

'In other words, you lied. To me and presumably to your chief super, since I heard the same story from him. Do you know how potentially serious that is?'

'Seriously? What harm did it cause? Was Gina the mole? Of course she fucking wasn't. And I knew it. All I did was divert attention away from her so people weren't pissing about investigating an innocent officer while the real informer was carrying on their filthy trade and we were all distracted from finding out who they really were.

'Are you saying you wouldn't go out on a limb for one of your team if they were under suspicion and you knew, without a doubt, that they were completely innocent?

'Because if that's true, then fuck you, Ted. I'm glad I was never on your team and never will be. Because if officers can't rely on their own boss to have their backs then we might as well all hand our warrant cards in and leave the villains to it.'

With that he turned on his heel and strode away, pausing only to throw another 'Fuck you,' over his shoulder as he went.

* * *

Trev was speaking Welsh on the phone this time when Ted got back in from work, feeling world-weary and thoroughly demoralised by his encounter with Ian Bradley.

It had raised a huge moral dilemma. One he'd never before had to consider. He'd always supported his team in their work. They needed to know he had their backs. But could he visualise himself doing as Bradley had done? Telling an outright lie? Could there ever be justification for that, in any circumstances?

Trev switched to English and started to wind up his conversation when Ted went into the kitchen.

'Ted's back now, Annie fach and he says hello. He looks like a man who's had a hard day and is in need of some food and TLC, in no particular order.

'I'm so pleased you got it so quickly and easily. It's going to be so much fun, and I'm really looking forward to it. Hwyl fawr now, and give Cariad a cuddle from both of us.'

He ended the call and moved to give Ted a hug, saying as he did so, 'I sorted out a passport for her. I knew you wouldn't have the time.'

'You must have done that some time ago, knowing how long it takes to get one issued these days.'

'Stop being policeman-like, Ted. I did it when she first told me she'd never been abroad and I could tell by her voice she would like to. I helped her with getting one so if ever the opportunity arose for her, she'd be all ready to go.'

Then he changed the subject, scanning Ted's face as he did so.

'You really do look like you've been through the wringer today, which is why I thought you might prefer not to chat to your mother. Is there anything I can help with? You know I'm quite good at brainstorming.'

Ted looked directly at him and asked, 'Am I a crap boss?'

Trev's eyes widened in surprise.

'You? No, of course not. Quite the opposite. That's why your team think the world of you. Firm, yes, but fair, always. What's brought this on?'

'I was posed one of those moral dilemma things today, by an officer not on my team, and it seems I came up sadly wanting. He asked me if I would ever go right out on a limb for one of my team. Far enough to bend the truth, not just the branch.'

'Well, I know you're a stickler for the truth. But I could never imagine you leaving one of your team hung out to dry if a small white lie might save them.'

'That's the sort of boss I always hoped I was. Listening

to this DS ranting and telling me exactly what I could go and do made me question my values. Really question them.

'I hope I can get the answer straight in my mind before ever I might be put to the test.'

Chapter Six

'There, if you looked any more gorgeous you would totally outshine the groom, and that would never do, on his special day.'

Trev finished tying Ted's tie for him, smoothed down the lapels of his jacket and planted a kiss on his cheek. Thankfully the dress code was lounge suits at the most, and Ted was prepared to make that effort for the day.

Ted was Oliver Burdon's best man, but it was Trev who had completely taken over making the day as special as he could for Oliver and Mary. And he'd overlooked nothing.

'Have you got the ring safely?'

Ted patted his inside breast pocket as he confirmed, 'Got the ring.'

'Right, let's get going. We don't want to have either of them panicking, thinking we're running late, or we've forgotten all about them or something horrendous like that.

'Drop me off at Mary's flat and we'll see you in the church. I can't wait to see Mary's face when she sees that the taxi she thinks she's getting to go there has been swapped for a stretch limo, full of flowers, which we've paid for.

'Well, strictly speaking, which you've paid for, for now, but I promise to pay up my contribution as soon as I can.'

'I know I've paid for it. I do check my credit card statement, you know,' Ted told him, but he was smiling fondly as he said it.

One of the things he loved about Trev was his unreserved kindness, even to people he didn't know well, or sometimes not at all. Once he'd heard that Mary had no family, no one to give her away, he'd offered his services not only to do that but to add a whole host of special extras to make the day unforgettable for both of them.

Like Mary, Oliver had no family, and seemed to have difficulty making friends, due in no small part to his learning difficulties. Which was why he'd latched onto Ted, who had shown him kindness in the past.

Trev had used his considerable charm to visit the hospital where Oliver worked and persuade two of his fellow porters, who would be off duty on the wedding day, to attend in their uniforms to form a small guard of honour. Seemingly no one at work had taken the initiative to arrange anything like that, but he appreciated they may simply not have thought of it.

One of them, Josh, with a sense of humour and of occasion, promised to 'borrow' a pair of crutches to hold aloft above the happy couple's heads.

Next, Trev had arranged a small but hilarious hen night for Mary with some of the other volunteers from the café for the homeless where Mary and Oliver had first met.

Oliver's stag night had consisted of Ted inviting him to The Grapes for a pint and patiently going over all the plans and procedures for the big day. He knew how anxious the man could get if he felt he didn't know what was happening or what he was supposed to do.

Trev had helped Mary choose her dress, her hairstyle and her make-up, determined that the day should be perfect for her, with lots of photos for lasting memories.

When he'd seen the dejected state in which Ted had come back from work the night before, he was even more pleased with his efforts. A wedding wasn't going to solve all of Ted's troubles and self-doubts, but hopefully if everything went off really well, he could have a few hours of enjoying a special occasion rather than being a policeman. Always trying to do the right thing and beating himself up mercilessly on the rare occasions he may have got things wrong.

* * *

Jo Rodriguez was in early on Saturday. Filling in for the boss, he thought he'd better follow his example on punctuality. In all the time he'd worked with him, he could never remember Ted being late for anything, except in a real crisis.

DS Rob O'Connell wasn't far behind him. Again leading by example. The team were once more trying to ensure everyone had at least some free time over the weekend, whilst not leaving the enquiry short-handed. It suited the budget better, for one thing, to try to run things that way.

At least they had their principal suspects in custody and likely to stay that way, for some time. With such serious charges, and the horrendous details surrounding them, few magistrates would be likely to grant bail, not even with the strictest of reporting restrictions, and no matter how hard defence lawyers fought for it.

'The boss has left me notes, but is there anything you can think of which I could usefully do to help with this one, Rob, using any of my meagre skills?' Jo asked him. 'I was thinking perhaps of the religious angle. I know the boss is bothered about the use of the word shaman. I've been checking and that seems to apply principally to North America and northern Asia, which doesn't seem to fit our particular profile of suspect, so he may well be right on that.

'I know Jezza's been suggesting some sort of lesser-known cult. We're not short of Catholic churches here and if anyone would know about such things, it would be a good parish priest. I wondered if it was worth an hour or so of my time to talk to some of them, see what I can glean. I know there's at least one locally who's made something of a study of such things and written some acclaimed papers on them. Worth a try? If nothing else to stop us blundering in and offending, therefore alienating, some groups.'

'My view, for what it's worth, is that anything's worth looking at, at this stage, if only to stop us making fools of ourselves by spouting the wrong stuff and, worse, letting the press get wind that we were going off in the wrong direction, like a bunch of headless chickens.

'I'd say give it a go. Presumably you'd only be a phone call away if I needed you, unless you'd need to turn your phone off.'

Jo laughed at that.

'I'm not planning on making my confession at the same time. There's not enough time for that. I'm only deputising for one day.'

* * *

Parts of the evening out with his workmates had been better than she'd dared hope. Some of it had been worse than her wildest imaginings.

There had been no serious damage to the dress. Simply a few stitches gone in some seams, which even she had managed to put right without it looking too bad. And it had washed better than any of her expectations. She found herself frequently running her fingers over the fabric, loving the opulent hand feel.

She hardly dared hope that they might, for once, go and have a nice night out together, like any normal couple. A meal in a decent restaurant with his workmates and their wives. A few drinks. Perhaps some dancing.

The wives didn't bother with her much. They were always a bit of a clique, and even without her poor grasp of English, they didn't seem interested in talking to her. The most they did to show any form of solidarity was to let her go to the restroom at the same time as they did so she wasn't left alone at the table with the men, which she would have hated. The way some of them looked at her made her feel very uncomfortable.

For once, she actually felt she looked quite attractive in the new dress. A couple of the other wives had even complimented her on how nice it was. One asked where she'd bought it, so she explained, as well as she could, that it was a present from her husband. She didn't mention the charity shop. She instinctively knew he would be angry if she told them that.

The only thing which had spoilt it for her was that she was wearing absolutely nothing underneath the dress. That had been at his insistence, of course. She would never have dreamed of doing such a thing.

He'd made her parade for his inspection before he left the house. He studied her for a moment then grabbed her arm and yanked her towards him, his other hand going straight between her legs, right up to the top.

He twanged the elastic of her underwear, hard enough to make her flinch, as he shouted into her face, 'What's this shit? I didn't buy you a dress this sexy for you to cover yourself in fucking granny pants. I want to spend the evening sitting where I can cop an eyeful and think about what we're going to get up to the minute we walk through the door together tonight. Get them off. The bra, too.'

She opened her mouth to protest, finding courage from somewhere, which quickly shrivelled as he lifted a threatening hand.

He made no move to look away as she did as he told her, slipping off the dress and putting it carefully onto the bed while she removed her underwear. When she bent slightly to pick it up again, he slapped her, hard, with the flat of his hand, across the buttocks.

'You'll get more of that if you don't do exactly what I tell you to tonight. And especially when we get back home.'

She tried her very best all evening. Tried to reply politely and as well as she could manage to anything anyone said to her. Danced with any of his workmates who asked her to, although that made her uncomfortable when one of them ran his hands over her and discovered she was wearing nothing under the dress.

There'd nearly been a violent scene when her husband looked across at that exact moment, and came rushing across, shouting the odds.

There was a bit of a scuffle, raised voices, some chairs knocked over, drunken punches thrown but mostly missing their target. Then the older workmate who seemed to have some sort of control over the others, at least, came racing in to separate them, to calm things down, and then to talk to the manager who came hurrying over.

She saw a banknote change hands and all seemed to be smoothed over and forgotten about. Except by her. She knew she was going to pay for it later. To be accused of having led the man on.

For the rest of the evening she refused to dance with anyone and sat quietly at the table. Mentally composing the letter in her head. In Russian.

'Dear Yulia,

Please can you help me? I think my life may be in danger and I don't know anyone else I trust to ask for help.

You have always been so very kind to me and I think I can trust you.

I am being physically and sexually abused. And mentally, because I am told if I try to leave the relationship, I will have no rights to remain in Britain and I could be deported.

I am so afraid as I don't know if this is true or not and I don't know anyone to ask for help.

Please Yulia. Please help me. Tell me what I can do and where I can go to get away from the violence without being sent away out of the country.

Please. I am begging you for help.'

And then she would sign it, and somehow she would find a way to give it to the kind young man, with the beautiful blue eyes. And he would know what to do.

She felt sure he would.

* * *

'Wasn't that just the sweetest thing you've ever seen?'

Trev was still misty-eyed with emotion after the bride and groom had left for their honeymoon – Southport, because it turned out Oliver had never seen the sea – and he and Ted had taken the opportunity to slip away.

'It was, I have to confess. Thanks for all you did for the two of them. It was largely thanks to you that they got their dream wedding. The stretch limo was perfect, but your master stroke with the guard of honour was amazing. Especially the crutches.'

'Oh, I can't take the credit for that, that was entirely down to Josh. As soon as I told him what it was all about, he came up with that idea.

'Oliver might think he doesn't have any real friends where he works but it's clear that quite a few of them think highly of him. Some are just not confident about how to interact with him sometimes. But I think he'll find himself going back to more of a welcome than he expects, and the possibility, at least, of a few doors opening to him.

'Mary definitely won everyone's hearts. I can't remember when I last laughed so much. Probably that time when we first met her.'

Ted was quiet for a moment whilst he changed down to bring the car to a halt at a red traffic light. As it changed and he moved off, he asked, 'Do you fancy going for a walk somewhere next? If you're not too full of cake and sparkling wine. It's a nice day, and I could really do with a leg stretch and a bit of a blow.'

Trev had, as usual, drunk a fair bit and was pleasantly merry, but he was still sharp enough to recognise the question for what it was. It was classic Ted-speak for saying he had something on his mind which he wanted to talk about. Something he was only ever comfortable doing, even to Trev, outside in the open. Preferably up on a mountain, or a decent hill, at least.

Trev sat up straighter in his seat and rubbed his hands over his face.

'That sounds like a very good idea to me. Change of clothes, cup of tea, feed the boys and girls, then off out for a blow. What level of a "needing to talk" scale is this one? High Peak? Kinder Downfall? Or Lyme Cage?'

'Are you up for the Downfall? Or is that a bit much after today?'

'If that's where you need to go, I'm up for it. As long as you solemnly promise that you will talk to me. Properly. Especially tell me why on earth you think you're not a good boss. And if you don't know by now that you can trust me not to say anything to anyone of what we talk about, then we have a serious problem.'

Chapter Seven

Sunday morning. Ted wanted to go in for a catch-up on any developments since he'd been out of contact for the wedding. He knew everything would have run smoothly in his absence with Jo at the helm, but he needed a clear desk on Monday morning when he would be welcoming DC Alison O'Malley to the team first thing.

As he'd anticipated, Jo had left him full details of everything significant, starting with his visit to a local Catholic priest to ask about possible religious cults, and the advisability or otherwise of using the term 'shaman' in connection with the murder case.

'Almost certainly best avoided, from the advice I was given,' Jo had written in the report Ted was now reading. 'We both know that religion is often one of the biggest minefields for sensitivity issues, and that was confirmed by what Fr Callaghan told me.

'He knows of no specific religious community for that area, even a minority one, for which the term would be appropriate and warned that public use of the term might hamper us more than help.

'He also doesn't know of any group where it would be standard to have any form of 'holy man' (temporary term, until we find the right one!) present for the birth itself, although there are several where one might be called very soon after. Nor one where the extended family would all be there for religious reasons, and he is something of a specialist on minority religions.

'Sorry it's not much to go on but we at least now have it on good authority that we shouldn't be using the word 'shaman', although we probably shouldn't go so far as redacting witness accounts which mention it. Simply take it out if a witness hasn't specifically used it, so that's over to interpreters and translators, in a way. It might be a dodgy interpretation by one of them or more likely, something a witness has said because they didn't know the correct term.'

Ted was taking the opportunity of it being quiet to catch up with anything new the team had come across in his absence. Still nothing significant to advance them very far, but at least their suspects were still in custody, with no immediate chance of bail on the horizon.

He'd promised Trev he'd try to be back in time to take him out to lunch somewhere nice, but not to book anywhere, in case he couldn't get away as early as he hoped.

He got a jolt when he checked the time on his phone and saw it was later than he'd intended. Definitely too late to think of finding anywhere decent with room for two for lunch on a Sunday, with no prior booking.

Feeling guilty, he dialled Trev's number and began, as usual, 'Hi, it's me.'

'So you remember me, do you?' Trev sighed. 'The hungry person, sitting here forlornly expecting to be taken out to lunch?'

'I'm really sorry, I lost track of time. Would afternoon tea, somewhere nice, your choice, no stinting, in some small way make up for it? If you can find somewhere to book at short notice. I'll be on my way in about half an hour so we could still have a run out and a nice tea somewhere.'

'Really no stinting? Or is this going to be another of your chips-in-a-bag sort of a date?'

Ted laughed at that.

'You're never going to let me forget that one, are you? No, no limit on cost, wherever you fancy and we can get in. I think the credit card can still run to a nice treat, even after the stretch limo.'

He knew he owed a lot to Trev for his endless patience and support. Ted found it hard to talk to anyone about feelings, even the kind and patient woman he'd seen before for counselling sessions, and occasionally returned to if he felt things getting on top of him.

Sitting up near Kinder Downfall the previous day had helped him so much after his unpleasant experience with the Drugs DS. He still thought the DS had been wrong to invent a lie by way of an alibi for Gina Shaw. He felt it damaged the man's own reputation, having done such a thing without seemingly batting an eyelid. He could surely have found a better way to stand up for her than a calculated lie.

'Come on, Ted, he did the wrong thing for the right reasons,' Trev had told him. 'He saw a way to deflect suspicion from someone he knew to be innocent so they could all concentrate on finding the real informant. Isn't that what friends do? Even police officers? Could you never see yourself doing something similar for one of your team, if you knew they were innocent but couldn't prove it?'

'But if I knew with such certainty, there would be proof there somewhere, so no need of a lie. I'd certainly help to dig out that proof.'

Trev gave a small tut of annoyance.

'Ted, for an intelligent man, you can be annoyingly obtuse sometimes. Aren't you always telling me how hard it is to prove a negative? Unless there is cast iron proof by way of a substantiated alibi or something, you can't prove someone didn't do something, surely? And are you even required to, under the law of England and Wales? Surely it's up to the prosecution to provide proof positive?

'Are you saying you really wouldn't step in to help one of your team if you were convinced of their innocence and they were struggling to prove it?'

'That's what the DS threw at me, in slightly more colourful language. He said all he did was divert attention away from a colleague so people weren't pissing about investigating an innocent officer.'

One thing Ted hadn't done was to name the officers he was talking about, although he had indicated their genders. He knew Trev was no fool. As soon as he'd heard mention of Drugs involvement he would have had a good idea of what and who it was all about. It just made Ted feel slightly better not to mention their names.

'He asked me what hope there was if officers can't rely on their own boss to have their backs in tight situations. He also said they might as well quit the force and leave the villains to it.'

'But would you really not? Say it was someone like Jezza who needed you to at least plant a doubt. Not even to tell a lie, just to make a diversionary tactic to save them. The classic "don't look here, look over there instead" sort of thing.

'And what about me? What if it was me in that situation? Are you really saying you'd do nothing like that to save me from a terrible fate?'

Ted heaved a world-weary sigh as he said, 'I honestly don't know the answer to that and probably wouldn't unless and until I found myself in that situation. Of course I would do everything I possibly could to help you. I hope you know that. And the same goes for any of my team. I would try everything I could. But I can't swear that I would go for an out and out lie. I simply don't know if I could.

'That's why the DS told me, in no uncertain terms, how glad he was not to be on my team, nor ever likely to be.'

* * *

Ted was relieved when he got home to find Trev was in smart casual, without a tie. He still looked stunning, as ever, but Ted had been worried they'd have to dress up in shirt and tie once more, something he always resented doing in his off-duty time.

'Did you find somewhere for us?' he asked him, leaning in to kiss him through the waft of expensive aftershave.

'I did, and I shamelessly played the double-barrelled card to guarantee us a table. I bet whoever took the booking has been frantically searching 'Mr Costello Armstrong, without a hyphen' online to see if I'm someone noteworthy,' Trev replied with a laugh.

'And I definitely don't have to dress up like a dog's dinner? I was just going to have a quick wash then put something else on, but definitely no tie.'

'I told you, they clearly think I'm at least a minor member of the aristocracy, so we can be as casual as we like without being thrown out.'

'And where are we going? Will I faint when I get the bill?'

'The posh spa place and restaurant, out near Macclesfield, and yes, quite likely, knowing how you like to count every penny, Mr Scrooge.'

Ted looked at yet more paperwork chaos strewn all over the kitchen table, with senior cat Queen sitting on one pile, and asked, 'Is this more work for your English students? Do you think you better put it away safely before we go, so it doesn't get shredded?'

'Oh, I will do. I thought I'd put together a little quiz for my students, to get to know a bit more about them. To encourage them to talk more about themselves, so I can help them better; respond to some individual needs, perhaps.

'We've been doing simple family vocabulary, so building on from that. There are a couple in my group who are a bit shy when it comes to talking about themselves and I think some of them may need to do that. I thought they might find it easier to put things in writing.'

Ted frowned at his words.

'Are you sure you're not crossing boundaries with that? Risking getting too personally involved? Would you not be safer sticking to "the bear is eating a mouse" instead?'

Ted had come home from work one day to find Trev giggling hysterically whilst researching what sort of online language courses were available and finding one which had that as a very early phrase to learn.

'Don't worry, Mr Policeman. I always tell them that for any such work I set them that they don't have to write the reality. They can make up anything they like as long as they use the right vocabulary. I thought it might be both helpful to them and revealing for me. Then I can offer a bit more help to those in need of it.

'Right, go and get washed and changed. I was reduced to beans on toast for lunch when my date stood me up so by now I could eat a scabby donkey.'

* * *

After a night of heavy drinking, he was still fast asleep when she slid as quietly as she could out of bed and went to make herself some coffee.

Her lips were split and sore where he'd hit her as soon as they'd got through the front door at the end of the evening, shouting in her face that she'd been encouraging his workmates. Flirting with them, showing them what was rightfully his and only his.

No point her even trying to point out he was the one who had made her wear such a revealing dress, and remove her underwear, leaving little to the imagination. She hadn't felt at all comfortable, sensing the eyes of most of the men present, all people he worked with, constantly swivelling in her direction to size up what was on offer.

She'd loved the dress when she had first seen it. Wearing it like that, the way he had made her, had left her feeling cheap. As if she was deliberately offering herself to the highest bidder, when nothing could have been further from the truth.

After the scuffle at the restaurant, he'd settled into a sullen silence, ignoring everyone, and proceeded to get himself as drunk as he could. They hadn't taken their own car, instead getting a lift with another couple, who had also driven them home. Some in the group were sensible, at least, always car sharing or ordering taxis for their nights out, never putting any of them at risk of prosecution, and worse.

She had been sitting in the back on the drive home, next to the other man's wife, while her husband was sitting in front, next to the driver. At least the driver seemed to have some ability to calm him down and make him behave. He'd been the one who had broken up the fight in the restaurant and handed over money to quieten things down. He seemed to be the most senior of them, to have some sort of control outside the workplace as well as inside.

She sat stiff and tense behind her husband, trying not to start shaking in anticipation of what lay ahead when they got home. She'd barely exchanged a couple of words all evening with the woman now sitting next to her, behind her own husband. But she was at least one of the quieter ones, one who didn't seem to be constantly judging and sneering, making fun of her poor accent and pathetic attempts at speaking English.

She was observant, too, as she saw that their passenger's hands were trembling in her lap, no matter how hard she tried to control them.

She gave her a look of compassion and mouthed silently <Are you all right?>

She nodded, frantically, not wanting to give anything away. Not wanting to make any waves which could come back to submerge her in the future.

<Yes thank you> she mouthed back, trying to find a smile somewhere to paint on her face to show she meant it.

The woman was still staring at her, clearly not believing her. Then she mouthed again and made a gesture with her hand.

<Phone. Give me your phone.>

She froze. Wanting to refuse. Desperately wanting to accept the unaccustomed offer of help.

The woman made the same gesture again, so she complied, fishing into her bag and handing over her phone.

She knew the number wouldn't stay there long. As soon as he did his usual checking on all of her phone activity, he'd delete it. At least it was a woman's name, one he knew they'd been out with, so he might not be too angry about it. It was the sort of thing people did, when they went out together. Exchanged phone numbers.

It was what normal people did, she mentally corrected herself. She knew her life was anything but normal.

She would never phone the number, even if he left it there, she knew. The woman was married to one of his colleagues, who was also a friend of his. She'd be bound to say something to him, and then it would get back to her husband that she'd been talking out of turn about him. And she dreaded to think how that would turn out.

He wasn't working over the weekend, unless he got called in for an emergency, but she would be spared his presence for much of it, hopefully. They didn't do the normal weekend things other couples did together.

She'd listened to what some of the other women in the group last night were talking about, by way of their weekend plans. Several of them had children of various ages so they had talked about their ideas. All of them had sounded so interesting and exciting to her, compared to what she knew hers would be like. Trips to adventure activities. Visits to family. Perhaps a trip to the nearest seaside resorts. For the couples without children, going to retail outlets, planning new furniture for their houses, going to garden centres for plants and outdoor furniture.

It was all a million miles from what she could even imagine. Her best-case scenario was him going off out with friends to all the sporting events he followed and leaving her at home alone. He'd watch anything competitive. Especially anything on the violent side. He loved contact sports, anything with an element of real danger.

He'd dragged her with him to watch a cage fight one time. It had both repulsed and terrified her. Worse had been the realisation that the more afraid she became, the more he enjoyed it.

But at least he was likely to be out of the house for most of the weekend. Which meant that not only was she relieved of the constant tension of dodging the next blow, but she could also spend her time perfecting the 'Dear Yulia' letter she'd been composing. To make sure it was absolutely right.

Every time she ripped up one draft to start again, she was so careful to tear it so it couldn't be read and hide it deep inside the recycling bin. He never looked in there. He left all that sort of thing to her to see to. Even though she was writing it all in Russian, she was terrified that if he found a piece of it which had enough words to piece together the gist of it, he would find someone or somewhere to get it translated. And if he knew what she had written, it would be very bad for her.

But if she could write it well enough, then keep her head down for just a few more days, she could hand it over to her teacher at the next evening class.

He would know what to do, she told herself. He was clever, as well as kind. He would help her.

Because if he couldn't, she had no idea who else could.

Chapter Eight

Alison O'Malley was already waiting in reception when Ted went down to find her. He wanted to welcome her in person and was pleased to see she was early on her first day.

He found her talking to retired sergeant Bill Baxter, now fulfilling a vital role as gatekeeper between the public and busy officers. No one knew better than Bill which cases needed urgent referral and to whom, and which could be dealt with by some form-filling and a bit of diplomacy from him.

Once again Ted stood aside to allow her to start up the stairs before him, but then fell into step beside her so they could walk and talk.

'We still have this triple murder ongoing and we've not made as much progress as I would have liked since we last spoke. I know you said you haven't worked a murder case before, and this is a complex one for all kinds of reasons, so how would you feel about starting on it? And what do you consider to be your best skills for a case like this?'

'Well, sir,' she began, before Ted interrupted her with a smile and said, 'Boss is fine, no need for formality. Are you happy to be called Alison?'

'Perfectly, boss, or even Ali, if that's all right. And I'm not bad in interviews. I know from what I've read around this case that there are a lot of female witnesses, so would it help if I took on some of those interviews? If you're sure I'm up to it? I know you currently only have one other female DC on the team.'

'The senior of our two DS's, Mike Hallam, is allocating tasks, so I'll discuss that with him. Meanwhile, let's find you a desk, at least, then you can meet everyone once they're all in.'

Introductions made, Ted asked for a round-up of any new information, turning first to Jezza.

'Any developments on the religion/ethnicity front, Jezza?'

'Nothing with legs to date, boss, and I did get Tommy to help with some of the research for me over the weekend.'

She turned to Alison O'Malley to explain.

'Tommy is my kid brother. On the spectrum, obsessed with fact-finding. Probably better than many of us here, except Steve, at online research. No social inhibitions at all, though, so often wakes me in the wee small hours to give me his findings. Hence me often looking like the undead first thing in the morning. Oh, and he's totally discreet too. Spooks couldn't prise information out of him if I tell him to keep something to himself.

'Boss, there are various cultural superstitions involving twins, of either gender, being a bad thing, bringing ill fortune on a community. Just as a for instance, some indigenous people in Madagascar believe that twins should never stay with their birth parents as they bring bad luck and violence to the community. They are put up for adoption, at least, there, whereas the outcome is a lot worse in some ethnic communities. But in terms of our case, it doesn't advance us much as I can't find any such information relating to any of the different nationalities we seem to be dealing with.

'So is it possible we're getting distracted by looking for

something from a particular race or religion when it might be simply some strange cult which potentially attracts followers from anywhere and everywhere? Maybe this is simply extreme domestic abuse. Equally abhorrent, but statistically speaking, sadly not all that uncommon. Jealous husband can't believe the twins could be his so in his anger he kills them and their mother, who he thinks has been unfaithful to him.'

'Jo said similar in the report he left for me from Saturday,' Ted told them, then added an explanation for their new team member. 'That's DI Rodriguez, Ali. He was deputising for me on Saturday and is our on-call religious expert, especially for the Church of Rome.

'I'll circulate his full report to all of you but one of the main points from it to consider when interviewing anyone is to avoid the use of the word shaman, please, as it's likely to be incorrect. If any witnesses use it to you, please try, without leading questions, to query why they're using it.'

'Boss, sorry, someone's bound to have suggested this already but I'll ask it anyway.'

DC O'Malley once more. She certainly wasn't hesitant of speaking up in front of her new team members. Ted didn't miss the admiring look she was getting from DC Steve Ellis. He was an excellent officer, but still so shy and unsure of saying anything in front of strangers, unless pressed to do so.

'What about schools, if there are children within the group of people we're talking about? I don't have children but I'm from a big family, with lots of nephews and nieces, so I know how observant they can be, and the sort of things they pick up on.

'Also, if there is some religious sect or another involved here, then might any of the children from this circle have been withdrawn from compulsory Religious Education in their schools? We might possibly be able to find out, even in vague terms, if there is mention of some specific religion regarding any of them.'

Ted and Mike Hallam exchanged an appreciative look.

'A very good suggestion, Ali, and one we haven't yet started on. Are you happy to make a start on collating that information? Once you have the details, I'd suggest you take either a PCSO or an officer from Uniform with you when you start visiting the schools. I'll arrange something with Inspector Turner. It makes it look official and can, sometimes, help to loosen tongues.

'On the other hand, if we're dealing with a secretive closed cult of some sort, it might just have exactly the opposite effect. In which case, it's entirely my fault for the wrong judgement call, no one else's.'

* * *

The weekend had been better than she'd dared hope because she'd seen very little of her husband. Far less than she'd expected to.

She knew it would in no way indicate any sort of remorse on his part for his behaviour. Far from it. He would have been busy convincing himself that she was the one at fault. Deliberately flirting with his mates from work. Being provocative and dressing like a tart.

He didn't even offer any explanation for his extended absence. Sometimes he would at least say where he'd been. If he was in a mellow mood he might even give her an in-depth account of some sporting event or another he'd been to.

Such things didn't interest her at all so she didn't know most of the sporting vocabulary in Polish, or in Russian. She certainly didn't know it in English and wasn't interested enough to learn it.

She'd made his favourite meals over the weekend for whenever he deigned to show up. He usually gave her the housekeeping money on Fridays, so she could buy something a bit better, in the hopes they could pass a weekend like any other couple; eating evening meals together, perhaps watching some telly afterwards. The best she could hope for was a respite from the violence. His only other setting towards her was a seemingly profound indifference.

She kept consoling herself with the thought that she only had two more days to get through, when he'd be working on both of them, before she could hand over the letter on which she was pinning all her hopes.

Hand it over to Yulia.

She was training herself always to refer to her English teacher by the name she'd made up. Even to herself. That way she would be much less likely to slip up and blurt out the young man's real name to her husband when he was in a violent mood.

He hated being lied to. He boasted how easily he could tell when someone was lying to him. Sometimes he spoke to her about aspects of his work. He'd sneer about the liars and said the only way they could convince him they were telling the truth was if they lived the lie, all the time. Twenty-four/seven, as he put it. Only if they believed it themselves could they possibly hope to make anyone else believe it.

So she trained herself to believe it. Her teacher was a kind middle-aged lady called Yulia. Julia, she corrected herself quickly. She had to get this right. Not make any mistakes.

She'd spend much of the next day perfecting the letter. She kept the final copy in a place she was sure he would never think of looking. She'd take it out and hide it in her bag on Tuesday, before he got home from work, and in plenty of time for her to go off to the class.

That was the one potential flaw in her plan – if for some reason he decided to go through her bag as he sometimes did before she went out. She wasn't sure she could stick to her cover story of it being a piece of fiction. Not to his face. Especially when he got angry. It was always when, with him, rather than if.

If she deliberately left early for her class, before he got home, without saying anything to him first, he might get angry enough to drive round to find her. Perhaps even to come storming into the room where the class was held. He would almost certainly come to pick her up afterwards and then he would see for himself who Julia really was.

She would just have to hold her nerve and trust in some divine being she'd long since ceased to believe in, with all that had happened to her in her short life.

* * *

Finally, it was Tuesday evening, and time for her English class. She'd thought the time would never pass. She'd been so worried her husband would see her rising tension and know that something was going on.

For once, luck had been on her side and he'd been working some overtime so she'd seen very little of him and he'd had no chance to search through her bag before she went out.

She was so eager to get to the classroom she didn't even bother to wait for a bus. She simply walked there as fast as she could, arriving slightly out of breath, her heart racing as much from the anticipation as the exercise. She was the first to arrive.

She usually sat towards the back, trying to be as quiet and anonymous as possible. Always seeking not to draw attention to herself. This time she chose a seat at the end of the front row. The tables and chairs were arranged in a horseshoe shape so the front row was the widest. That meant there was no one sitting directly behind her who might possibly catch a glimpse of the letter she was going to hand over, when the opportunity presented itself. The desks were spaced out to the sides, so there was no danger from that direction.

She knew there were at least a couple of people in the class who spoke some Russian. In the early lessons of introducing themselves and where they were from, they'd touched on what other languages people spoke. Their teacher seemed to be fluent in quite a few of them.

Several of the students were there before their teacher, as usual. He was almost always on the last minute, full of apologies, striding in still wearing his motorbike leathers, greeting them all with his usual dazzling smile as he peeled off his biker clothing.

'Hello, everyone. One of these days, I'm going to surprise you by being here before any of you!'

He was pulling papers out of his bag as he went on, 'This evening I want to start with an exercise to practise the family vocabulary we've been learning. Some simple questions for you to answer, if you want to. You don't have to answer all or even any of them. You don't have to give real details. It's just for me, no one else will see your answers.

'Is that all right for everyone? Do you all understand what you have to do? Please ask me if you need any help at all.'

She couldn't believe her luck. She'd been worrying about how she was going to give him the letter without drawing attention to herself. Now she had the perfect excuse as she was actually going to have to hand in the answers to the questions. She could simply put her own sheet of paper with the one he had handed her and hope he didn't say anything about it.

There was no reason anyone there should know who she was married to, or anything else about her. Her circumstances had simply made her so paranoid she trusted no one and didn't want anyone to know anything about her or her home life. Not that she had much of one. Cleaning, shopping, cooking and watching daytime TV in an effort to improve her English about summed it up.

She almost smiled to herself as she bent over the exercise, determined to do it as well as she possibly could, as if that might somehow make him take her letter more seriously. Almost smiled. Because she was still taking a huge risk in trusting someone she didn't know.

She felt her heart pounding in her chest once the exercise was finished and he started collecting in the papers, smiling at each student in turn, saying 'thank you' and adding their name. Her hands were trembling, not with her usual fear, but with a hope she had never before dared allow herself to feel.

She lifted the two sheets of paper up herself to hand to him, eyes riveted on his face. A kind, smiling face she instinctively felt she could trust. Trying to signal to him how important that second sheet of paper was to her. To her safety. Willing him not to make any comment which would draw other eyes towards them both.

He seemed to understand. He did no more than give her a warm smile and another 'thank you' then go on his way, her precious lifeline tucked safely in amongst the others.

Now all she could do was wait. And hope.

* * *

'I put the shepherd's pie in the oven as instructed, so it should hopefully be ready very shortly. How were your students?' Ted greeted Trev as he came into the kitchen, noting his partner looked more serious than usual.

Normally after one of his classes he would come bouncing in, smiling, full of enthusiasm, clearly having enjoyed himself. This time he looked uncharacteristically sombre, distractedly stroking the nearest cats as he hung his bag from the back of his chair and fished out his paperwork.

'Is everything all right?' Ted asked him. 'You don't look as happy as you usually do after your class. Did it not go well?'

Trev held up the sheet of paper he was looking for and turned it towards his partner.

'It seems my instincts were right about thinking at least one of my students might have something they wanted to share with me. One woman handed me this, with her completed answer sheet.'

Ted frowned at the unfamiliar letters and asked, 'Is that Russian?'

'It is. She's one who has quite good Russian so we can communicate in that if she gets stuck. It starts with "Dear Yulia, Please can you help me? I think my life may be in danger and I don't know anyone else I trust to ask for help".'

'Yulia?'

'I'm guessing that if this is someone in fear of their life, they might write in such a way that if an abusive partner saw it they could say it was a translation from something they were working on. Or even a piece of fiction they'd been told to write.'

'And is it?' Ted asked him? 'A piece of fiction? To get your attention, for some other reason than being in danger?'

'I honestly don't know, but I couldn't live with myself if I did nothing and something terrible happened to her because of my inaction. Can you do something? Send an officer round to at least check? Please, Ted. I have her address, from the records.'

'There are all sorts of ethical pitfalls if I wade in and we've got this wrong. Not least the question of you giving out students' confidential information if this is nothing but a piece of creative writing.'

'But she was one of the ones I already had some worries about. She always looks so nervous. And she always wears very long sleeves, pulled right down over part of her hand.'

'There are all sorts of cultural reasons why that might be perfectly normal.'

'But I have seen bruising to her wrists before, when a sleeve slipped back as she was handing some work in. Please, Ted, can you at least get someone to go and check it out? Please? I'll take the consequences if I give you her address and it's all a false alarm.'

'All right, I'll see what I can do. Because you're right. If this is genuine and I do nothing, that makes me culpable for anything which might happen which I could possibly have prevented, and that wouldn't be an easy thing to live with.'

Chapter Nine

She tried not to let her face betray her but she kept smiling to herself with a rare optimism, now she'd handed over the letter. Her teacher would know what to do about it, she felt sure. He must know. She was counting on him.

He was very clever; she knew that already. It showed in the way he carefully didn't react at all when he realised she'd handed him two sheets of paper when everyone else before her had given him one.

She'd felt those incredible blue eyes scan her face for a moment. Then he somehow seemed to know not to react, so he simply thanked her as he had the others.

'Thank you, Anna.'

On the bus on the way home she felt happier than she had for some time. More optimistic and relaxed now she felt she had finally shown some initiative and tried to do something to change her situation.

She was not stupid enough to think it meant the end of all her troubles. She was painfully aware of how it could all backfire on her if her teacher said the wrong thing to the wrong person. She pushed thoughts of what the possible consequences could be right to the back of her mind.

But she had finally done something. For once she had stopped being a doormat and putting up with everything he did to her without so much as trying to do something about it.

If she got nothing more out of it than finding out what her true rights were as his wife, that would be something, at least.

Usually, on the bus, she sat with her head down, not looking at anyone, eyes studying the bag in her lap which she clung to as if her life depended on it. She'd never spoken to anyone, other than for the essentials. It was almost always the same driver on that route, but she'd never so much as found the courage to look at him, never mind to speak.

This time, she felt brave enough, as she stood up and moved to the door for her stop, to say a 'Thank you. Good night,'

'You're all right, love. Mind how you go now. See you next week.'

* * *

'There is no one currently available to deal with your request. Please leave a message which we will continue to ignore for as long as possible, along with all the others.'

Inspector Kevin Turner didn't so much look up at Ted as he made his ironic comment, wrestling as he was with a pile of admin which seemed to occupy more and more of his time of late.

Undeterred, Ted pulled out a spare chair and sat down opposite him as he said, 'One of these days you'll get it wrong and it will be the Ice Queen on the other side of your desk and not me, which might leave you with a bit of explaining to do, since she's not known for her sense of humour.'

Kevin looked up at that as he retorted, 'Well, unless she's suddenly started borrowing your aftershave, I knew it was you. Is that the only one you have?

'But seriously, Ted, if you've come cadging for more officers for your triple murder, even for that I've none left to offer you. And you surely know I'd give you everyone available for something as bad as that.

'Are you any nearer nailing the bastard who did it?'

'Not anything like near enough yet, but not for want of trying, from all angles. And for our latest line of enquiry, I only need one more of your officers. A PC or a PCSO, whichever you can spare.

'We've got a new DC, Alison O'Malley, who started today, and she had a good idea. One none of us had thought of exploring up to now, and it's certainly one worth following up.

'We're hampered a bit by not knowing what, if any, particular religious sect we're dealing with, and it might possibly be helpful to know.

'Ali suggested she could go round the local schools, find out which children have been withdrawn from compulsory RE and see if there's any mention of an alternative religion or cult they belong to. If it is anything official, it's worth looking into. It was my idea to have a Uniform presence as that might possibly have more of an impact, visually, on teachers and pupils alike.'

Kevin was looking at him sceptically.

'Is anyone really likely to tell us that? Whoever we send to ask? Surely if it's some weird secretive sect, it will be drummed into the children not to talk about it to anyone? And if that's the case, might the sight of a uniform make them less likely to say anything rather than more?

'Aren't most of these closed religions a bit secretive? Not open to sharing anything with outsiders? Bearing in mind that my knowledge of such things is based entirely on reruns of that old Harrison Ford film set in an Amish community, and I assume that's not what we're talking about here. Do they still go round with a horse and carriage? We'd probably have noticed if they did that round here. If we even have any in this country.'

'My thinking was more for the school itself. Teachers and headteachers might possibly be more forthcoming with a Uniform officer present, although that's just a hunch. I know they'd face the usual ethical dilemma over personal information, but in circumstances as bad as these they might unbend a bit, at least. Especially if we hinted at being prepared to get warrants for their records, if that became necessary. '

Kevin sighed. In an ideal world, he'd have enough officers at his disposal that lending just one to Serious Crime would make no difference to his staffing levels. But he was far from being in an ideal situation. He was constantly scratching around to deploy officers as best he could, and constantly being told he couldn't have any more in the current financial climate.

'All right, if it will help you on this one, I'll find you one officer to go round the schools with one of yours, but that's your lot.'

'Aah.'

Classic Ted stalling sound. Kevin knew him well enough to know by now that meant he hadn't yet put away his begging bowl.

'Seriously, Ted, that's it and you're lucky to get the one. I'll have to do some shuffling about to make even that happen, and it leaves us stretched to the limit. Again.'

'I really do need another one, I'm afraid, Kev, for

something else. And this is something of a special request. A fairly urgent one. I need a female officer who speaks either Polish or Russian, because it's a potentially serious domestic abuse case.'

Kevin lifted his face towards the ceiling, sighed and rolled his eyes.

'Well, you should have asked for that first, Ted. Stockport nick is full of fluent Russian-speaking female officers. How many would you like?'

Then he looked directly at Ted once more as he asked, 'Are you being serious or is this some strange sort of a wind-up? I do have a couple of officers with some Polish, at least, but no one I know of with any Russian. Are you sure this is something urgent? Would it not be easier to bring in a civilian interpreter? At least that way it would come off your budget, not mine. Especially if it comes to nothing.'

'I'm taking a massive gamble as it is so it would help me a lot if we could keep it in-house for now.'

'At least tell me what it's all about and why you can't simply send your own officers.'

Ted gave him the broad outline of what the letter Trev had showed him had said, without mentioning where he'd seen it nor in what connection. Kevin was no fool, though. He was a good, astute officer, as capable as anyone of making four from two twos. But he could also understand Ted's reticence to divulge the source, in the probable circumstances.

'And you think it's credible, do you, this letter?' Kevin asked. 'You've seen it yourself? Do you have a copy?'

'I've got one for you, to put on file. Like I said, it's in Russian, but I've had a translation made, and not by Google, a copy of which you can also have. It specifically mentions a possible threat to life, which is why I don't think I can afford to ignore it. Justin.'

Kevin was used to Ted's verbal shorthand by now. Justin. Just in case. Covering his back. Thinking of the possible consequences if he took no action in response to such a letter and if it later turned out to have been a genuine and prophetic cry for help which went unanswered.

If there was a violent death, and if any whisper of the plea for help to prevent it being ignored got out to the public via the media, it would be catastrophic for already delicate relations between police and public.

'So, assuming you're sure this isn't some kind of fantasy, fiction, creative writing, something like that, do you really think it's a good idea to send an officer in Uniform to go knocking on the door of a potential domestic abuse victim? What if the alleged abuser is at home, or has spy cameras or anything? Would we not, in fact, be potentially signing their death warrant rather than helping them?'

'Ah, but I have a cunning plan,' Ted told him. 'At least I hope it's cunning enough. We send two officers, one of mine, one of yours, armed with a sheaf of suitable pamphlets. Neighbourhood Watch, Remember to Lock Your Car, Witness Appeal, anything you currently have lying about gathering dust but still looking official.

'Our respective officers visit every single house in the road together ...'

Seeing Kevin's horrified expression, he went on quickly, 'Don't worry, it's not a long road, not too many houses, so it won't take all that long. They knock on every door, with some plausible story about preventive policing, hand out the leaflets, and give householders a card with a suitable direct contact phone number.

'So if the writer of the letter is at home and will answer the door, they will at least have a card with a phone number to call for help, and a hopefully convincing reason for the visit.

'I know it's a very long shot, but surely it's got to be better than doing nothing then having another murder case on our hands because the domestic abuse ends in a death – a possibly preventable one – when we've already got one big as yet unsolved triple killing on our hands?'

Kevin gave a weary sigh as he said, 'I suppose so. All right, you can have Barbara Kowalski. She's a fluent Polish speaker and a good, experienced officer. I'll let you know when I can free her up, and yes, I know you want her soonish. Which one of yours will she be working with?'

'Maurice Brown,' Ted told him without hesitation. 'If someone won't talk to Maurice in Daddy Hen mode, they're not likely to talk to anyone. But at least we'll have given it our very best effort to prevent a violent crime.'

* * *

DC Maurice Brown and PC Barbara Kowalski were proving to be the ideal team to gain the public's trust as they went door-to-door with their crime prevention leaflets.

Despite his bulky build, people instinctively trusted Maurice. Saw no threat in him, just a kindly, caring person. They were constantly being invited in for a cup of tea and a biscuit which Maurice, reluctantly, kept refusing, knowing they weren't supposed to drag their task out any more than was essential to find out what was going on in their target household. Assuming that he could work up enough charm to be allowed entry there, or even get the occupant to open the door so he could try to assess the situation.

'Looks like it's this one,' Barbara told him as they reached a neat semi-detached house towards the end of the short road. 'Let's hope someone opens the door to us, at least. Paint on your friendliest smile, Maurice.'

Maurice stood aside to let her go first up to the front door and ring the bell. They exchanged a glance as they saw the set-up. Doorbell CCTV. Anyone inside the house could be watching them. That was why the DCI had wanted an officer in uniform to accompany Maurice, so it would be obvious at a glance the visit was from the police.

It also meant anything they said could be sent remotely to a smartphone belonging to the owner. And they might find themselves talking to whoever that might be, and not to the occupant of the house.

There was no immediate response. No voice over the intercom, no sound of the door being opened. Yet both officers formed the distinct impression that there was someone behind the door, watching them without wanting to show themselves.

They exchanged a glance then Maurice knocked on the door with his hand, rather than using the bell again, as he said, 'Hello, it's the local police. Nothing to worry about. Just a routine visit to give you some crime prevention leaflets. We're visiting all the houses in the road. Have you got five minutes to talk to us, please?

'I'm Detective Constable Maurice Brown, this is Police Constable Barbara Kowalski. I'll show you my warrant card, over the camera. If you want to check, you can phone the police station in Stockport and ask about us and the reason for our visit.'

No response, but still the strong impression that there was

someone behind the door.

She was there. Her whole body shaking with a deluge of different emotions. Surprise and elation that something had happened so quickly.

Panic about what the consequences might be if they didn't believe her story.

Terror at the thought that whatever the outcome, her husband would know about their visit because she had no knowledge of how to wipe the evidence which was being filmed.

She had no idea of what she thought might happen after her 'Dear Yulia' letter. Two police officers turning up on her doorstep the very next day, one in uniform, had never even occurred to her as a possible outcome.

'Can you at least open the door to show us that you're all right, please? I promise we'll go away if you don't want to talk to us. But now we're here, I think there's someone behind this door so it's my duty to try to find out why you won't open up to us. To two clearly identified police officers.'

Maurice was patience personified in any such situation. Barbara knew him well but was still looking at him admiringly for his efforts. She felt sure if she had been the one behind the door, no matter how frightened, she would have opened up to him.

'I'm concerned now that you might perhaps be injured in some way and unable to open the door so I need to satisfy myself that you're safe and unharmed. I'm also worried that you might perhaps be a young child alone in a house.

'If you don't want to open up, can you please indicate by whatever method you can that you are in fact all right. If not I think I'm going have to call someone to help us gain entry to your property to check on you.'

A quiet, wavering voice spoke up at last. It was the voice of an adult, which removed one of Maurice's concerns.

'I sorry. I not understand well English. All is good.'

'What language do you speak?'

'Polski. Polish.'

Barbara Kowalski took over now, speaking quietly and calmly to the woman in that language.

'Hello, I'm Barbara. As my colleague said, this is simply a routine visit to give you some leaflets about crime prevention. Can you please open the door then we can see that you are all right. Then I promise we'll go and leave you alone if that's what you want us to do.'

There was another long pause then, slowly, the door opened a crack and a thin face with a scared and worried expression peered out at them.

'I am Anna Wójcik. Everything is all right, thank you. I am all right. I was just a bit worried to see police officers outside the door. But everything is all right. Thank you.'

Maurice was studying her face and her body language – what he could see of it – not believing a word of her assurances which Barbara was translating for him, but aware of the sensitivities around the situation. The wrong word or action by either of the two officers at this point could destroy any hope of giving the help and support he was now convinced that the young woman needed.

He spoke and let Barbara simultaneously translate his words.

'Here are the leaflets we wanted to give you. There have been some burglaries and car thefts in the area so we're asking everyone to keep an eye out and report anything suspicious which they may see. And here's my card, with my direct number on it. You can call me on that at any time, for anything you think I can help you with.'

He was looking directly at her as he said that, willing her to understand that he was there for her. If she was in some kind of danger and didn't dare speak now, all she had to do was call him.

Walking away and leaving her like that, so clearly terrified, was one of the hardest things for Maurice to do. But he knew it was all he could do in the circumstances. Walk away and report his concerns to the boss.

As he got into the area car next to Barbara, who was driving, he said, 'If that lass is fine and not in any kind of trouble, then I'm the Pope.'

Chapter Ten

DC Alison O'Malley was starting to feel a little discouraged after visiting the third school and getting nothing to show for her best persuasive efforts.

She wasn't naïve enough to think every school was going to tell her everything she wanted to know immediately, but a part of her wanted some small crumb of a lead to take back to the boss to show she merited her place on the team. This triple murder was a particularly complex one for her baptism of fire into Serious Crime.

The officer from Uniform who had been sent with her was young and keen but with no more experience of such a case than she had.

Jonathan 'don't call me Jon' Kelly had a pleasant manner about him, polite and smiling, but even that hadn't succeeded in tearing down barriers to get them the information they needed. He'd started out as enthusiastic and optimistic as she had, telling her it was a good idea of hers and well worth the effort by both of them.

He'd even set great store by the old superstition of third time lucky. But his optimism was now clearly beginning to desert him.

'I can understand the need for some things to be kept confidential in schools, but if we have to wait for approval from school governors for every one, we're going to get nowhere fast,' he told her, his expression glum, as they parked the car at the next school for another attempt.

This time they were at least shown straight to the headteacher's office, without having to wait as they had elsewhere. Ali wondered if it meant that this head had received a tip-off from one of the others that the police were on their way, and what it was about. In which case, this was probably going to be their shortest visit yet, with still nothing to show for their efforts.

The woman who rose from her desk to greet them was at least smiling and looked welcoming. She also looked young to be head of a largish school, although Ali had learned never to judge by appearances.

'Linda Ranken. I'm the head here. Do please take a seat and tell me what I can do for you, officers.'

Her opener, after Ali had introduced both of them and shown her warrant card, was at least encouraging. At one school they hadn't even got as far as being offered a seat.

'Thank you, Ms Ranken,' Ali began, scanning the woman's hand for a possible clue to marital status and not seeing anything.

'Do please call me Linda. Unless you've come to arrest me,' she added with a laugh.

'Hopefully not, although we know already that you may not be in a position to answer our questions immediately, without, perhaps, reference to your governing body.

'It's a bit of a delicate topic. We're currently investigating a serious crime which we believe might involve a religious movement, sect, cult, or something along those lines, of which we're not yet aware.

'I appreciate you're constrained by issues of confidentiality, but I wondered if there was anything – anything at all – which you've come across which might at least point us in the right direction, please? Perhaps through pupils who have asked to be excused from RE studies?'

'If you're asking me as headteacher of this school, I'm afraid you're right. I couldn't comment in that role without seeking authority from higher up, which may take time.

'However, I'm also a mother, with a daughter at this school, and we all know how mums like to gossip outside the school gates.

'I'm due a cup of coffee and something sticky, which I usually take at my desk. If you would indulge a seemingly bizarre request, there's a pretty decent place five minutes up the road – you might well know it – for such a thing. Could we meet there, very shortly?

'I know it sounds ridiculous, but I feel I could talk more easily and with a clear conscience there than here. Is that all right?'

Ali and Jonathan exchanged a look. Both had received some strange requests in the past when trying to interview people. It would mean information which couldn't be on the record at this stage. But Ali in particular wanted to go back with something – anything – by way of a lead on this, as it had, after all, been her idea.

'All right, and thank you. We'll see you there shortly. And we are in an unmarked car, which might help, so PC Kelly could simply be having a break.'

'Or he could, perhaps, even take his coffee and cake to eat in the car,' the headteacher suggested. 'No offence, PC Kelly, but I would simply feel more comfortable with no chance of anyone knowing that I'd been talking to the police.'

* * *

'Linda Ranken was the only head who would talk to us at all without authority from the governors, and even then it was all a bit cloak and dagger, boss. PC Kelly had to sit in the car round the corner and out of sight, while I spoke to her in the café, strictly off the record. I thought even that might be better than nothing, which is what we have if we discount what she told me,' Alison O'Malley told the DCI when she got back from doing the rounds of the schools.

'I think you did the right thing, Ali. Even if it's simply hearsay, it's more information than we had before you went out. Did you consider her to be credible?'

'I did, boss, yes, very much so. Apart from anything else, I couldn't see what she would possibly have to gain by inventing something like this. I know some people make up things to say to the police. Effectively coming up with a pack of lies to make themselves feel important; but that's not how she struck me.

'She's quite young to be a head of a school like hers. Because I did check her out. She was brought in to sort out a failing school after a very bad Ofsted report. Bad enough for the previous head to jump before they were pushed. And things have gone from strength to strength there under her leadership. So much so that the school was taken out of special measures after just one term after she'd taken over.'

Ted knew that all sorts of people could turn out to be not as they appeared. But if this teacher had convinced the official government standards monitor that hers was the right steadying hand on the school's tiller, he was inclined to at least consider that what she'd told the officers was worth listening to, if nothing more.

'There are two specific children in the school who she mentioned, a brother and sister, who've been taken out of RE lessons on the grounds of incompatibility with their own family religion. And family seems to be very much the keyword.

'She said it's generally considered too much of a minefield to ask for much detail as to why there is a request to withdraw a child from RE. It can be perceived as too intrusive, so a lot of schools simply follow the line of least resistance. But occasionally, cultural issues, different ways of life, can come up spontaneously when teaching other subjects, which is what happened in this particular place. It's potentially relevant to us as the children live not far from where our murders happened.'

Ted had brewed up for her when she'd come into his office, so she paused for a quick swallow of the tea he'd made for her. It was a pleasant novelty. Where she'd been stationed before, few of the male officers would ever voluntarily make her a brew, and she'd never had a senior officer make her one before. Caveman rules still applied in some places, despite all the talk of equality within the service.

'Linda told us that the girl, who's very young and quiet, never says anything at all unless asked a direct question. Even then, she can struggle to answer, and it appears to be more than shyness. Linda said it's as if she's not used to being allowed to voice an opinion on anything. She also always wears a headscarf, with her hair covered, although they are definitely not from a Hindu, Muslim or Sikh background, for instance.

'The brother, on the other hand, is not backward in coming forward, as she put it. Assertive, sure of himself.

They've also had to correct him a few times when he talks across any girls who are speaking, as if he thinks he has the right to do that. It makes the school think that may possibly be a part of his culture.'

Ted had been listening in silence, impressed with the information she'd obtained and how she was presenting it, but he interrupted her quietly at that point.

'I think we need to be a bit careful of assuming the boy's attitude is in any way to do with any religious factor. I'm sure we both know all too well that there are still too many serving police officers, for instance, who show misogynistic tendencies, sometimes quite openly. As well as things like racism, homophobia, and so on.'

He was thinking back to his own early days in the service, and some of the comments and reactions he'd encountered as a short, skinny, gay policeman called Darling.

'Sorry, boss, noted for future reference. Anyway, in short, the little girl hardly ever speaks, the boy does, although not much about their religion. He hasn't given it a name, but he has said they don't have a church, mosque, temple, or any other the usual sort of buildings associated with religions.

'He says they hold gatherings in each others' homes, although he wasn't clear on what the exact term should be in English. They hold hands in a circle, anyone can speak and say whatever they like, as long as they don't interrupt one another. Sometimes they might sing something, but not like hymns in a church, and again he lacked the right vocabulary.'

'The going to each others' houses and sitting in a circle like that could be quite benign. Don't Quakers worship like that? I do know of a Quaker officer within GMP so I can give you his contact details to ask him. I don't somehow see anything as violent as this being related to Quakers, but we do need to check out each and every lead.

'And as for this boy, he does seem to have said a lot, if it really is a secretive sect of some sort. That seems out of keeping somehow.'

'Oh, this has all come from different snippets over some lengthy time. Because the little girl is so very quiet, almost cowed, the teaching staff have been keeping a careful eye on both of them, from a welfare point of view, and noting any information at all in case it helps.

'One thing which might be relevant to us is there seems to be one central male figure who is always there for these gatherings. And the no interrupting rule applies rigidly to him. Once he speaks, everyone else must be quiet instantly and listen, apparently, no matter how important what they were saying might be.

'Again, the boy wasn't sure of the right terminology in English but says the person is always called Uncle, by everyone, and he is their leader.

'Boss, might that possibly be the so-called shaman, and if he does hold such power over them, could it be the case that he not only remained present during the killings but may perhaps even have instigated them? Or possibly carried them out himself. So should that line of questioning now be put to him, if we can identify him?

* * *

'Boss, to sum up, that young lass says she's fine but both Barbara and I agreed that she doesn't look it. She seemed terrified. And very surprised to see us on her doorstep.'

'That might, of course, suggest that what she wrote was

never intended to be taken seriously. A piece of creative writing. Was there any sign of physical violence?'

'She had a split lip which was healing, but nothing else that we could see. We didn't get to see much of her, though. But she did look scared. Really scared.'

'But she spoke to you? Once she'd opened the door? She didn't refuse to talk to you?'

'She said her English was bad but she talked a bit to Barbara. She kept saying everything was fine, but neither of us believed her. There's CCTV on the door, so she knew we were the police. She could see Barbara was in uniform, and I showed her my warrant card.'

'That might be part of the problem, though,' Ted told him. 'I seem to recall reading somewhere that the Polish police haven't always had a glowing reputation. Allegations of brutality, heavy-handed tactics, that sort of thing. Certainly in the recent past. Like too many police services recently, including in this country. Or maybe she's worried about her status here? Is she here legally, do we know?

'And I take it you've checked if there have been any incidents at the address? Even call-outs where there was no evidence so they were NFA. And what do we know of the husband or whoever she lives with? Someone known to us? Any form?'

'No calls from that address at all, boss, so no visits until ours, official or unofficial.'

Maurice stopped and looked sheepish.

'I haven't checked on other occupants, boss. Not yet. It's clear Anna, the woman, wasn't going to talk to us any more so we couldn't ask her. And it gets a bit complicated with Polish names, Barbara told me. The spelling of the ending of a surname depends on whether it's for a man or a woman, but Anna gave her name as Wójcik, which is the same for either gender. So we don't yet know if that's her married name or not. It's also one of the most common Polish surnames. Fourth place, I think.'

Ted managed to stop himself just short of an eye roll. Maurice was a kind man, not a bad officer, although a plodder, but on the lazy side by nature so would often follow the line of least resistance when it came to the amount of work he did.

'Check, Maurice, please, and soon. You have the address. That should be all you need to find out if anyone other than Anna living there has any cautions or convictions for anything, or any other details on record about them, then we can work from there.

'You can also check in more detail if there's any history of such complaints for that address, perhaps something previously from a neighbour or someone, which might help us work out how credible that letter is.

'It's something you should have been all over from the start, and not something I should have to be reminding an officer with your length of service to do. Go and do it now, please, and report back.'

Ted's tone softened slightly as he said, 'Is there anything going on I should know about, Maurice? Trouble at home to explain your lapse? I hope you know you can always talk to me.'

Maurice could be a skiver, always doing the bare minimum he could get away with. He'd come perilously close to losing his place on the team once before when Ted was faced with having to axe one of them.

One thing Ted had never known him do was to lie himself out of trouble. He could so easily have come up with a tale of his young twin sons disrupting sleep. He didn't.

'Nothing at all boss, thanks for asking. And sorry, you're right, I should have checked. I will do now. I'm sure that young lass is in genuine need of help so I should have done a thorough job.'

He went back to his desk to run the checks, let the boss know there was nothing recorded about that address, then went to write up all his notes.

He was genuinely worried about Anna Wójcik, convinced there was something going on. So convinced that he couldn't stop himself.

Instead of going straight home to his partner as he always tried to do, he made a detour back to the same road he'd visited earlier with Barbara. Parked his car outside the same house as before.

There was no sign of a vehicle there. Everything was as it had been on his earlier visit. Hopefully he could speak to the young woman again and reassure her that she only had to phone him, at any time, and he would do whatever he could to protect her.

Remembering the CCTV, he avoided the doorbell and again knocked instead on the door.

'Anna? It's DC Maurice Brown again. I really want to check if you really are all right, pet. Can you open the door for me, please?'

Chapter Eleven

'Well, this is a nice and most unexpected surprise,' Trev told Ted when he found him waiting outside the dojo, in good time for their usual self-defence session for youngsters. 'I'd called in Terry as back-up, thinking you weren't coming but it's lovely to see you here.'

'I didn't know I was going to come myself until not long ago. I decided I needed a break before I did something drastic which might see my own team having to arrest me. But I'll just stay for the kids' club, then I better go and finish off the work I was intending to do before I left.'

They fell into step across the car park as Trev asked, 'As bad as that? Are you not making any progress on the murders?'

'Nothing to shout about. At least the new DC is showing some initiative and looking promising. Maurice, on the other hand, seems to have relapsed into plonker mode, with a side helping of doing the bare minimum so missing vital stuff. Well-meaning, but corner-cutting if I don't watch him like a hawk.'

Before Trev could reply, they were interrupted by a joyful shout of 'Ted!' and the sound of running feet behind them.

They stopped in unison and turned to see Ted's number one fan, young Philip, known as Flip, racing towards them. He stopped with a parade ground stamp which would have impressed even ex-Military Police DI Oscar Smith, then lifted his chin, and snapped a proud salute to his hero.

'Very nice, Cadet Atkinson, at ease,' Ted told him indulgently.

'We've been doin' drill in Cadets. It's great! Was that all right?'

Flip's adoptive mother had caught up with him and was smiling apologetically at Ted and Trev.

'I'm sorry about that, inspector. Philip, you need to go in and get yourself changed ready for your session, and let Trevor and Mr Darling do the same thing.'

Trev was looking fondly at Ted as they made their own way into the building, heading for the changing rooms.

'No matter how crap a day you're having, that boy can always put a soppy smile back on your face. He really does worship the ground you walk on. And speaking of the therapeutic effect of young things, Rhian phoned me to ask if she can visit this weekend. It's genuinely an exeat, she assures me.'

He left a pregnant pause before he added, 'With her girlfriend.'

Ted stopped walking and turned to face him.

'Girlfriend? Is this your sister being serious now, or more experimenting? And are we back to Rhian? Will she be Eirian again by the weekend? Or Siobhan? Or something entirely different?'

'Who knows, with teenage things. It could be anything,' Trev laughed.

'What will we do about sleeping arrangements? There's only the double bed in the spare room. Put one of them on the sofa?'

Trev shook his head in mock despair.

'You can be so stuffy sometimes, Mr Policeman. Let

them sleep together. Where's the harm? It's probably their only chance to do so and let's face it, neither of them is going to risk pregnancy. And if it is a passing phase, or some rebellious statement to provoke, us being totally cool about it should make them think twice.

'Leave me the car for the weekend if you can – they're coming up Friday evening – and I'll look after them and keep them out from under your feet, for the rare occasions you might appear at home. Taking two young, newly out lesbians shopping and dining is the stuff of any gay man's dreams.'

* * *

Ted let Alison O'Malley present her own findings from the school visits at the following day's morning briefing. It was another chance to see how she acquitted herself. So far he was impressed by her. She seemed like a good fit for the team.

'So the question is, do we already have this Uncle person in custody, or did he leave the scene? Sarge?'

She looked at Mike Hallam for a possible answer.

'Impossible to tell at the moment. First responders found the back door wide open, as was the garden gate, so there's a possibility, at least, that some people may have left the scene before the emergency services arrived.

'Now we have the word uncle to go on, which is something new, I can at least pass that to all the interviewing officers for them to mention in questioning.'

'It might be more a hindrance than a help, perhaps,' Jezza put in. 'Don't a lot of families have friends who might always be called uncle, especially by the children, and who might not be a relative at all? And again, that might be a cultural thing. An honorary title for someone held in esteem within a circle.'

'Steve, that's one for you, please. See if you can find any references to such a thing anywhere. Because I agree, Jezza. That is a distinct possibility. And yes, I know your Tommy could do it for us but we need it soonish, and I presume he's not allowed to be using his phone all the time when he's at school'

'Officially, he's not, no. But good luck to anyone who tries to separate Tom from his mobile when he's determined to do some research. It's not pretty, and it seldom ends well.'

'Boss, we've also had the results through from the professor on the chance of any potential DNA from the killer having been left on any of the bodies,' Mike Hallam told him.

'She said that from the way in which the babies were killed, it's highly likely that their killer would have had some blood splatter on themselves. We've assumed up to now that the father was the killer, but we've no firm evidence to confirm that yet.

'We know the mother was strangled by strong bare hands. There were some faint traces of blood on the woman's clothing. At the neck, where you could quite reasonably expect wrists to be positioned whilst hands were round her throat, doing away with her.

'The professor warns it's only faint, and so far what she has managed to extract has not been matched to anything on record. But with rare optimism, for her, she has said there are still some enhancement techniques which might yield a bit more for us to go on. It might, of course, be blood from the babies, but it needs checking.

'We've of course tested everyone we currently have in

custody but are still waiting on results.

'All signs so far would suggest that the same person killed all three victims and could therefore have transferred some of their own traces – hair, sweat, that sort of thing, to the mother during that killing.'

'Thanks, Mike. And how are the interviews going, with our suspects? It's getting time critical, as far as holding them goes. We've nothing in the way of solid evidence to show any of those we have is the killer. Especially when we consider that open back door, and the mysterious, possibly missing person known as "Uncle".

'I can keep haggling about a potential flight risk, if we bail any of them, but I can't keep that up forever, unless we apply to confiscate passports, which might be a tricky one. So let's crack on hard, please. Anything and everything you can find to justify extending custody, at least for the principal suspects. Especially the father, if he's the killer.'

Alison O'Malley was impressed. Not only a senior officer who didn't consider himself too grand to brew up for his team members, but who included plenty of pleases and encouragement in his briefings. That was certainly a novelty to her, compared to where she'd been before.

'Meanwhile, so you're all in the picture, I received information about a possible domestic abuse case with the potential to develop into a serious assault or perhaps even a fatality.

'I judged the potential risk sufficient to send officers round to the house, initially, on the excuse of leafleting the whole road for crime prevention, which they did. I sent Maurice, with PC Kowalski – Barbara – whom most of you will know. That was based on being told that the possible victim is a Polish speaker with not very good English.

'I know it's not something which usually comes under our remit, but I thought it was at least worth looking into. Maurice, tell us your findings, please.'

'The person who opened up to us, eventually, although they weren't keen to do so, was a young woman, around mid-twenties. Her English is certainly not very good. Without Barbara translating, I don't think we'd have got anywhere.

'There's doorbell CCTV so she could clearly see who we were. She looked scared, but that might be natural. She might not know what the police are like here. She insisted she was fine, not in any danger. The alert came from something she'd written and passed on to someone who thought it worth reporting to us. But she stuck to her story that she wasn't in any immediate danger.

'She did have a split lip, which was healing, but no other visible signs of abuse.'

'Even a split lip is not necessarily a sign of abuse in itself,' Jezza put in. 'When Tom is in one of his most difficult moods over something – frequently not wanting to get in the bath – he's like a madly spinning windmill, with arms going in all directions. I thought he'd broken Nathan's nose one time because he managed to whack him so hard, although he didn't mean him any harm. He never does. He's knows any sort of violence is unacceptable.'

'We left her with a load of crime prevention leaflets and I gave her a card with my direct number on it, in case it was a genuine cry for help. My gut feeling tells me it was.'

'We've done as much as we can for now, if she's denying there's a problem,' Ted put in. 'You checked and found nothing reported from that property. I know neighbours often prefer to stay out of any domestic incidents but unless and until she contacts us again and will agree to talk, I think that's as much as we can do for now.

'That means no one goes there again for now, without a very valid reason, and without running that reason past me for approval first of all. Is that clear, everyone? Maurice? You in particular. That means stay away. We've tried, the potential victim says they're fine, so we have to leave it at that for now. Clear, Maurice?'

'Clear, boss.'

Jezza, sitting close to her best friend as she often did, was studying him, hard, while the boss was marking his card. She knew him well by now. Knew he was a rubbish liar, for one thing. She could tell from his body language that he had no intention of letting the matter drop whilst he thought a defenceless young woman's life might be in danger.

She would make it her personal mission to keep an eye on him; to stop the big soppy idiot she knew him to be from getting himself into serious trouble.

'So let's concentrate on our triple murder. There's plenty there to keep us all busy, and we badly need a result on it, soon as.

'Thank you, everyone.'

* * *

She'd known the consequences would be bad. Very bad.

Even in her wildest fears she couldn't have imagined just how bad. For the first time in her marriage to him, she actually believed he was going to kill her.

She'd never imagined for a minute that police officers would come to the house in response to her letter. Even assuming her teacher passed it on to someone who could make such things happen.

She'd somehow thought that nothing would happen at all before next week's evening class, when perhaps her teacher would tell her that he'd passed on her message to someone in authority but they'd said there was nothing they could do to help her. It was a domestic incident, so it was up to her to sort out her marital problems herself, or find someone in her own family or community to do it for her.

At her most optimistic, she hadn't imagined anything would happen at all until then, and perhaps it would be just someone coming to the centre to ask her a few questions, then tell her there was nothing they could do.

She'd panicked completely when she'd seen the two officers on the doorstep. That was not meant to happen. Not with the doorbell video he'd installed so he could spy constantly on anyone who came to the house, convinced she was seeing other men when he wasn't there. Eaten up by jealous rage, furious at her continued seeming inability to give him the child he so badly wanted. The baby he seemed convinced would put their marriage onto a more normal footing.

At least she knew that he was currently working somewhere he wouldn't be able to have his phone on at all during the day, so there was no danger of him seeing anything the camera might have sent. That meant he couldn't have heard what the police had said to her.

He wouldn't hear it until he switched his phone back on. Then he would see and hear everything, because she didn't know how to delete anything.

At least she had the leaflets the officers had given her. Crime prevention, they'd said. That would show him that it had been a simple routine visit, going to other houses in the road. Because she'd been so worried that her visit might have been the only one of all the houses in the road that she'd stood in the upstairs front bedroom window to watch them after they left. And they did go to other houses, as they'd said. That part at least was true. All the better for her.

He did speak to some of the neighbours sometimes, although she wasn't allowed to. He could at least go and check if they'd also had a visit, and what it had really been about.

She wasn't sure what time he'd be back from work, but she was already dreading how angry he might be, especially if he'd somehow been able to watch and listen to what the camera had recorded whilst he'd been out.

She knew he would immediately be suspicious that the police happened to send round a Polish-speaking officer. He would take that as evidence they had some prior knowledge of who lived in the household and what problems there might be. It would suggest she had somehow signalled to them for help, and that would be bad for her. Very bad.

She thought she'd better make a start on preparing the best meal she could make for him, in the hopes that might at least distract him. And she'd have a shower, put something nice on, and try her best to play the part of a loving wife pleased to see her husband back from work and preparing the best welcome she could.

This first thing he usually did when he walked through the door was to throw his car keys into the bowl which sat on a small hall table, just inside the door.

She decided to put the flyers the police officers had given her into that bowl, on full view. They would hopefully be the first things he saw, and she could even make something of a joke about the police visit. She'd try practising saying it in

English, so he wouldn't mock her attempts too much.

'Today was funny. Policeman and lady come to house ...' she began, speaking aloud, then made a sound of annoyance and corrected herself.

'Came to house for give papers. People steal cars. We must to take care.'

It didn't sound too bad. She tried it a few more times. Then her mouth dried totally and her heart began to pound as she heard a car screech into the driveway, squeal to a halt, then a slam as its door shut viciously.

She went to open the front door, trying to find a smile of welcome from somewhere to fix on her petrified face.

The door opened violently as she was still in front of it, knocking her backwards clean off her feet. He paused only to kick it shut with a loud noise.

Then he was on her in an instant, one hand hauling her up by the hair, the other slapping any part of her he could reach, despite her vainly trying to protect her face with her arms.

'What have I told you about speaking to strangers, you stupid bitch? And what were they doing her? Did you call them? Did you? Are you really stupid enough to think I'd know nothing about it?

'I may have had my phone off for part of the day, but now I've seen and heard everything and you're going to pay.'

He was shaking her now with a powerful hand. Like a terrier shaking a rat.

'You are so fucking going to pay.'

Chapter Twelve

The more Ted read up on the statements taken to date, the more he watched parts of the interviews, through interpreters, the more he became convinced they might not yet have got the real killer in custody.

From observing the husband and father, he wasn't at all sure the man had carried out the murders himself, but had been present and in all probability had played some role, if only as a passive observer.

There was a sort of resignation about him. An acceptance of something meant to be. Something he'd known would happen and had felt powerless to prevent. Possibly enough for a joint enterprise charge against him, depending on what CPS advised. If he'd been present and done nothing to prevent the killing of his wife and babies, he could still face serious charges which could lead to a long custodial sentence.

Ted was making himself notes as he read through everything. Points he needed clarifying before he could decide what things needed to be followed up. The first one was whether or not the man knew or could have known that his wife was expecting twins.

Jezza was still looking into superstitions surrounding the birth of twins which might be a factor in their particular case. If they could find something which strongly indicated the babies' fate would have been sealed as soon as both were born alive, it would be powerful evidence. Knowing what lay in wait for his newborn babies and doing nothing about it, even if he didn't physically carry out the killing himself, would be bound to weigh heavily against a father with any jury, if they could get the case as far as trial.

Any member of the public sitting as a juror would certainly be asking themselves why the man hadn't simply taken his wife to a place of safety to give birth. He could then have arranged safe adoption for one of the babies and reappeared with the other, claiming it had been the only child.

Even if his beliefs dictated the birth should be in public with whoever the elder, 'Uncle', was being present, it surely wouldn't have been that hard to invent a plausible excuse like the woman going unexpectedly into labour, before he could summon anyone else.

The man was showing little emotion when interviewed, as Ted had picked up from watching him. A sort of passive acceptance of his fate. A sense of the inevitability of it all. No doubt any defence counsel would simply claim his client was suffering from shock and grief and his detachment was merely his coping strategy.

Ted had been sufficiently impressed with the work of DC Alison O'Malley so far to send her out again, as well as anyone else he could spare, to see what else they could find out about 'Uncle'. His instincts were telling him that whoever he was, he needed interviewing, if only to eliminate him from their enquiries, if they could.

This time he'd sent Jezza with Alison, armed with the information she'd found out so far about superstitions involving the birth of twins. The two of them were planning on trying to visit as many different denominations of worship as they could find in the area they were investigating – churches, chapels, temples, synagogues and anything else they came across.

As ever, Jezza was on the ball regarding dress. She insisted both of them went with the means to cover their hair where needed. She didn't follow any particular religion herself but she knew better than to antagonise someone who might be able to give them information vital to their case by refusing to respect their traditions.

Jo Rodriguez hadn't found any specific details from his Catholic contacts, but Jezza and Ali were planning to ask around closer to where the incident had happened, so they might do better. Ted was also keen on seeing how the two of them would work together.

On her own admission, Jezza could be territorial about new females joining the team, although she had finished up becoming friends with Gina Shaw. Hopefully she would get on as well with Ali. There was no room for friction in the team at the best of times and certainly not with such a difficult and sensitive case to investigate.

'So do you know where we have to don our headscarves, or do we play it by ear?' Ali asked Jezza as they pulled up outside their first destination.

'I've researched online, of course, but I'm honestly not sure about all of them. I imagine if we get looked at as if we should be at home cooking and producing babies, we'll probably need to cover up.'

Ali laughed at that.

'My last boss was a bit of a religious nut. Heaven help anyone who made any kind of a crack about religion. In fact I wouldn't have dared say "religious nut" within his earshot. As far as he's concerned, he and his fellow worshippers are the sane ones. It's us heathens whose sanity is in question.

'So as well as your research assistant brother, do you have a significant other? This is not just me being nosy but testing the waters so I don't put my foot in it by saying anything inappropriate. In case your other half is also deeply religious.'

It was Jezza's turn to laugh.

'Not Nat, for sure. He was a high-flying financial trader. Made a big mistake, lost a fortune and finished up on the streets for a while. If he'd ever had any faith I think he would have lost it at that point. You? An "Other Half" at home?'

'Well, your story takes some beating, that's for sure. I have a nice, trouble-free man who's a builder so he can turn his hand to pretty much anything. I'm sure he might count as boring on some people's scales, but he's solid and dependable and at least he works sensible hours.

'My last one was a copper. A secretive and off-the-radar one. I never did know the half of what his job entailed. I tried to find out one time but came up against a brick wall so decided it would be sensible to give up. I thought I might be better off not knowing the full story.'

'Is that why you're no longer together?'

'No, not really. I thought I might be able to live with that, working for the same firm but not at the same extreme level. But he was obsessed with having kids. I mean totally obsessed. I've never wanted any and made no secret of the fact. But you know how some men can be. They seem to think you're just saying that and they can persuade you. So I ended it. It was a while ago and I did hear he's married someone else now.

'Right, so heads covered here, or not?'

'Definitely not. This is one of those happy-clappy groups

where pretty much anything goes. Whether or not they'll be able to tell us anything about any more sinister cults in the area remains to be seen.'

* * *

Sometimes, no amount of knocking on doors and speaking to no end of people brought any significant breakthrough. Occasionally, if the fates were feeling kind, one small snippet could set a chain in motion and produce the results they so badly needed.

DS Rob O'Connell had been out on the knock for so long his feet were starting to hurt and he was feeling dispirited. He was on his own for this, as were the other officers doing the same thing. Looking for witnesses had been deemed low risk. They weren't expecting any of the officers taking part would somehow come face to face with the mysterious 'Uncle'. That would only happen in bad crime fiction.

Certainly in response to his latest knock on a door, it was a somewhat harassed-looking woman, probably in her mid thirties, who opened the door to him.

'Detective Sergeant O'Connell, Greater Manchester Police. It's just routine enquiries; we're asking everyone, in connection with a recent serious incident,' he told her, holding up his warrant card.

Before he could answer, a boy of about ten appeared from an open doorway in the hallway, looking excited.

'You called them then, mum? You said you weren't going to.'

'I didn't call them, Ethan. I told you it was just gossip, what you told me. Not worth bothering anyone with.'

She turned back to Rob then, holding the door open a bit

wider and saying, 'Sorry, officer, do you want to come in and ask us whatever it is you want to. You'll have to put up with Ethan, though. He wants to be a policeman, he's off school for an inset day, so he might ask you a lot of questions.'

She led the way to a light and welcoming kitchen at the end of the hall and went straight to put the kettle on.

'Would you like a brew, if you've time? Tea? Coffee?'

Rob opted for coffee as she went on, 'Ethan told me he knows a lad at his school who has an uncle ...'

Her son interrupted her immediately.

'I didn't say he had an uncle. I said he knows someone everyone calls Uncle. You have to get information right, in witness statements and stuff.'

His mother glanced at Rob, rolling her eyes in a see what I have to put up with gesture, then busied herself making the coffee.

'You're right, Ethan. Accuracy is important,' Rob told him. 'Thank you. What can you tell me about this person known as Uncle? Why do you think it might be linked to what I'm here to ask about?'

'Kids at our school have all heard about a murder, because it's not all that far from our school, where it happened, and it's been on the telly. This lad, Zac, goes to, like, some sort of prayer meeting thing. His parents make him go, a couple of times a week. He doesn't want to. He's not really into that stuff but his whole family are. The bloke in charge is this "Uncle".

'He's not a priest or a vicar or anything like that. But he is sort of in charge. Zac says no one is allowed to speak if he's talking. Not for any reason. Anyway, Zac never usually talks about the group much. He says they're not allowed to. It's private. He talks to me a bit sometimes and he said no one's seen "Uncle" for about a week and no one knows why or where he's gone.'

His expression turned earnest as he looked hard at Rob, clearly wanting him to understand the importance of what he was saying.

'That means since the murders happened, doesn't it? No one's seen him since then. That's why I wanted my mum to tell the police about it. I know Zac won't say anything to anyone else, but he does talk to me, so I wondered if he thought I might say something for him. Like, that way, if anyone asks him if he said anything to the police, he could say no, and that would be true.'

'You did the right thing, Ethan, thank you.'

'Does that mean I should have contacted you straight away, like Ethan wanted me to?' his mother asked. 'I'm sorry about the delay, if so, especially if it might be something important.'

'No worries, we've got the lead now so we can follow up on it. So, Ethan, can you give me more details about this Zac? Full name, where he lives? Anything at all you can tell me. Don't worry, you're doing the right thing, and I won't mention you in connection to this. Not to Zac, at least, or anyone connected to him or to the group he attends.

'Would he talk to the police, though, if we approached him in the right way? We wouldn't, of course, tell him our source for this information ...'

Ethan interrupted him at that point, 'Oh, I think he wanted me to pass it on to someone, that's why I wanted mum to call you. He was really shocked about what had happened, with people he knows, but too scared to say anything himself. I don't know what he thought might happen to him, but if the group he goes to has done murder and stuff, that would frighten him, for sure.

'I think he thought if he told me and I told someone else, that wouldn't count as him telling anyone.'

'I really am so sorry, officer. Ethan, I should have listened to you and taken you seriously.'

'Really, don't worry about it, I'm here now. Did Zac tell you anything else about this Uncle person? Where they live? A description? Anything?

Ethan shook his head.

'He doesn't know where exactly he lives, just the area. None of them go to his house, he always goes to the others. But I got a description of him. I wrote it down in my notebook.'

He trotted off into another room and reappeared swiftly, clutching the book, then opened it and read what he'd written there. He was certainly into correct technology as he used PNC code for ethnicity. IC6 for Arab or North African. He also said the man was taller than average height. How accurate any of it was Rob had no way of knowing, but it was something, at least. A new potential lead when they were desperately in need of any such thing.

He thanked the boy for his help and told him, 'In a couple of years, when you're old enough, if your mum agrees, you should look at joining the Police Cadets, if you're serious about going into the service when you leave school. It can be a good place to start.'

* * *

Ted called the team together as usual for an update at the end of the day. Rob fed back what Ethan had told him, Jezza and Ali nodding in unison at what he was saying.

'We didn't get all that much from visiting other places of worship around the area, but the physical description, the ethnicity certainly, fits with what little we were told. Uncle is certainly known of in the area, although with little real detail,' Jezza told them.

'Most of the people we spoke to know very little about the cult with the Uncle figure. And cult was the word most of them used, not always with a pejorative sense behind it. More as a catch-all for something they know little about. All of them knew of its existence, mostly through hearsay, and again some of that came via children, from snippets mentioned at schools, so how much is correct remains to be seen.'

'At least now, with what Ethan has told Rob, we're gradually narrowing down where this Uncle might be based, assuming he's still in the area,' Ted told them all. 'So that's the target as of now, please. Find him, and bring him in for questioning.'

Jezza went over to Maurice's desk when everyone was starting to get their things together to leave.

'Now then, bonny lad, I want a few words with you before you disappear off home. So let's go round to the The Grapes and I'll buy you a beer.'

She was sharp enough not to miss the fleeting guilty look which crossed his face at her words. She could always read him like an open book and he knew it. It didn't stop him from sometimes trying to fob her off with a half-truth, or worse, when he thought it was in her best interests not to know something.

* * *

'Right, Maurice, it's just you and me now, so don't try and feed me any bullshit. I know you too well,' Jezza began as soon as they were sitting in a corner of the still quiet bar, with only a few of the regulars occupying their favourite seats.

'I know you're worried about this possible domestic abuse but you've been round and done what you could. If it's genuine, the alleged victim now has various ways of contacting us, including your direct number. You've done all you can, and if she's really genuine, she'll surely find a way to make contact somehow.

'Promise me you aren't going to go blundering in like the big soft lump you are. And swear to me that if you go anywhere within half a mile of her house again, for whatever reason, you'll take someone with you as a witness. Preferably someone with a body cam, or at least someone with their mobile on and filming.'

For a moment, Maurice shifted in his seat and looked uncomfortable at her words, so she pressed on, hammering the point home through genuine concern for Daddy Hen.

'I mean it, Maurice. You'd be leaving yourself open to all kinds of allegations. Not to mention running the risk of bumping into a violent husband who might beat the crap out of you, at the very least.

'Stay away.'

Chapter Thirteen

'Priority for today, and for as long as it takes, is to find this person known as Uncle. Still nothing showing up anywhere on the system, Steve?'

Ted asked the question at morning briefing more in hope than anticipation, knowing DC Ellis would have notified him immediately if he'd tracked down so much as a faint whiff of the person who was becoming their prime suspect, by default, if nothing else.

'Nothing so far, sir, and I'm running out of searches to try. As soon as any new intel comes up, no matter how vague, like the IC6 suggestion from DS O'Connell's interview, I've searched on it straight away but nothing's shown up so far.'

Steve was the only one of the team who used Rob's rank since he'd been promoted. To everyone else, he was still Rob. Steve always struggled with informality. It seemed to take him too far outside his narrow comfort zone.

'At some point we need to speak to the boy Zac, who Ethan mentioned, but in such a way there's no comeback on either Ethan, or on Zac for having said anything to someone outside the circle. In other words, we can't simply go straight round to Zac's home asking questions. We'll need to go in gently and visit other homes in the same road.'

'The other problem is Ethan didn't know Zac's exact address, although he knows roughly the area he lives in, and possibly the right street, which is not all that far from our scene of crime,' Rob put in.

'If you know what school Ethan and Zac go to, Rob, I can tell you if it's one I visited and therefore tell you how likely we would be to get an address out of the headteacher without a court order,' Ali told him.

'It would be exactly the bit of divine intervention we need if it turned out to be Linda Ranken, the one helpful headteacher we came across.'

'Failing that, we'll use the same tactic Maurice and Barbara used on the suspected domestic abuse case. If we can find out the rough area, we'll put some officers in going door-to-door with leaflets again. Any other directions we should be looking in?'

Virgil Tibbs spoke up, with his usual ironic humour.

'Because I is black, boss, I've tried some of the gospel congregations nearby. None of them seem to be aware of this small cult, whoever they are. But if, and it's a big if, its leader is possibly IC6, there's the possibility, at least, of a cultural divide. Most of the people I've spoken to today are IC3. It depends, of course, if Ethan is right about his IC numbers, although there's a big difference between three and six.'

'Ethan struck me as pretty switched on,' Rob replied. 'I could always visit him again and get him to describe people based on IC numbers, but I got the feeling he does his homework and is probably spot on with them. He's certainly very keen on joining up so he's mugging up on absolutely everything to do with policing.'

'Right, everyone, let's please focus on finding this Uncle. Make that our short-term priority, so we can at least rule him in or out as a suspect. For one thing, I would be very interested to get his DNA to test against what was found at the crime scene and particularly on the bodies.'

'And Rob, if you're working at all over the weekend, can you go round to see Ethan once more, please, and make absolutely sure he knows not to go off trying to be a detective and getting too close to a potentially dangerous suspect we know insufficient detail about for any kind of a risk assessment.

'Do you think it would be worthwhile to get him to come in with a parent and look at some faces to see what ethnicities he knows? Rather than you visiting? He's not seen the man, but the description he gave you from what Zac told him was quite detailed. He could be asked to select images which he felt matched closest to the description he was given. That exercise of itself might tell us whether or not he does use IC numbers correctly. Otherwise we risk going off in the wrong direction and potentially stirring up mistrust.

'Maurice, regarding your possible domestic abuse case, I'm assuming if you'd had a call from the woman you visited, or any further news, you would have reported back to me?'

'Nothing, boss. She hasn't phoned me, although I was really hoping that she would, because she looked so scared, poor lass. And yes, I'll let you know straight away if I do hear anything.'

Jezza's eyes were on Maurice as soon as the boss posed his question. She was still far from reassured by his body language, nor by what he said. He was hiding something, she felt sure.

'See that you do. If I'm tied up for some reason, speak to Mike or Rob, or phone Jo at Ashton and follow instructions. Don't whatever you do go round there on your own. You'd be putting yourself not just in a compromising situation but quite possibly a dangerous one, if the partner really is as violent as the alleged victim said in her letter.'

Ted was tidying up in his office, putting his things together to head home, when there was such a timid tap at his door he knew it could only be one person.

'Come in, Steve.'

'Sir, sorry to bother you ...' DC Ellis began timidly.

Ted wondered again, as he so often did, how Steve had got through selection, never mind training. Yet he knew he had done so with outstanding marks in everything. He had definitely grown in confidence since arresting his own bullying father, but he still seemed permanently worried about saying or doing the wrong thing. The scars of growing up in an abusive environment seemed never to heal completely.

'No bother, Steve, it's what I'm here for. What can I do for you?'

He didn't bother offering him a seat, knowing how that would make him more fidgety and nervous than ever.

'Sir, the more I look into the religious angle, the more I'm wondering if that's leading us off in the wrong direction, or at least in a misleading one. If it was an actual religion, even a small break-away cult of some sort, surely more people would know about it?'

'Is the distinction all that vital to enquiries, though?' Ted asked him, as ever playing devil's advocate.

'I think it might possibly be, sir.'

Steve had his slightly stubborn look on now. The look he got when he thought he was onto something. He frequently was, so he was always worth listening to.

'All right, give me your reasoning.'

'Well, sir, statistically speaking, interest in religion is on the decline in this country. More than fifty-five per cent of people polled don't believe in any form of deity. So as soon as we start asking them about religious groups, we probably risk losing their interest from the outset.'

'That's true enough. I'm one of them,' Ted told him. 'But does that advance us at all in our line of questioning?'

'I think it does, sir. I'm also in that percentage. Apart from research for work, if anyone asked me anything about local religious groups, I wouldn't have a clue and frankly wouldn't be interested in finding out. I suspect a lot of people would be like that.'

Ted had to smile at that.

'You're right, of course. I'd be the same. So what do you suggest?'

'We try to drop any leading words from questions posed when going door-to-door. We need a ball-park figure for how many people we're talking about in this group, whatever it is. Perhaps Rob could ask Ethan about that specifically, in case Zac mentioned it to him. Then we simply ask people about houses where they might have noticed groups arriving from time to time, on a regular basis.'

Steve had found his confidence and hit his stride now.

'We'd need to be very careful about vocabulary, though. Some seemingly anodyne words can be misleading. I think, for instance, that words like Friends and Meetings have special significance to some groups. Like Quakers, I believe, but I need to check. I can easily do some internet searches from which to produce something of a script, with sensitive words listed. I could do that this evening, at home, because I'm not on the rota for tomorrow and this might be important ...'

'Steve, this is very good work. Thank you. But now I've

heard what you've said, I think even I might be able to brief those who are on tomorrow about the likely pitfalls. Take yourself off home and do whatever it is you spend your leisure time doing normally.'

Steve gave him a definite grin as he said, 'That would be researching information on my computer, sir.'

* * *

Violent sexual assault cases always went up at the weekends, for so many reasons. The main one was often alcohol.

End of the working week for many. Time for a few drinks with friends and colleagues, winding down before the return to the daily grind of having to earn the money to be poured down throats on the next weekend. A few drinks could so easily become too many, often leading to domestic abuse behind closed doors.

Stranger rape, too, tended to be higher than on weekdays. So many unknowns mingling together in pubs and clubs.

Young people in particular were getting wise to the risks of drink-spiking, and spiking by injection. They at least tried to watch out for one another. Bar staff were being trained to help, too, with code words for anyone ordering drinks and wanting to signal they were in danger or thought they might be, without giving anything away to someone they might be with. WAVE training, Welfare And Vulnerability Engagement, for hospitality staff, was helping. But there was nothing solid in place for the increasing numbers of violent assaults in the home, where there was simply no chance of signalling to anyone, in a large number of cases.

Staff in Sexual Assault Centres saw all sorts of people coming through their doors, seeking immediate help soon after an attack. Women, children, men, all of them often the victims of unimaginable trauma and violence. So many of those working there had developed the ability to assess without judging. Rapidly sizing up what was in front of them whilst hurrying to give vitally needed assistance to anyone who came in. Because it was the sort of attack which could impact on a wide circle around the principal victim.

The woman who hurried towards the latest couple to come in grabbed for the nearest folded wheelchair because she could see at a glance that without the powerful arms of the man holding her upright, the battered and bloodied woman, trailing her feet and looking on the point of collapse, was clearly not going to make it any further without support. And she wanted that support to be completely neutral. Whoever the man was – husband, partner, sibling, helpful passer-by – she would always prefer to hear the victim's own account first.

'Help me, please. My wife's been attacked. Raped. In our own home. I've been working away and I've come home to find her like this. I brought her straight here, but she's been in this state for a few days now, poor love. Oh, and she doesn't speak much English, so she'll need me to translate for her.'

That was a red flag going up immediately. It could very well be a protective husband, trying his best to look after his wife. It might, on the other hand, be the attacker in person, wanting to be there to hear and to counter anything the victim might say.

The staff member spoke immediately to the woman who had now slumped into the wheelchair and was sobbing. That might have explained why some of the cuts and splits around her mouth were now weeping fresh blood. But there could also be an altogether different reason for that.

'Hello, my name's Suzanne. Can you tell me your name, please?'

Again it was the man who answered. Up close, she could see how powerfully built he looked. Someone who kept himself fit, by all appearances. Not overly tall but his bulk had made him look bigger on first impressions.

'It's Anna. My wife. Her name's Anna. She speaks Polish and some Russian, but her English isn't very good. That's why she needs me to stay with her, to translate for her, don't you, kochanie?'

'Don't worry, we have staff available who speak several languages,' she spoke slowly and clearly, scanning Anna's face to see if she was being understood.

'I'm sure I can easily find a Polish speaker quite quickly. Anna, the best thing now is if I take you somewhere safe and private. I'll find someone to speak to you, and your husband can wait here for you and have some coffee.

'Is that all right for you? Did you understand all right? Are you happy to come with me for now? I promise that you will make all the decisions now. We won't do anything you don't want to do. So are you happy to come with me?'

For the first time, the woman lifted her chin and made fleeting eye contact. Even setting aside the clear evidence on her face which spoke of a savage beating, there was emotional pain etched there too, together with raw terror. Whatever had happened to this woman, it was something she was unlikely to forget in her lifetime.

'She needs to be seen as soon as possible. Like I said, the rape happened some days ago so it's not going to be easy to find traces on her of who did this to her.'

So far it was the husband who was doing all the talking.

The woman had not said a thing.

She was so weak and her mouth so dry she wasn't even sure if she could speak. In the three days since the police visit he'd kept her securely imprisoned in the house. He had special locks on all the doors and windows, which he sometimes applied. Ones which could only be released with a specific key, of which he kept the only copies.

He'd removed almost all food from the house, leaving her only some already no longer fresh bread which quickly became hard and unpalatable, especially without even a bit of butter to spread on it. Nothing to drink, either, except water from the tap. It had left her feeling feeble, light-headed and utterly defeated.

'We need the police here, too. As soon as possible,' the man was speaking again. 'We want this reported as a serious crime, and we already know who the rapist is. He's a police officer. I've got footage of him from the doorbell CCTV coming to the house on a pretext, with a woman officer in uniform.

'That was clearly just a way of finding out what women were living in that area on their own, and which of them would be an easy target, because there's more footage of him coming back later in the day, on his own, and with absolutely no valid reason to do so.

'The attacker's name is Detective Constable Maurice Brown, based at Stockport.'

Chapter Fourteen

Ted had left his car with Trev on Friday, as promised, so he could go and pick up his sister, Siobhan Eirian, under whatever name she was going by the time she arrived, together with her girlfriend.

It was later than he'd planned when he finally finished for the day. Mike Hallam was just as late leaving so had been happy to drop the boss off on his way as he lived not far away.

Trev had promised to cook in the hopes that his partner would be back in time to eat with them, to meet their new house guest. Ted had at least phoned him with an update on when he hoped to be back.

Unusually, none of the cats came to greet him when he let himself into the house. Not even his number one fan Adam.

He could hear talking and some laughter from the living room so went in there first.

The two girls were sitting close together on the sofa, with the television on in the background. Trev was in the kitchen, with the door open so he could talk to them as he cooked. The lack of cats was explained by all seven of them being piled on top of the sofa occupants, with normally one-man-cat Adam curled up on the visitor's lap, purring away happily.

'Oh, hi Ted. This is my girlfriend, Faith, and this is my

brother-in-law, Ted. Like I told you, he's a copper, but not a bad one, if a bit boringly predictable.'

Ted had to smile at that. He decided not to embarrass her with the peck on the cheek with which he would normally greet her.

'Please excuse me for not getting up, Mr Darling, I don't want to disturb this cute little cat because he seems so comfortable.'

'Ted, please. It's nice to meet you.'

Even looking at her sitting down, Ted could see that Faith was well above average height and with the long, toned limbs of a dedicated athlete. He'd heard via Trev that she was not into horses to the same degree as Rhian but played basketball to high level as well as doing track and field events.

Ted excused himself and went through to the kitchen which was, inevitably, looking like a bomb site with Trev's culinary efforts, although the aromas suggested it would, as ever, be well worth the amount of washing up and tidying away Ted would need to do afterwards.

Trev paused to proffer his cheek for a kiss and to mouth a quiet, 'Well?'

Ted always spoke quietly. The girls wouldn't hear him above the television, even with the sound turned down.

'She seems very nice. Polite, certainly.'

Trev laughed.

'Ted, you are funny. She's an absolute stunner, and you comment on her manners. She is polite, though. I think she'll be good for Rhian. Despite my sister's brash outer layer, she's quite vulnerable under all the bravado. Especially after the bad experiences she's had with men. I think Faith might be exactly what she needs.

'You will try to get back in time to eat with us again tomorrow evening, won't you? I know it's difficult, with a big case, but I really think it's important we show we're supportive of Rhian and her choices. She hasn't told the Olds yet, and I know she's dreading it, after how they treated me. Pa might be all right, now he's mellowed a bit, but Her Ladyship will never change. She'll always be a malicious old bigot towards anything and anyone which falls outside her religious constraints.'

'I can't promise to be here, you know that. But I promise I'll try my very best, barring any developments on the current case, or anything else turning up in the meantime.'

* * *

'So Steve emailed me a list, late last night, of his suggestions of what words are best avoided in looking for where these gatherings, for want of a better word at the moment, are taking place, which I'll circulate,' Ted told the team at Saturday morning briefing.

'He suggested, and I agree, that we should avoid getting too hung up on religion as a factor. There may well be something else behind it all. Something we've not yet identified, so we need to cast a wider net in what we're looking for. We might possibly miss vital intelligence if we're not careful about the terminology we use.

'Rob, can Ethan come in today, with a parent? On the off chance that what he tells us might advance us. We're definitely at the stage of following up on everything we can. Please update everyone if and when there's anything new. But be aware that we need to protect the source of such information. Is Zac the same age as Ethan?'

'They're both ten, coming up eleven.'

'Right, so in this case more than ever it's vital we protect our sources of any information we get from them about our suspect. So far we've gone on the basis that some religious or other beliefs were behind the killing of this mother and her babies. But it's also possible that whoever this group is, they're simply people who would think nothing about removing anyone who spoke up about them.

'Three violent deaths is already too many. Let's not potentially put the lives of two young boys in danger as well.'

* * *

Trev and the two girls were in the kitchen when Ted finally got home on Saturday. Judging by the number of full bags from most of the best shops at Trev's favourite retail outlet which were cluttering up the hallway, a good time had been had by all.

Ted knew Rhian had a more than generous allowance from her parents, which she always referred to as conscience money, to make up for how little they saw of her.

From the sounds of happy chatter and frequent laughter coming from the kitchen, it sounded as if the day had been a resounding success.

The cats had been temporarily banished to the garden so no one risked falling over them. Trev, as ever, had a large glass of red wine in one hand as he cooked, but Ted noticed that both girls appeared to be drinking sparkling mineral water. He imagined Faith wouldn't drink much, if at all, if she took her sports seriously. She might hopefully be a good influence on Rhian, who had always liked to drink wine, even before she was legally allowed to in restaurants.

'Fantastic! You're back. Thanks for making the effort,' Trev told him, proffering a cheek for a kiss. From the sound of him, it was not his first glass of wine of the day, although hopefully he wouldn't have been drinking when out driving Ted's car.

Ted greeted the girls, who looked as if they'd enjoyed themselves, before asking what he could do to help with the meal preparation.

'We'll eat in the living room, then we can shut the hooligan cats out and have a bit of peace, so why not set the table for us? The meal won't be long now. And I hope you're going to turn your phone off, at least while we eat.'

'Sorry, can't do that. With a case this big and complex, I need to be on call. We'll just have to cross our fingers and hope for a quiet night.'

He actually made it to halfway through the dessert before his phone rang. The screen told him it was Kevin Turner calling him. With any luck, it would be nothing all that urgent. Something which could at least wait until he was back in the office the following day.

He excused himself and went out into the hall to answer the call, shutting the door behind him. Whatever it was, there was no need to disturb anyone else's enjoyment of the rest of the meal.

'Ted? Kev. Duty inspector, and I bloody wish I wasn't for this one. And please don't shoot the messenger. There's no easy way to say this, but Maurice Brown's been arrested, on suspicion of rape.'

For one optimistic moment, Ted thought it might be some sort of sick wind-up. A joke in very bad taste which was going to turn out to have some stupid punchline to it.

As if he was reading his thoughts, Kev went on, 'I know, it's so far-fetched I didn't believe it either, but the arrest part is true so there must be some basis, at least, to give enough cause for an arrest and interview under caution.'

'So where is he now? Where did the alleged offence take place?'

'That's where it gets complicated. The alleged offence happened on our patch, on Wednesday, but it was only reported today. At the rape centre in Manchester, where the woman was taken, in a shocking state, by all accounts, by her husband. He'd been working away and only knew about what happened when he got back home and found her.

'The police were called to the centre and it's snowballed on from that. Maurice has been taken to Stretford for now, because clearly it wouldn't be appropriate to bring him here initially, where he's a serving officer, so that was the closest neutral territory, so to speak.

'I'm only telling you all this unofficially, Ted, because I know you'd do the same for me if it was one of my officers. And no, I'm struggling to believe any of it myself, probably just the same as you are. Just don't, whatever you do, go wading in like an avenging fury. I don't want any of mine to have to arrest you for interfering in the course of justice.'

'Look, I'd better come in …'

'Don't be daft, Ted. There's nothing you can do, officially or unofficially. And didn't you tell me you had visitors this weekend? Trev's kid sister, wasn't it? Stay there and enjoy whatever you were all doing together. Having your tea, I imagine, at this time. Whatever's going on with Maurice will keep until morning.

'I imagine they'll do an initial interview, put the facts to him, hear what he says and then bail him, probably until

Monday, with a bit of luck. I doubt he'd be considered a flight risk. Not a family man like him, with little twins at home. Not to mention a serving officer. Although I suppose he'll have to be suspended immediately, if only for form's sake, and his reporting conditions are likely to be much stricter than normal.'

But Ted had the angry words of DS Ian Bradley rattling around in his brain all the time Kev was talking.

'Are you saying you wouldn't go out on a limb for one of your team if they were under suspicion and you knew, without a doubt, that they were completely innocent?

'Because if that's true, then fuck you, Ted. I'm glad I was never on your team and never will be. Because if officers can't rely on their own boss to have their backs then we might as well all hand our warrant cards in and leave the villains to it.'

So now he was facing the ultimate test. One of his own officers, almost certainly wrongly accused of a serious crime, with the possibility of a sentence of life imprisonment. What could he do to help Maurice? One person he would wager his career on not being capable of any kind of violence towards a woman. Certainly not rape.

The one thing he could, and should, do, he decided, was to make a public show of his faith in and support for him, right from the outset. But there was a little niggle he needed to clear up first.

'There must be something solid enough to have got an arrest warrant that quickly, though.'

He posed it as a question.

'You absolutely did not get any of this from me. At all. I didn't even call you. But they've got CCTV footage. Of him going to the house where the incident took place.'

'If it was Wednesday, Maurice was out door-to-door. You know that, Kev, you lent us Barbara Kowalski to go with him as the suspected victim of domestic abuse needed a Polish interpreter. I know all about that visit. Maurice reported back to me and flagged up the strong likelihood of the domestic abuse allegations being true.'

'Ted, this is the part you certainly didn't hear from me. I'm risking all sorts of grief myself for breathing a word of it. There's CCTV of Maurice going to the house twice on Wednesday. The second time he was alone. Barbara wasn't with him. Nobody was.'

'I'm on my way in.'

'I should warn you that I called the Ice Queen before I called you, Ted. Sorry about that, but you can imagine the bollocking I'd have let myself in for if I hadn't. You know she likes to know everything that goes on and I'm not brave enough to be the one who decides not to tell her when something as big as this happens on my watch.'

'So how am I going to explain my presence, without dropping you right in the shit for tipping me off?'

'You're the clever detective, Ted. I'm just the humble Woodentop. I'll leave that one to you.'

* * *

Ted was still fishing for a plausible excuse for being there as he pulled into the car park at the nick, noticing as he did so a leather-clad figure on a red motorbike turning into the parking space next to him.

A red Ducati.

The Ice Queen in person.

Inwardly cursing, Ted got out of his car as she was

pulling off her helmet and unzipping her leathers.

'Ma'am.'

'Chief inspector.'

Her greeting was no frostier than usual. Ted fell into step half a stride behind her as she headed for the station.

'I don't intend to compromise you by asking who tipped you off. I'm pleased someone took the initiative to do so and I would prefer not to know who it was. I take it you don't believe the allegations against DC Brown?'

'I would find it very hard to do so, ma'am. He has his faults but I could never imagine Maurice committing an act of violence against anyone. Especially not a woman. After all, he got himself very seriously stabbed once by trying to prevent a young woman from being raped at knifepoint, or worse.'

'Indeed.'

They'd reached the entrance now and let themselves in, heading straight for Kevin Turner's office. When he saw who swept in together, after the briefest of knocks, he shot to his feet, looking uncomfortable and guilty in equal measure.

'Please sit down, inspector. It was a welcome surprise, and most fortuitous, for me to find that the chief inspector had come in to finish some paperwork. It saved me from having to summon him.

'Whilst we cannot be seen to show any special treatment for DC Brown, we must ensure that the premise of innocent until proven guilty is rigidly applied in his case. We all know that the fate of any police officer who is unfortunate enough to find themselves remanded in custody for any reason is not good. With such a serious charge, implying, if true, a total abuse of power and breach of trust, the consequences don't bear thinking about.

'As the DCI and I, in particular, know from our recent meeting at Central Park, public confidence in the police service has seldom been lower. The last thing we need, therefore, is any hint of one of our own receiving preferential treatment in any way.

'I'm rather taking it as read that neither of you gentlemen believe the charges levelled at DC Brown, unless substantive proof is produced?'

'Maurice? Hurt a woman? Or anyone, come to that? Not remotely, ma'am,' Kevin Turner told her emphatically. 'Skiving? Yes. That I could believe. But nothing else. Barbara, PC Kowalski, who went out with him on this particular job, was telling me how very good he was with the woman in question. How kind and calm he was, and patient in getting her to open the door to him. And she said the woman did look very scared about something when they got there.'

'And yet there is apparently CCTV footage of him returning to the same property, alone, at the end of the day. Chief inspector, were you aware of that second visit?'

'Not at all, ma'am. In fact knowing what a big softy Maurice is I specifically cautioned him against going back there and certainly not alone. At the most he was supposed to be checking on other occupants of the property and reporting back.'

'So at the very least, he disobeyed his senior officer, thereby putting himself in a compromising situation. But that's an internal disciplinary matter. What we need to concentrate on now is how we are collectively going to help him out of this situation he's got himself into, without denting our public image any further.'

Chapter Fifteen

Ted took the first brief chance he got to send a quick text to Trev to tell him he'd no idea when he'd get home but he'd try to get the car back to him at some point. Trev would need it to take the girls out to lunch then deliver them safely to the station in time for their train back to the West Country and their boarding school.

He also took time to call Mike Hallam. Knowing how the jungle drums could work, he wanted to be sure that none of the team went off on some ill-advised crusade to show solidarity with Maurice if they got any hint of what had happened. He knew hot-headed Jezza, who thought the world of Daddy Hen, was quite capable of doing something stupid to show her support for her best friend.

'Mike, we have a delicate situation. I'll tell you now, but make sure it goes no further at this stage, please. I want everyone in for briefing first thing tomorrow morning. Forget the rota. Everyone, from our own team but no outsiders, no exceptions. I'll inform all of them at the same time what I'm about to tell you. That way we should hopefully keep any unhelpful leaks or actions to a minimum.'

Mike was usually mild-mannered, not prone to swearing. When he heard what the boss had to say, he couldn't help himself.

'Bloody hell, boss! This is surely someone getting their

wires crossed somewhere in a big way. Our Maurice? Assaulting a woman? I can't think of anyone less likely to do such a thing.'

'Nor can I. But the daft idiot seems to have put himself in a very dangerous situation, despite me warning him not to. So for now, he's currently at Stretford, under arrest and being interviewed, so I'm here with the super trying to see what, if anything, we can do to help him.

'But so that no one, especially Jezza, tries to do something daft to save a mate, I would like to be the one to tell them all, in person, at the same time. So, early doors tomorrow, please, and not a hint of what it's about before then.'

Back in Kevin's office, Superintendent Caldwell had decided she should be the one to make the first contact with officers at Stretford to get an update on Maurice's current situation. She put the call on speaker as she asked to be put through to their duty inspector.

'Superintendent Caldwell, from Stockport, inspector ...' she began, but got no further.

'Ma'am, let me stop you there,' Inspector Esme Lee cut in, her tone determined. 'I've been anticipating your call, or one from someone there. My answer is the same as it would be for any member of the public. I can confirm that Maurice Brown is currently being interviewed under caution at this station. He has been informed he can have a close relative informed as to his whereabouts, but that's as far as his rights extend, so that's as much information as I'm required, or prepared, to give out to anyone for now, ma'am.'

'He's one of my officers ...' the Ice Queen tried again, sounding ever more frosty, but got no further.

'At the moment, ma'am,' there was an increasing note of

irony to the word each time she used it, 'he's being treated the same as any other member of the public would in the circumstances. I'm sure you can understand why it's important for us to do things that way.

'The most I can offer you, as a courtesy, is that you will be kept informed as to whether Brown will be bailed or remanded in custody, after initial questioning. Best I can do for you. Good evening. Ma'am.'

Ted had certainly never seen his senior officer at a loss for words, but as the call was ended abruptly, she sat for a moment looking at the blank screen, collecting her thoughts.

'Well,' she said finally, 'Inspector Lee is, of course, right in what she said. But I have to confess to have been hoping for a little more in the way of cooperation between divisions.'

'Ma'am, all may well not yet be lost,' Kevin told her. 'I know Esme. I've met her many times, and I know she is an absolute stickler for equality and fairness. Her roots are in the traveller community so she's passionate about there not being one rule for minority groups like that, and something completely different for the police policing themselves. She's bound to be more by the book on this one than anyone else would be, and I doubt any of us can get her to shift on her stance.

'But I know a good few officers at Stretford. With a bit of luck and a following breeze, the duty custody sergeant might even be someone I know, and I'm sure I might be able to get a bit more out of them than any of us are going to get from Esme.'

He also made the call on speaker phone, praying silently, when he was told who the custody sergeant on duty was, and being transferred to him, that he wouldn't start off with his

155

usual foul-mouthed greeting to an old friend.

'Kevin, you tight-fisted old bastard, when are you going to buy me that pint you owe me?'

'I'm here with my super and with DCI Darling, Sergeant Adams, and hoping you can help us,' Kevin cut across him before he said anything worse.

He heard the muttering under the breath from the sergeant, who switched into formal mode.

'Always happy to help, sir. I'm taking it as read this call is about your officer, DC Brown. In which case I can't unfortunately tell you a great deal other than that I booked him in and he's here being interviewed. Best I can do for you is to give you a little tinkle if that situation changes, and I'm not even meant to be doing that, of course. There's a three-line whip on any deviation from standard procedure.'

'Appreciate it, but I need another tiny little favour, and this time I will remember to pay up, in drinks. Has he got, or asked for, legal representation?'

'More than my job's worth to tell you that, sir. I can tell you, though, from what I've heard, that he doesn't need it.'

'Thanks, Paul, I really do owe you one.'

He ended the call then looked at the other two.

'I'm taking that to mean he's heard on the grapevine that Maurice is refusing to say anything for now, which is probably the best we could hope for in the circumstances. So what's the plan next?'

'I don't know about anyone else, but I think what I need to do now is to go over to Stretford to see what the chances are of getting Maurice out on bail for now,' Ted told them. 'Clearly he can't continue working for the time being, with all of this hanging over him, but he should at least be at home. He's no flight risk. He would never leave his family.

But we all know the inordinate amount of time it takes to get DNA results back for rape cases, and he certainly can't be sitting waiting in custody for anything like that length of time.

'If Stretford would agree to daily reporting here as part of bail, and if I assure them we'll be all over Maurice like a rash the minute he's as much as five minutes late attending, they might hopefully agree to police bail for now.'

'If you would give me a few minutes to change into something slightly more suitable, I will accompany you, chief inspector. And I suggest you take your service vehicle. Perhaps a few hints of how seriously we are taking this unfortunate situation might help us somewhat,' the super told him as she left the office.

Kevin leaned back in his seat and blew a large sigh in the direction of the ceiling.

'Bloody hell, Ted. I always knew Maurice was too soft for his own good. But how in hell has he got himself into such a bad situation? And how on earth are you going to help him dig himself out of it, if they've got CCTV evidence?'

'I only wish I knew the answer to that, Kev. But I'm counting on you to keep a tight lid on all of this. We both know how the jungle drums work. Gossip isn't going to help anyone, certainly not Maurice. For the moment, I can't think of much that will help him. But we'll find it. And we will help him, because I don't believe this of him. Not for one minute.'

Ted grabbed the time whilst waiting for the Ice Queen to reappear to make a quick call to Trev.

'Sorry I had to bail on you and I've absolutely no idea how long I'm going to be. A bit of a crisis situation which is going to take some sorting, and I really can't talk about it.

But I'm fine.

'I'll get the car back to you somehow at some point for you to take the girls to the station.'

'You're definitely all right, though? You sound worried.'

'Remember me asking if I was a good boss? It's one of those situations where I'm about to find out the stark truth in answer to that.'

* * *

'Ma'am, I'm not sure why you felt the need to make the journey in person. My answer remains the same as when we spoke earlier. DC Brown will be treated no different to any member of the public, so you know perfectly well how long we have the right to hold him here for. And that time is nowhere near expired yet.'

DI Lee was nothing if not dogged. Ted admired her standing her ground, especially as she was quite short, shorter than Ted, and dwarfed by the imperious stature of the Ice Queen. He'd encountered her in the past but never to speak to, and had certainly never seen her in action.

'You are right, inspector, I do know. But at the end of that initial period, you are going to have to either remand him in custody, if you think you have sufficient evidence, or release him on bail.

'In the latter case, he is going to need a lift home, so the DCI and I are happy to be his taxi service. Should you decide the risk of bailing him is acceptable, I can give you my personal assurance that I will oversee his reporting conditions, which can hopefully happen in Stockport. That way, I can give you my word that should he be late at all to report, I will have him immediately arrested and delivered back to you.

'For now, if someone could kindly point us towards some coffee, I assure you we will sit here, quietly and patiently, and not interfere in any way.'

Ted had seen her in that mode before on another case. It was no less impressive the second time round. Whether or not her presence had any effect on the outcome, it was not as long as Ted had feared it might be before Maurice appeared, looking white and drawn. If he was surprised to see the super and Ted waiting for him, he showed no sign of it, just relief to see someone he knew. Anyone.

'Ma'am, boss, I didn't do it. Honestly I didn't. I never touched her. I would never do anything like that. Boss, you know that, surely?'

'Unfortunately, DC Brown, you're going to have to come up with something much more solid than that, facing such a serious charge,' the Ice Queen told him.

'I would suggest that we all now go back to Stockport where you can initially tell us your version of events, then we can advise you of the best way to proceed. You cannot, of course, be on duty until all of this is sorted out and you must follow all of your bail conditions.

'Once we have done that, I'm sure the DCI will be happy to drive you home to your family, which is probably the best place for you to be at the moment.'

* * *

'What I'm about to tell you goes no further than this room. It is not for discussion outside this team, and preferably not even talked about between yourselves. We all have more than enough to do with this triple murder still a long way from being solved.'

Ted's sounded more serious than usual as he addressed the team early on Sunday morning, after apologising for having to call everyone in, not just those on the rota.

He'd told Mike he only wanted the regular team in, none of the other officers who'd been drafted in from elsewhere to boost numbers for the murder case. He was determined to keep a lid on this for as long as possible.

It was going to be hard enough for any of them to concentrate, knowing what Maurice was going through. It would be much worse if the whole of the station was gossiping about the case as well.

'Superintendent Caldwell and I went over to Stretford station yesterday after being informed that Maurice Brown had been arrested and was being interviewed there.'

'Maurice? Arrested? What on earth for?' Jezza cut in.

'Please let me finish, DC Vine, I'm coming to the detail. As you all know, Maurice recently attended at the scene of a suspected domestic abuse. He went to the house on Wednesday, with PC Barbara Kowalski, as the informant about the situation had indicated that a Polish translator would be necessary.

'Maurice left his card with the female occupant, but she insisted she was all right, not in any danger, so there was nothing else which could be done for the moment.

'Yesterday, the woman was taken to the Sexual Assault Referral Centre in Manchester showing signs of serious assault. She was with her husband who spoke for her because she was in such a state she was struggling to say anything.

'He said that Maurice returned to the house later in the day, alone. His wife opened the door to him because she had met him earlier and saw no reason not to trust him. She thought he was just being persistent because she'd told the officers earlier that she was fine. She simply hadn't opened the door to them on the first visit because she had been worried by an unexpected visit from the police but she assured them she was all right and not in need of their assistance.

'This time, she claimed, Maurice pushed her back into the house, shut the door and violently raped and assaulted her.'

Jezza gave one of her characteristic snorts as she said, 'Maurice? Daddy Hen? No way on this earth. He hasn't got it in him, and I know him better than anyone else here. He's not capable of such a thing.'

'Jezza, there's CCTV of Maurice returning to the house, later in the day. On his own. At a time when he had no reason to be there, and certainly not without another officer, a female, present. And he's never mentioned that visit. It's not in his report, anywhere.'

There was nothing more he could usefully tell them, except that Maurice was on police bail, with a requirement to report twice daily at their own nick, and that for obvious reasons, none of them was to make any kind of contact with him until further notice.

After that, he took himself off to his office, glad, for once, of all the admin tasks he had to distract himself with.

He'd only just begun when, after the briefest of knocks, Jezza came into his office with her familiar determined expression.

'Boss, the footage is clearly fake because Maurice was with me on Wednesday. From when we finished work to later in the evening ...'

Ted looked up at her over his reading glasses, his

expression sad.

'Jezza, please don't. I know how much Maurice means to you, and all of us are having difficulty believing any of this. But please don't perjure yourself, thinking you're helping him. You're not. If he's innocent, and I'm sure he is, we'll find the right way to clear him. But not by lying.'

Jezza slumped into the spare seat and burst into tears. It was so rare for her to show such emotion that for a moment, Ted had no idea how to react. Then he got to his feet and went to put an awkward arm round her shoulders.

'We'll prove his innocence, Jezza. We're trained to get at the truth so we'll do it this time, for Maurice. We will clear him.'

Chapter Sixteen

Ted was feeling in desperate need of someone he could talk to – really talk to – about the situation he was facing with such a serious sexual allegation having been levelled against Maurice.

The Ice Queen was still doing her best to be supportive. She'd phoned him earlier to see how he'd got on with telling the rest of the team, and had assured him she was always available. But he seldom felt totally relaxed in her company, no matter how much she attempted to unbend.

There was only one person he would feel completely at ease with when speaking about such a difficult situation. Someone he realised he'd been rather neglecting for far too long. And someone who wasn't usually available until much later on a Sunday morning.

Ted's call, when he did make it, was answered on the second ring and Big Jim Baker's voice boomed at him so loudly that Ted needed to hold his phone away from his ear.

'Ted? This is a surprise,' then as an even louder aside, 'It's Ted, dear. I'll try not to be long.'

Then he went on before Ted had chance to say anything much, 'Well, of course I'm available, if you need me, Ted. We're not long back from church and we were just going out, but it's nothing urgent. I can postpone.'

'Trouble is it's nothing official, Jim, so there's no consultancy fee on this. But I'd really appreciate your help and guidance on something that's left me feeling right out of my depth and going down for the third time.'

He heard an aside from Jim, apologising to his wife and saying he was being unexpectedly called in to help with a case. There was no sound of dissent. Bella knew that Jim may be officially retired, but he was always ready to jump back into work mode, if summoned to consult.

When Big Jim spoke again it was more quietly.

'Does Dave still let you use the back room when needed? If so, I can meet you there in half an hour or so, and you can buy me lunch. Bella will understand, when I explain. I'll get her to drop me off then she can take the car and still have a nice trip out. You'll need to drive me back afterwards, though. Deal?'

'Definitely a deal. Thanks, Jim, I'll see you shortly.'

Ted received the usual warm greeting when he walked round to the local pub to ask about having exclusive use of the back room for a meeting.

'We hardly ever need the extra seating of a Sunday lunchtime these days, Ted,' Dave, the landlord, told him. 'But even if it was full, I'd kick them all out for you. I'm forever grateful for your kind sensitivity, both me and the wife. No news yet on the extradition, I suppose?'

Ted had recently had an eventful trip to Germany to sort out getting the leader of a gang who had seriously sexually assaulted a number of victims, including Dave's wife, sent back to Britain to stand trial.

'Not yet. These things take forever. Even ours, which is on fast-track. But I promise to keep you informed, as soon as I hear anything.

'Now, what's on the lunch menu today? I'm meeting Big Jim here shortly and we both know he's not exactly the salad bar type.'

'We've got a lovely cut of beef today, with Yorkshires and all the trimmings. And Susan's famous apple crumble with thick cream to follow. Does that fit the bill?'

'It sounds perfect, thanks. And we're definitely all right for the back room? I need to pick Jim's brains about something and I don't want any word to leak out anywhere.'

'Worst case, you can use our living space upstairs while we're down here, and very welcome. But you should be fine in the back. A Gunner while you're waiting for Jim to join you?'

Jim Baker had been Ted's immediate boss for some time before health concerns made him take the retirement he'd long been dreading. Ted still had a lot of respect for him, so he stood up when he came into the room.

Jim's wife Bella had been keeping a close eye on his weight since his heart attack and he looked better for it. He was still a big man, who towered over Ted.

'Sit, Ted, for goodness' sake. How long have we known one another? And didn't we once dance together when your Trev was teaching me, ready for the wedding dance? I say that puts us beyond the formalities. Sit down and tell me what the problem is, and why it's so cloak and dagger.

'But before you do, tell me what we're eating today. Is there a Sunday roast on?'

'There is, so I took the liberty of ordering that for both of us, with apple crumble and cream to follow. Is that all right for you?'

Jim settled himself into a seat with a contented sigh of anticipation but gave Ted a conspiratorial wink as he said, 'Perfect, as long as you get the cover story right for when you see Bella. I had the mixed salad and a low-fat yoghurt.

Oh, and mineral water instead of this pint which seems to have been put here in error, but it's a shame to let it go to waste.'

Ted took a mouthful of his Gunner before he began. He presented Jim with all the facts as he knew them then waited for his reaction.

It was delayed when Dave appeared with their food. Dave had the same attitude to anything he heard whilst serving his pub customers as a priest did to whatever he was party to in the confessional. It simply went in one ear and out the other, never to be repeated.

On this occasion, with something so delicate, both men instinctively waited until he had left the room.

Jim cut a piece of succulent beef, smeared it with the home-made horseradish sauce, put it into his mouth and chewed appreciatively.

'Now that's what I call a proper Sunday lunch, instead of the usual rabbit food Bella is convinced is better for me.

'Right, we both know Maurice is a total plonker who needs a kick up his lardy arse and a very sharp reminder about his boundaries. But we also both know he isn't capable of anything like that, although if he's on camera as going back there, that was bloody stupid, especially if he tries to deny it. So clearly someone is lying. The wife? The husband? Which one, and why?

'And in case it's relevant, where did your tip-off come from? You mentioned getting a letter which you took seriously, hence sending Maurice round in the first place. How did that reach you? What was the source?'

When Ted hesitated fractionally, Big Jim growled at him, 'For heaven's sake, Ted, if you want me to advise you on this one, which is, I presume, why you brought me here, I need all the facts, not just a watered-down version of them.'

Ted abandoned his meal for the time being. His appetite was not there, with the worry of the situation, so he let Jim carry on relishing his plateful while he gave him the unabridged version about what had started the chain of events which had ended in Maurice's arrest.

'This better not all be about someone with a vivid imagination writing a piece of fiction to try to impress teacher. But your Trev's always struck me as someone sensible enough, so let's assume it was a genuine cry for help from an abuse victim, and Maurice was stupid enough to forget his boundaries. Then let's assume he did go back to the house, but that he didn't carry out any attack.

'We need to know what's on that film footage, before we can do anything,' Jim told him. 'That's critical. If it exists, and if it's not somehow been doctored, we need to know exactly when and why Maurice went back there, and if he really did go on his own, the big daft barmpot.

'Now, you and your team clearly can't look into any of this. You're only going to make things a whole lot worse if you even try. I'm hoping I can take it as read that none of you are going to do anything stupid.'

He looked hard at Ted and waited for his nod of agreement before continuing, 'I, on the other hand, still have a few useful contacts who might give me a nod and a wink if I ask the right questions in the right places.

'The second visit film footage is critical. Assuming it really does exist, and it's not techno-trickery, put together from the first, official, visit, somehow. That definitely needs checking for.

'If it does show Maurice going back there on his own and, crucially, the woman opening the door to him, then he's probably stuffed, even if none of his DNA is found on the victim.

'And that's the other thing. That convenient time-lapse between the attack and presenting at the rape centre. Of course, anyone with a computer these days could discover what the window is for taking samples from a rape victim. But coppers know. You and I know information like that, so someone else in the job might know and have been counting on that. Keep that in mind. It might well be relevant.

'So what do you know about the husband, partner, or whatever of the unfortunate victim?'

'Well, so far, nothing. The alleged rape isn't our case, for obvious reasons, so I've been told to back off.'

Big Jim shook his head in disbelief and made a tutting sound.

'Well, that's a novelty. You playing by the rules. Especially when one of your team is in the shit. Not at all like you to roll over at the first obstacle.

'You can't go near the rape case. Of course you can't. But what about the original domestic abuse intervention? I'd bet good money Maurice didn't write up all his notes on that before going off duty. It would be a first if he did. So that needs finishing off for him, to put on file, even if it does go down as an NFA.

'You said he went with a PC? Which one, and have you at least got their notes?'

'Barbara Kowalski, and I've not yet checked her notes.'

This time Jim responded with a loud snort.

'For goodness' sake, Ted, what the hell is wrong with you? This is one of your team. It's Maurice, of all people. You should have his back. Think of all the things he's done for others, including you, without a second thought.

'You can't break the rules – of course you can't – but you can and should be bending them as far as you can to look after one of your own. And you shouldn't need to be buying me lunch to get my permission to do what you should have been doing anyway, and that's whatever you can to sort this.'

He was spot on. Ted knew it. There were things he could and should be doing, and he had no idea why he'd hesitated. Maybe Ian Bradley was right. Maybe he was a long way short of the sort of boss he tried to be to his team.

At least Big Jim was simmering down, now he'd had his rant. His tone was softer when he spoke again.

'Seriously, Ted, you know what you need to do, without making the situation any worse. Get on and do it. And if you really have lost your appetite, pass me the rest of your beef and Yorkshire. It would really be a serious crime to see that go to waste.'

* * *

Ted arrived back at his desk with more resolve after Jim's pep talk. There was a lot he could be doing which might be of some help to Maurice, and he should have been all over it himself, instead of taking the "hands off" order too literally.

Once he'd cleared the admin backlog he'd been determined to shift, which was the main reason he was in all day on a Sunday, he went over the notes which had been put on file after the home visit on Wednesday following up on the letter about alleged domestic abuse.

PC Barbara Kowalski's notes of the visit where all there, as he'd expected. Clear, concise and mirroring Maurice's impression that, despite her denials, the young woman had looked frightened by their visit. She described her behaviour as not untypical of an abuse victim in denial.

Her report included a suggestion of a possible follow-up, but more for form's sake. It was not feasible to check up on every potential victim, especially those who simply refused to talk.

Amazingly, Maurice's initial notes were also on the file. Light on detail, as he often was, but again a mention that things might very well not be as they appeared. He'd highlighted the fact that there was a doorbell CCTV system in place. Nothing sinister of itself. They were popular for so many valid reasons, although controlling behaviour could, on occasion, be one such reason.

Ted stopped reading for a moment at that point, frowning to himself. He got up to put his kettle on whilst he thought about the implications.

Maurice was many things, but he wasn't a particularly stupid man. Unwise, yes. Often. Doing daft things for noble reasons. But still a trained copper, with powers of observation. He would know that going back to the house a second time and ringing the bell would trigger the CCTV, so he'd probably knock instead of ringing. So if there was footage of his return, that meant there must be another camera somewhere covering the front door, and that suggested some higher than average surveillance for the main entry point to a domestic dwelling.

His train of thought was interrupted by Steve's signature knock on his door.

'Come in, Steve. Sit down. The kettle's just boiled, if you fancy a brew.'

'Nothing, thank you, sir,' he replied, as Ted expected he would. But he did at least sit down this time.

'I've been looking again for anything about Uncle, sir,

for the murder case, and I think I might have got somewhere, with a bit of lateral thinking.'

Ted took a sip of his tea, nodding to him to continue.

'I've not been finding anything relevant to date, so I decided to try different search parameters. I started with the Arabic word for uncle, as our only information to date suggests our suspect might be IC6, but I couldn't find a way to drill down on that locally enough to be of use to us.

'Then I decided to try the French word for uncle, tonton, for any mention in our specific area or the Greater Manchester area, going over into the fringes of Cheshire. Because French is a second language in some Arabic-speaking countries. And I found something, sir.'

It was never quick, getting anything out of Steve. It was always worth the wait, Ted reminded himself.

'A small group, on social media. Closed, so you have to answer questions to be admitted. I didn't break any rules or guidelines, sir. I simply said I was interested in exploring spirituality beyond the boundaries of established religions. So I'm in. I have access to a list of when and where their gatherings will be held in the coming weeks. And I specifically know which ones Tonton will be attending. And I don't think I've crossed any lines in getting such information, sir.'

He was looking anxious, hoping for approval but, because of his history, always expecting the worst by way of a response.

'I don't think you have either, Steve, from what you've told me. Very good work. Make sure you write it up in detail and at tomorrow morning's briefing we'll discuss where we go from here.'

Steve was still hesitating, clearly with something else on

his mind. Ted invited him to share it, whatever it was.

'I did the next part on my lunch break, sir. Not in work time. But because I'd found the trace to Tonton quicker than I thought, I decided to take a look at something that's been bothering me, although I know you told us all not to do any such thing.'

Ted was surprised that it appeared to be Steve, of all his team members, who'd decided to look into Maurice's case, if that's where he was heading, against a direct order not to. He'd still be interested to know what, if anything, he'd found out.

'Go on,' he told him, keeping his tone neutral.

'Well, sir, I've been wondering about this so-called camera footage of Maurice's second visit, alone, to the home of the alleged domestic abuse victim.

'Maurice told us there was doorbell CCTV, so if he did go back for whatever reason and he didn't want anyone to know about it, he surely wouldn't ring the bell. So I can think of only two possible explanations for the second lot of footage. Either there's another camera near the entrance somewhere, well hidden, which is an unusual level of security for most domestic dwellings. Or that footage has been cleverly doctored, cobbled together, from the first lot by someone who really knows what they're doing.'

Ted sensed there was more to come so he said again, 'Go on.'

'I tried to find out a bit more about who lives at that address, apart from Anna Wójcik. The only other resident who is listed anywhere is an Eric Leader.'

'So they're not married and he used the term "wife" in a liberal sense. Nothing wrong with that. A lot of people do the same.'

'That's true, sir. Except that Eric Leader doesn't appear to exist. I can't find anything about him anywhere, except a brief listing of his occupation being given as "government employee".'

'There could be any number of reasons for that with, again, nothing to raise any red flags.'

'There could sir, but it did increase my curiosity. And I was doing all of this in my own time, sir.'

Steve was sounding on the defensive now, but his ideas were always worth listening to, at least.

'All right, tell me what else you found out.'

'Well sir, I started with the name. Eric is a name which is not uncommon in Poland, but spelled Eryk. And people do sometimes anglicise foreign names, for ease. I looked at the translation of Wójcik. It means a village headman. So, someone who is a leader, perhaps.

'Then I started to wonder about what sort of occupation someone might have where it would simply be listed as government service. I thought about the various intelligence services. And I also thought about some branches of the police service where deep cover might be needed. Counter Terrorism, perhaps.

'And then I thought that anyone in any of those categories would definitely know how to alter camera footage to show whatever they wanted to. The only thing I've not yet come up with, sir, is why anyone would want to do that, in this case.'

Chapter Seventeen

Ted had lost all track of time since he'd returned to his office after lunch with Big Jim. It had been exactly what he needed to get him back on track. He could always rely on his old friend to make him see the bigger picture. There was still a lot Ted could do which might help Maurice, without crossing any boundaries, and it was time he started doing that.

First off, he needed to clear every bit of outstanding admin work from his desk so he could start in fresh the next day. With Steve's latest lead to run with, they might finally make much-needed progress on the triple murder, for one thing.

When Mike Hallam put his head round the door to ask if Ted needed dropping off at home Ted was surprised to see what the time was. With a guilty start, he realised that he hadn't found the time to phone Trev to ask him to apologise on his behalf to the girls for not seeing much of them, and to wish them a safe trip back to school.

'You're all right, thanks, Mike. I was planning on walking back. I think the exercise might do me good, after all the paperwork.

'Steve's bit of work looking for the Uncle character looks hopeful but I will need to check the ethics of how he's come by the information and what use we can put it to that CPS aren't going to quibble about, if we ever get to the stage of charges.'

'And is there anything any of us can be doing to help Maurice, boss? Legitimately, I mean. None of us want to make a difficult situation even worse by doing the wrong thing.'

'None of us can discuss the charges against Maurice with him. Nor anything else relating to the case. But I don't see anything wrong with the odd personal phone call, not from a work phone, to wish him well and let him know we're all thinking about him.'

'I can't begin to imagine how he's feeling, the poor bloke,' Mike told him, shaking his head. 'I'd say he was the least likely person of anyone I've met to be a violent rapist. But we know innocence is often a lot harder to prove than guilt.'

'We need to keep a close eye on Jezza, to make sure she doesn't do anything stupid. She's already tried to give him a false alibi, but I treated that as exactly what it was. An ill-informed but well-intentioned effort by one friend to save the skin of another.'

Mike went on his way and Ted made a rather guilty call to Trev to update him on when he'd be back.

'Did the girls get off safely? Sorry I didn't call before to say goodbye. I'll be setting off home shortly. Walking back. I feel as if I need the exercise to clear my head a bit. There's serious stuff going on at work at the moment. I can't discuss all of the details, but I promise to tell you as much as I can when I get back.'

'Did you eat properly at lunchtime? On a scale of one to ten how hungry are you likely to be this evening, so I know what sort of a meal to make?' Trev asked him.

Always the nurturer; thinking of his partner's needs rather than complaining about not having seen much of him.

'I had lunch with Jim because I needed to pick his brains, but I didn't have much of an appetite. He ended up eating his own roast dinner and half of mine, but he doesn't want Bella to know that. I could eat something light though, if that's no trouble?'

'The girls opted for a deli picnic lunch in the garden after we'd been out, whilst it wasn't raining, for once. The cats joined us, of course. Faith absolutely adores cats but none of her family do, so with her being away at school, and all the competing she does taking her away even in the holidays, she's not allowed any. There's plenty left over for us. We went a bit mad with what we bought.

'Faith's so lovely, and so good for Rhian. Even if it never goes further than friendship, I hope it lasts. My sister needs someone like that in her life. She deserves it.

'I'll see you when you get back, and you can tell me as much as you're able to.'

Ted's next call was one he now realised he should have made the day before.

Maurice's voice, when he answered, sounded defeated. A man at his lowest ebb, not knowing where to turn to find a way out of his current pit of despair. Not even knowing if there was one. Hesitant, too. Sounding unsure as to whether this was going to be a friendly call of support or yet more kicking of a man who was already down as far as he could go.

'Boss, I'm sorry about all this, but I hope you know I would never harm anyone, certainly not a vulnerable woman ...'

'Ted, Maurice. It's Ted. This isn't an official call. In fact, it never happened. And I'm sorry. I should have called you straight away to find out how you were and if you had all the help and support you need.'

Ted could hear that Maurice was crying now. He shouldn't have let things go this far before contacting him. Bradley had been right. He had been a rubbish boss on this one. Trying to play everything by the book and failing to understand that in doing so, he'd left a good-hearted man feeling abandoned and hung out to dry.

Time to put things right.

'If anyone's made an error here, Maurice, it's me. I should have done a more diligent risk assessment on the potential situation before I sent you in. And I'll say that to anyone who needs to hear it.'

'I did go back, though, Ted. On my own. And I shouldn't have done. I put myself in danger. I just never thought it would turn out as bad as it has.'

'I can't discuss any of the details with you. Nor can any other members of the team, and I hope they'll know better than to try. But we can look further into the original complaint which started this whole chain in motion, as it's on our patch, and we are already doing that.

'Meanwhile, we need to make sure you have all the help and support you're entitled to. Have you had legal advice? What about your Federation rep? Have you spoken to someone?'

'I've just been sitting here cuddling the bairns and Megan, not knowing what to do. It's hit me like a steam train. I'm only just beginning to realise that innocence is a lot harder to prove than guilt. I know I'm innocent of any crime. I just don't know how to prove that.'

'Maurice, I can only apologise again. I let you down. Getting the right sort of advice is something I can sort for you with a few phone calls, and I will do that. Probably not easily on a Sunday evening, but I'll make it my priority in the morning.

'And don't forget, you don't have to prove your innocence. It's up to the prosecution to prove your guilt based on any evidence the investigating team give them, if it even gets that far. And they're going to have an uphill struggle to do that.

'For now, make sure you turn up promptly to report for your bail conditions. Always. Get here early, every time. Don't run the risk of being late or you could well find yourself re-arrested and remanded in custody.

'Again, none of us can really come and talk to you while you're in the station to do that, but no one's going to ignore you if they happen to walk past. Passing the time of day is fine. Just nothing at all to do with the case.

'We've got your back, Maurice. All of us. And I'm sorry I left it so long to let you know that in person.'

* * *

'I'm in the garden, protecting our picnic from a horde of marauding cats, all claiming they haven't eaten all day, the shameless fibbers,' Trev called out when he heard Ted open the front door.

Ted paused in the hall to dump jacket, tie, and even his work shoes, before padding out to the patio to join him, sinking gratefully into one of the pair of steamer chairs which had been the first bits of furniture he and Trev had bought together when they'd originally moved in.

'The girls told me to thank you for letting them visit and being cool about them. Faith is fabulous. I have to confess, when I first saw her, to thinking my sister was deliberately

178

trying to be provocative, choosing a black lesbian to come out over. But I can really see what she loves about her, and I hope they stay together for a while. Faith is a really good influence on Rhian.'

Now his new best friend had gone home, youngest cat Adam was back to trying to climb into Ted's lap once more.

'Faithless feline,' Ted told him sternly, picking the little cat up and installing him on his legs, rewarded by ecstatic loud purring.

Trev was studying his partner's face as he asked, 'Are you all right?'

Then before Ted had time to reply, he went on, 'You're not all right, are you? Is this to do with whatever you had to rush off to yesterday? Is there anything I can do to help?'

'I need to tell you some things which are strictly confidential. Not for repeating anywhere, please, but I do think I should put you in the picture.'

Ted knew he could trust his partner but he needed to stress the seriousness of the situation. He wasn't worried about them being overheard. The neighbour in the adjoining semi, an elderly woman, increasingly heard less and less. The couple on the other side were hardly ever there, and certainly never at home at the weekend.

'I've not had time to tell you much about the follow-up to that letter you were handed in your evening class. I told you the woman had denied there was any problem when Maurice and Barbara Kowalski went round there, so there was no further action we could take. And I reminded you about being careful over such situations yourself as occasionally, they can lead to trouble.'

'I was going to ask your advice on what I should say to her next Tuesday, if anything at all, about the letter she passed to me.'

'I think it's safe to say that she won't be there on Tuesday. Anna Wójcik was taken to the Sexual Assault Referral Centre yesterday by her husband. She showed signs of a violent assault. The husband claimed she'd been raped, and said her attacker was Maurice Brown.'

Trev was also lounging in a steamer chair. At Ted's words, he pulled the arms up to return it to the vertical, shedding a collection of cats as he did so, and put his feet on the floor, staring at Ted in a mixture of shock and disbelief.

'Maurice? The same Maurice who yomped up to Kinder Downfall with me to find you when you disappeared that time and had me worried sick? In his work shoes, so his blisters got blisters of their own? I can't imagine anyone less likely to commit any kind of assault on anyone, let alone on a woman, and certainly not a rape.

'What's happened to him? Where is he? Will you have to handle the case?'

Ted shook his head.

'None of my team can go anywhere near it. It's been referred to Stretford and Maurice is on garden leave until it can be sorted out. But that can take forever.'

'Ted, I'm so sorry I passed that letter on to you, which is what must have set all of this in motion. I honestly thought I was doing the right thing because Anna does so often look afraid, and I have genuinely seen bruises on her arms.'

'You did the right thing. There's still a possibility that the letter was perfectly genuine and that what happened since is a way for the husband to try to hide the truth by pointing the finger at an innocent man.

'But Maurice made a rod for his own back because he now admits he did go back to the house, later on Wednesday, when he had no business doing that at all.'

Trev was frowning now as he asked, 'But if he went there on Wednesday, why was the alleged attack not reported until yesterday?'

'The husband says he was working away and only found out what had happened when he got back, then insisted on taking her to report it.

'And therein lies part of the problem. There's probably too long a time-lapse to get any DNA evidence from a rape victim, but there's apparently film footage of Maurice returning to the house alone.

'It's always harder for the defence to prove innocence. All the prosecution needs for a conviction on balance of probability is to show means, motive and opportunity. And that film very strongly indicates two of those, at least.'

* * *

'So no one is in any doubt, let me reiterate. The charges currently facing Maurice are being dealt with by Stretford, fairly and scrupulously, and are nothing to do with us. Not our circus, not our monkeys. Please remember that,' Ted told the team at the start of Monday morning briefing.

It was a full meeting, with officers present from other divisions, who had not previously been told officially about Maurice's arrest, although no doubt many had heard snippets. Any such news always spread like wildfire.

'What we can do, as time allows around the murder case, is to see what further light we can shed on anything surrounding the original complaint of domestic abuse which started this whole thing. The reason I decided to send Maurice and PC Kowalski round to the house in the first place to see if everything was as it should be.

'Maurice hadn't got round to finding out who else lived at the house where the complainant, Anna Wójcik, lives. But Steve has been doing some digging to see what he could find out. The only other person listed as living at that address is someone called Eric Leader ...'

Alison O'Malley sat bolt upright in her seat in surprise at that and said, 'Sorry, boss, but I need to declare an interest. I know Eric. We were together for a time. Well, we never quite got to the official moving in together full-time stage, but I'd say I knew him as well as anyone, and I've never known him to be violent. Certainly not to me.'

'What can you tell us about him? Steve's research shows him simply as a government employee.'

'He's one of us, boss. He's a copper. A DC. I never did find out exactly what branch. He was always a bit secretive. Some sort of special ops of some sort, I always imagined, but we never really talked about it. He always changed the subject if I tried.

'He kept himself in good shape. Certainly knew how to handle himself, but he never laid a finger on me.'

'If it's not too personal a question, would you mind telling us why you parted, in case it's relevant?'

'Oh, that's easy to answer and I don't mind. He was obsessed with having children and I didn't want any. And I mean really obsessed. It got to be almost all he talked about. We argued about it, but it never got physical. We parted on decent terms, but I haven't spoken to him since. But violent? No, never.

'D'you want me to contact him, boss? I could say I'd heard what happened on the grapevine ...'

She got no further before Ted interrupted her.

'Absolutely not, DC O'Malley. Any contact at all would be completely inappropriate. And please consider that a direct order.'

'And even if you did talk to him, could you rely on him to tell you the truth?' Jezza asked her. 'Because someone was certainly violent towards his wife, and I know it wouldn't have been Maurice. So one of those two is lying, and I know where I'd put my money.'

Chapter Eighteen

'That's all any of us can do or say for now on the subject of Maurice. It doesn't mean we're ignoring him or forgetting about him, of course. Just please, everyone, remember your boundaries, for your own sakes as much as his.

'Right, Steve also did some very good work in trying to track down the character we've been calling Uncle, up to now.'

Ted didn't leave Steve in the position of having to put his own findings forward in front of officers he didn't know well. Within his own team he was fine, but outsiders still put him on edge. Ted knew it would be quicker if he summed up himself, checking occasionally that he hadn't missed or misinterpreted anything.

'These gatherings seem to happen twice a week – I think you said often a Wednesday and a Friday at this particular house, Steve?'

'Correct, sir.'

Even that brief response made him go pink and look uncomfortable.

'Which means that the next scheduled one is the day after tomorrow.'

'Who are we sending to attend, boss?' Mike Hallam asked him.

'No one, yet,' Ted told him. 'All we know about this group is that they are already potentially implicated in three killings, so we need to know exactly who and what we're up against before we go in, to avoid any further casualties.

'We know the husband and father of the victims is still on remand in custody, with bail having been refused as he's deemed a potential flight risk. He's suspected of at least being present during the deaths of his wife and only children, if not having carried them out, so he would seem to have no reason to stay around waiting for trial.

'Regarding their presumed leader, who we've been calling Uncle. Again, Steve's skills found that he actually goes more often by the name Tonton within the group, which is familiar French for Uncle, according to what Steve's discovered so far online. And this Tonton is the one we need to talk to.

'Rob, it would seem that the boy who first mentioned this character to you, or the other one who told him about him, may have automatically translated the name when speaking English. But the social media group Steve has found is too big a coincidence not to be connected to the character in our case.

'We're fairly sure that whoever this character is, and whatever their role is, they were not any of the people who were still at the scene when the first responders arrived. Those responders reported that both the back door and the rear garden gate were standing open when they got there, so anyone could have left that way after the killings.'

'Is there anyone else left unaccounted for, boss?' Rob O'Connell asked. 'I'm still trying to get my head round so many people being present for a birth, especially in a smallish room. Steve, is there anything anywhere in this group you're in to suggest actual numbers?'

'I was surprised that the social media group has close to

three hundred members, sarge, but the gatherings – I'm still trying to find out what the most appropriate term is for them – all happen in people's homes, so I can't imagine we're talking more than a dozen or so at any one time, or surely they wouldn't all fit in.'

'That many members?' Jezza queried. 'I was thinking probably a dozen in total, which would explain why no one seems to have heard much about them. So they don't all go to the same gathering at the same time, you mean? And I wonder if there's any sort of subscription involved. Or if a collection of some sorts is taken when they meet. Because if so, I imagine this Tonton would be on a nice little earner for whatever his services are to this group.'

Steve managed to respond to that without prompting, as he could focus entirely on Jezza as he replied.

'I'd thought the same. The get-togethers I've seen mentioned happen twice a week. Sometimes two different houses within the same week, but often the same one twice, then move on to another, sometimes in a different area. I have some addresses, from the group posts.'

'Which is good news for us as it gives us chance to do a thorough recce on the houses before I decide on the best course of action,' Ted told them. 'If we can just get ahead of them and take them by surprise, we might start getting somewhere.

'Mike, let's start taking a look, discreetly, at the address for the day after tomorrow. Can you sort out some low-level obs for the property. We need to know entry and access points, front and back, in particular. Find out if it's even possible to watch from all sides at once, which we're going to need to do if we want to stand a chance of bringing Tonton in for questioning.'

'I'm really stunned that they seem to be going ahead, after what happened,' Alison O'Malley put in. 'Surely they can't think any of that was normal? Does that indicate there might have been more such things we know nothing about yet, perhaps in other areas?'

'Good point, worth checking,' Ted told her, then turned towards Steve, but he didn't get beyond saying his name before Steve was head down at his computer, fingers flying over the keyboard, as he said, 'On it now, sir.'

* * *

'We're going to need to find a way to get round behind these houses for some shots of any rear entry and access points, but at the moment I'm not sure how,' Rob O'Connell said as he drove past the target property.

Virgil was in the front passenger seat, taking photos, trying not to look too conspicuous. The house they were interested in was a modest semi-detached in a road of similar properties.

The small, gated front garden had been sacrificed to accommodate a vehicle in more safety than roadside parking might have given it. A few tall rose bushes just inside the retaining wall were all that now remained in the way of greenery.

'Because I is black, and only a humble DC, I wouldn't have thought of that for myself, sarge,' he told Rob jokingly.

Rob laughed, well used to his friend's self-deprecating humour by now.

'All right, I'll fine myself ten pounds for stating the bloody obvious. But it does look like back-to-back gardens, so we might need to think of using a drone to see better. We need to go back with the best intel we can. The boss seems to be on a bit of a short fuse currently, with all that's going on with Maurice, so I don't want to overlook anything.'

'Poor sod, I can't imagine what Maurice is going through. He did a daft thing but there's no way I believe the allegations against him at all. He looks lower than I've ever seen him.'

'You've seen him, then?'

'I just happened to be passing when he went into the nick first thing to answer to his bail,' Virgil told him.

'What a coincidence,' Rob replied ironically. 'Remember the boss doesn't like those, so be careful not to pull that stunt too often. Just like I'll be careful not to play the same card too often, after bumping into him in the car park when he was going home after reporting.'

They chuckled in unison then Rob said, 'If nothing else, we could always try going down the parallel road behind this one. Going on the knock, saying we're warning householders about an increase in burglaries in the area and asking about what security they have, especially to the rear of their properties.'

'Not sure I like the sound of that. Isn't that how things started to go wrong for Maurice? Door-to-door with a cover story? Can you imagine how many times I'll have people wanting to phone the nick asking if they really have sent a big black bloke built like a brick shithouse round door-to-door? Perhaps I better stay in the car to guard the hub caps and you do the door-knocking.'

'Don't even think about it. I'm the ranking officer here. I'm ordering you to get out there and pound the pavement, see what you can see.'

They were both laughing to themselves as they got out of

the vehicle. They needed the light relief, with all that was going on. Especially with Maurice. Neither of them could begin to imagine what he was going through. Nor could they think of anyone less likely to be facing a serious sexual assault charge which had the potential to put him in prison for a lengthy sentence. Possibly even for life. And for the moment, there was nothing either of them could do to help him.

* * *

Rob O'Connell got lucky at the fifth house he visited in the parallel road. Doubly lucky, as by his reckoning, it was one which was probably diagonally opposite the property they were interested in and should have a view of some sorts onto its back garden.

It would all depend on whether or not there was anyone at home and whether they would be a helpful citizen type, wanting to cooperate with the police, or someone who wasn't prepared to say anything for fear of making waves with their neighbours.

An older man opened the door to him. Seventies, at least, Rob thought to himself. There was a little yapper by his feet, doing its best to look and sound ferocious. It didn't appear to have many teeth but the ones Rob could see looked sharp enough for a nasty nip.

'Hello, I'm DS O'Connell, Greater Manchester Police. We're visiting houses in connection with a series of burglaries, to see if we can give any help or advice by way of crime prevention,' Rob told him, holding up his ID for inspection.

'Toby, be quiet, leave the nice man alone,' the man was

chiding the little dog, bending down stiffly to scoop it up. Once securely in his arms, it curled its lips back and made a threatening noise in its throat, like someone gargling.

'Come in please, officer. If you'd like to go into the living room, there on the left, I'll just put Toby in the kitchen out of the way. He doesn't like visitors very much.'

He wasn't long. Rob had remained standing until he came back, only sitting when he invited him to, then commenting, 'Well, you've certainly got a good little watchdog there.'

He launched into his spiel about proactive policing, helping householders to prevent crime like burglary with a few simple and inexpensive measures. He gave him his card and told him not to hesitate if he wanted to phone the station to check he was who he said he was.

'I suppose I should really, shouldn't I? You could be anyone. But then if you weren't genuine, I would imagine you could easily overpower me to stop me making the call, if that really is the police station number. Or it could be the number of someone who's working with you and then they would tell me anything I wanted to hear.'

Rob had to smile at that as he replied, 'You're very astute, Mr …?'

'Lawrence. And I haven't quite lost all my marbles yet. I'm a bit of a crime fiction buff. I read and watch practically nothing else. Fiction and drama, true crime, anything, really.

'But you won't have the time to hear of any of that, so please tell me what I can do for you.'

Rob asked him about security measures for his house and, after hearing what he said, was pleasantly surprised that they were better than he'd anticipated.

'What about the rear of the property? That's something householders can sometimes forget, but with your interest in crime, I expect you have that covered as well.'

'Come through to the back garden so I can show you. I'd be glad of your advice in case there's a weakness somewhere I haven't thought of. Don't worry, we can go out of the side door, so you won't have to face the ferocious Hound of the Baskervilles again,' he told him with a laugh.

Rob couldn't have hoped for better. From the back garden he had a decent view of the target property, masked only by a wooden fence and a few trees.

'That fence could probably do with being a bit higher, or maybe having some wire at the top. You might perhaps consider getting a quote for that.

'Do you know much about your neighbours, at the side of you, or any of these at the back? Have you had any sort of trouble with any of them? Unsociable behaviour, noisy parties or gatherings of any sort? Happy to help with anything I might be able to while I'm here.'

'I don't spy on my neighbours,' the man began, in a tone which suggested that might not be quite the truth, 'but my bedroom is at the back of the house, because of traffic noise, so if I'm up there, sometimes I do see and hear comings and goings.

'It's a reasonably quiet area, not many noisy parties, but that house over there,' he pointed straight at the one Rob was interested in, 'they have quite a lot of people round every so often.'

'When you say quite a lot …'

'At least twenty, I would say. Men and women. And they look foreign.'

Then he corrected himself quickly as he went on, 'That sounds awful, doesn't it? Makes me sound racist, and I'm not. I don't think I am, at least. But they all wear long, flowing clothes, men and women, and most of the women wear headscarves. Not hijabs. Just an ordinary headscarf. And I know at one time that was fairly common for women, especially in parts of the north. But you don't see it so much now, so it's always struck me as unusual. A bit old-fashioned.'

'I understand,' Rob reassured him. 'You say this happens every couple of weeks. So did they have one of these events last week?'

'I don't think so, no. So that probably means the next one will be this week. There's no nuisance factor at all. It just struck me because of the way they all dress. It always puts me in mind of one of those closed religions, or sects, like the Amish, or something like that.'

'Any idea of ethnicity?'

'IC6, in the majority,' the man replied, with no hint of hesitation.

He saw Rob's surprised expression and laughed as he said, 'I used to work in passport control at ports and airports. Predominantly IC6. I've never seen any IC3 there, certainly.'

Rob tried to keep his voice casual as he went on, 'Before I go, I wonder if it would be possible for me to have a look out of your bedroom window? Just to get a feel for what security is like at the back of the houses in this road. While I'm here.'

'Absolutely it would be possible. As long as you're not going to try convincing me that your interest in a predominantly IC6 possible religious cult has anything to do with burglaries in the neighbourhood. Your body language lets you down when you're not being entirely honest with me.

'If you'd have been in my line for passport checking, I would have clocked you straight away and earmarked you for further checking.'

Chapter Nineteen

'Mr Lawrence, Derek, was extremely helpful, and very observant. He's worked in passport control and he clearly doesn't miss much.'

Rob O'Connell was feeding back to the full team at the end of the day on what he and Virgil had found out about the target house and surrounding properties.

'He's more than happy to have someone on obs in his bedroom, which is at the back of the house with a very good view of the target property. With his background, and how he was with me, I'm happy that he wouldn't say anything to anyone about a proposed operation.

'The houses in both roads have back-to-back gardens, all with reasonably high fencing. It would be possible to climb over, but you'd need to be pretty fit and agile to do so. We'd definitely need to factor in that possibility, though.

'The gardens to the sides are all also separated by reasonably high fencing. That's easier to get over but it means a lot of climbing to get to the nearest road. If we had units at each end of both roads, they should theoretically be able to pick up anyone legging it that way.

'It's also possible someone would try to hide in one of the neighbouring gardens, hoping to wait until all units had left the scene before emerging, so I thought we might need dogs available for that eventuality, boss.'

'So can we go in on Wednesday, boss?' Virgil asked him.

'With the intel we have, can we set up in time to be sure of getting hold of Tonton? Because if we get it wrong, it's probably going to be a long time before we can get near them again.

'No offence, Steve, because you did a great job of finding them, but if this group get a bungled raid, they'll know we're onto them and the first thing I would do, if I was running the online group, would be to immediately block any members who've only just joined. And then I'd set up so many hoops for anyone new wanting to join that none of us would stand a chance of getting near them again.'

'You're right, of course, Virgil, which is why I want to go very carefully at this point. Steve, it might perhaps be best if you stay away from the group for now. As Virgil says, anyone new to the group might come under suspicion as soon as they get any hint that they're under observation.'

Steve's tone in reply was respectful and patient, rather than patronising.

'Sir, it would take the FBI to track me through the group, since it's largely what I've learned of their methods which is keeping me anonymous. But I will, of course, stay away.'

'How likely is this Mr Lawrence to start doing some spying of his own, or doing something else which might draw attention to himself and raise suspicions which might perhaps lead to the gathering being cancelled?'

'Very unlikely, I would say, boss. With his background in passport control, I'd say he's someone well used to knowing when to pass something up the line and show no reaction himself,' Rob told him.

'So can I leave it to you to come up with a plan of action, including what officer numbers you need?' Ted asked him. 'And don't forget to liaise with the dog section to see if they have available dogs and handlers to assist.

'I know it's getting late in the day and we all have homes to go to, but is there any chance of me getting that before you go home? Then I can start to put wheels in motion, so we have the best possible chance of success.'

'Every chance, boss. I was sure you'd say that so I made a start as soon as we got back. It should be with you shortly.'

'Right, thank you. Anything else, anyone?'

'Yes, boss. The elephant in the room. Or rather not in the room. Maurice,' Jezza began, with her familiar determined look on her face.

'You've told us what we can't do concerning him, but can you please tell us what any of us can do to help him? And please don't say nothing because there must be something.

'As you said yourself, the original report of domestic abuse came from our patch, so could we at least be looking to see if that has legs at all? What about this Eric Leader? The copper. Can we look into him? Find out if there's anything on his records about previous complaints of any sort of violence or abuse? Or even any complaints about misogyny in the workplace? We all know that can sometimes lead on to other more serious things, including abuse.'

Alison O'Malley spoke up before Ted could reply to Jezza.

'But like I've already said, I was in a physical relationship with Eric for some time and there was no suggestion of anything like that. I'd have ditched him straight away for any hint of misogyny, never mind violence.'

'Well, I've slept with Maurice and I know he's not a rapist!'

Jezza had flared up before she could stop herself. She

realised straight away that she'd gone too far. Way too far. She'd been totally unprofessional and she felt like kicking herself. Hard.

She could see the shocked look on many of the team members' faces. It was news to a good many of them. She'd lashed out trying to defend her best friend and had made a bad situation so much worse.

She hardly dared look towards the boss, fearful of his reaction. She knew he would never lose it in a team meeting but she had no idea how he was going to react once they were alone.

Ted's voice, when he broke the tense silence, was even quieter than usual. An ominous sign.

'Thank you everyone. Let's have some ideas for morning briefing tomorrow about how we need to proceed with this gathering on Wednesday. Rob, I'll wait for your report.

'DC Vine, DC O'Malley, a word, please, before you leave.'

Jezza mouthed a heartfelt, 'Sorry,' towards Ali as the two of them followed Ted to his office. He did at least stand aside and open the door for them to go in first. Even at his angriest, he seldom lost his manners.

He sat down behind his desk and looked up at them, standing on the other side of it, looking uncomfortable.

'DC Vine, that was totally unprofessional and unacceptable. I know you're concerned about Maurice – we all are – but that was way out of order.'

'I know, boss, and I'm really sorry. I just couldn't stop myself and I agree, it was totally unprofessional. Sorry, Ali. I shouldn't have said it. I wish I hadn't. The way some of the team looked at me I don't think it helped in any way.'

'All right, we'll say no more. Please remember to keep

your personal life out of the workplace as far as possible.'

'Sir, can I just say one thing, though, because it might possibly be helpful?' Ali asked him.

'Is it relevant to Maurice's situation?'

'It might possibly be. It's not official, so I don't know what you can do with it, but I really think I should tell you.'

'D'you want me to leave?' Jezza offered.

'No, stay, if that's all right with the boss.'

Ali posed it as a question, looking towards Ted, who nodded to her to go ahead.

'Well, when I was first thinking of taking my relationship with Eric to the next level and perhaps moving in with him, I thought I'd try doing a bit of digging into what exactly he does. He was always very dismissive of anything I asked about his role. Always jokey. The old "if I tell you I'll have to kill you" line. I know a lot of us don't like to talk about the job when we're at home, supposed to be relaxing off duty, so initially I put it down to that.

'But I am a copper. A detective. I like digging into things. So I dug a bit further. I did finally find a file with a brief mention of his name. That's literally as far as I got. The whole file was heavily redacted. I couldn't read hardly anything, certainly not enough to even get the gist of what it was about.

'I tried asking Eric about it. Asking if he was some international man of mystery because I couldn't find out anything about him anywhere. He laughed it off and said I clearly wasn't looking in the right places.

'The next time I went to look for the same file again, it had disappeared. Completely.

'I've still no idea of what branch he's in, but if he can cover his tracks like that, might that mean that he is beyond prosecution through the usual channels?'

* * *

Ted had at least phoned ahead to let Trev know it was going to be another latish finish for him, but that he would be home as soon as he could. Luckily Rob hadn't kept him waiting too long to submit his proposals for Wednesday which were, as ever, detailed and well presented.

Ted really fancied another walk, to work off his earlier anger which hadn't yet totally subsided. He was still annoyed by Jezza's lack of professionalism, although he understood the bond between her and Maurice. But he was seething about Ali's suggestion that Eric Leader might somehow be working the system to allow him to have possibly carried out an appalling attack on his wife then cynically set up Maurice to take the blame. And whatever branch of the police service he was in, he would certainly have the knowledge of how to do that. Which might of itself explain the time-lag between the assault and the visit to the rape centre.

It might also cast doubt on the authenticity of the later CCTV, although Maurice had now admitted to going back to the house.

Ted doubted he'd get much further than Alison had if he tried to dig into Leader's background. The first thing he would want to know was if the man had really been working away from home for those critical three days, as he'd said.

The Ice Queen had already left, so Ted left her a message that he needed to speak to her as soon as possible. She might perhaps get further, or if not, she would certainly support him going higher to get at information which could be the vital key to clearing one of their own officers of suspicion.

Ted would take it as high as he could to help Maurice, and he was sure his super would back him. To the ACC, or even to the Chief, if necessary. That was what a good boss would do for one of his officers and now, more than ever, after DS Bradley's stinging words, Ted wanted to show that he was a good boss.

Ted had the perfect card to play if he did have to go to the top brass. He'd been at the meeting at Central Park, to discuss the current lack of trust in the service as a whole. He'd been the one to bring up the issue of recruitment needing to be looked at. He was still waiting on a firm date to talk to the ACC about the selection process not being up to scratch, as well as what action to take about serving officers whose conduct was letting the side down.

That meeting had already been postponed several times. Ted had been kept informed, and told that the ACC wanted to bring in a higher-ranking officer from another division to oversee the way forward, to ensure impartiality, which was part of the reason for the delay.

Ted was sure that, after what was said at the earlier meeting, none of the top brass would countenance any officer, no matter how protected their role would normally be, being allowed to get away with anything like what Leader may have done, if it really was him behind it all.

He was halfway across the car park towards his vehicle when he had a lightbulb moment. One he was badly in need of. He'd already discovered that Inspector Esme Lee, at Stretford, who'd been duty inspector the night Maurice had been arrested, was rabidly opposed to any form of special treatment for any serving officer under suspicion of any kind of crime.

If he could find out if that was the case for Leader – and it was something he would look into himself: it was potentially too delicate to entrust to anyone else – he'd be very interested indeed to hear her views on the whole thing.

* * *

Trev was once more talking in German on his phone whilst randomly stirring things in pans on the cooker, when Ted finally got home from work.

He switched straight away to English and mouthed, 'It's Oscar. D'you want a word?'

Ted shook his head emphatically. The last thing he felt like doing was talking to Smith. He still felt a sense of being indebted to the man, but all he really wanted to do was to unwind after a bad day and that didn't involve any awkward chit-chat with Oscar.

'Well, I'll try asking again about dates, but he's up to his eyes in two very tricky cases at the moment. You know how it is. Booking leave is probably the last thing on his mind.

'But I will keep you posted, as soon as I have any news. Annie and I are really looking forward to it.

'Tchüss.'

Ted was rummaging round in the fridge, looking for the makings of a Gunner. He pulled out a bottle, looking in bemusement at the label.

'Ginger beer with hibiscus? What the hell is that? What even is hibiscus?'

His tone was unusually sharp, for him.

'It's something new. I saw it in the shop and thought you might at least like to try it. Sorry. There's plenty of your usual stuff if you don't fancy it.

'Oscar was asking again about our visit ...'

'I can't remotely begin to think about booking leave with all the crap I've got going on at work.'

It was nowhere near a shout but it was certainly louder than Ted's usual voice. Enough to send Barcelona, the most nervous of the cats, scuttling rapidly into the garden through the cat flap.

The eruption was over as quickly as it started. Ted immediately wrapped his arms round his partner and said, 'Sorry. I'm really sorry. I shouldn't have snapped like that. None of this current stuff is your fault.'

'But if I'd never mentioned my concerns about Anna in the first place ...'

Ted silenced him with a kiss.

'You did absolutely the right thing. You'd never have forgiven yourself if you'd said nothing and something terrible had happened to her at the hands of her husband. I should have managed the situation better. I know Maurice well enough by now to know he forgets all procedure when he sees someone hurt or in danger. I should have sent someone else, or marked his card for him much more clearly than I did. I'm sorry.

'Now, why don't you book the trip for you and mam and I'll come if I can. But if I can't, at least you'll have been able to take her on her first foreign trip and she'll love every minute of it.

'But first, I better go and apologise to Barcie, if she's still speaking to me. Then I must try this delicious new drink. I'm sure it will be lovely. It's bound to balance my chakras or something. Keep me more zen and less grumpy. Sorry.'

He was smiling again. Trev threw his arms round him in relief, hating any disharmony between them.

'No, I'm sorry. I should have read the mood music better. I'd just love you to be able to come with us. I'm really looking forward to seeing Oscar again.'

Chapter Twenty

Ted made a point of being in the car park at the time he knew Maurice would be arriving to answer to his bail the following morning. He was pleased to see that he was taking seriously the warning about never being late.

Maurice looked shocking when Ted saw him getting out of his car. He seemed somehow smaller, less bulky than his usual build, even in the space of such a short time. His hair clearly hadn't seen a comb and his morning shave must have been a cursory affair, judging by the number of places he'd missed.

'Hello, Maurice, what a coincidence, running into you. I'd just come out to retrieve a file I'd left in the car.'

It was a feeble bit of acting. Ted had never been known to accidentally leave a file anywhere, let alone in his car. But it somehow assuaged his conscience to have some sort of an excuse to trot out if needed.

'How are you doing?'

It was a daft question. Ted could see perfectly well how Maurice was doing, and the answer was very badly.

'Not good, boss. I can't sleep, I can't eat. I don't know what I'm supposed to do.'

'Have you had legal advice now? Spoken to your Federation rep?'

'Doing both later today. But what if they can't help me? How can I prove I didn't do something? Rape conviction rates are right down, we all know that. But what if the prosecution can make it look like I did it? Enough to swing a jury? We know how much the public hates a copper gone bad. And I did go back to the house, on my own, so I have no alibi.'

'I can't discuss any case details, Maurice, you know that. Talk to your lawyer and your rep, then feel free to call me if you need any more help of any kind. You know we'll all do anything we legitimately can to help you. You hopefully know, too, that none of us believes you capable of any such thing.'

His words made Maurice cry again, so Ted hurried away back to his office to save them both embarrassment, hoping he had at least helped in some small way simply by being there.

He headed next to see the Ice Queen. He knew she was in, and he hoped she would be available. He wanted someone, at least, to put the wheels in motion to find out as much as possible about Eric Leader. It could be the vital key to saving Maurice's skin.

He found her between meetings, so told her everything Alison O'Malley had said to him the day before.

Her expression was never easy read. This time it was at its most enigmatic.

'And DC O'Malley has no inkling of which branch Eric Leader is in? That seems both surprising and disconcerting. It suggests that we are likely to come up against a lot of obstacles in trying to get at that information. I can't think, offhand, of many officers who would have that degree of apparent protection. The only ones who would are likely to be ones who would certainly need it, so nobody would say anything about them without very good cause to.'

'Wrongful prosecution of a dedicated, decent, if misguided, officer would surely count as a good cause?'

'In an ideal world it would, of course,' she told him. 'And I will do absolutely everything within my power to prevent that from happening. I'll take it as high as I can to see what we can find out about this Eric Leader that would be helpful to the case. Specifically, of course, helpful to the initial allegation of domestic abuse, because the rape allegation is not within our remit. I hope you will keep reminding your team members of that.

'However, we have to stay realistic. Let's suppose for a moment that this officer, the husband of the rape victim, was involved in something to do with national security. Counter Terrorism, for instance. Would he be sacrificed in order to save DC Brown? I would like to think the answer would be a resounding yes. I think we both know that that would probably be wishful thinking.

'We must face the possibility that the best we are likely to achieve is the charges against DC Brown being quietly dropped and nothing further being said about it all.'

'Maurice deserves more than that. He deserves full exoneration. He shouldn't have to face the rest of his career being thought of as the copper who raped a woman and got away with it.'

* * *

Ted was at least able to tell the team he'd spoken to the super and they were both doing everything they could to help Maurice. He stressed once more that they were limited in what they could do without appearing to be seeking special treatment for a police officer.

'For now, we need to focus all our efforts on bringing in Tonton tomorrow. We have one chance at this, so we can't afford anything to go wrong. If we blow it, we've no idea of when we might get close to him again.

'We still don't have enough evidence for a murder conviction on the husband and father. None of the witnesses is saying anything at all, so without this Tonton's DNA, we don't know definitely who the actual killer was, or if it was the same person for all three murders.

'Rob, good job with your report. Very thorough. We'll go with that and I'll sort out and confirm the extra bodies we need. It's probably best if you're inside the house with Mr Lawrence, as you've clearly built up some sort of a relationship with him already. So you'll need to be there early enough to start obs on the target house in case people start arriving there ahead of time.

'Or, of course, in case they're doing their own bit of checking out if there's any unusual activity in the area. They must surely realise the seriousness of the situation, and they probably won't be naïve enough to think we're not getting close to them.'

'Unless it really is something they've done before and got away with,' Alison put in.

'Speaking of which, Steve, how have you got on with searching for similar cases anywhere?'

'Sorry, sir, it's taking me a bit longer than anticipated. I went off down a bit of a rabbit hole, because I thought there might be a connection to our case. I still think that's a possibility.

'I found a case over in Wigan last year, just over the force's western boundary with Merseyside. The death of a newborn baby, one of twins. It drew my attention as there was sufficient doubt as to whether or not it was a stillbirth or something more sinister for a full post-mortem to be carried out, and then an inquest. Both were inconclusive, so it was recorded as an open verdict.

'On the off chance that there was any connection to our case, I read the inquest reports. It was another occasion when there were more people present at the birth than would be normal. It never went any further because in this case the family themselves reported the death and by the time a doctor arrived for certification, there were only immediate family members present. Once again, nothing to raise any real red flags.

'The father said it was a tradition in their culture for people to be there to welcome a newborn, but when it became clear something was wrong, everyone left the room, out of respect. Nobody present would say who the others were. There was no mention of a Tonton or of an uncle, but some of those present said they were a group of close friends who met together for spiritual purposes.

'I've been running the names of everyone mentioned anywhere through the system, seeing if there are any crossmatches with our case. That's what's taking the extra time, as once again some of the names are duplicated. The equivalent of John Smith, in terms of frequency.'

Jezza had been looking at something on her phone whilst Steve was speaking. Once he'd finished, she looked up and said, 'All right, this is far-fetched. Very. But so is this whole thing, so I feel I should mention it.

'I was looking at the map for that area. There's a place called Billinge near to where this death occurred. Now Billinge, as I know through Tommy's research, has several witchcraft rumours swirling about it.

'We've been talking about cults, religions, strange beliefs, possibly being behind this case. Is this just complete coincidence, or might it be a belief in witchcraft behind the killings? Always assuming there is any link at all between the two cases. So would it be worth liaising further with Merseyside, to see if there's any crossover between our cases? Should I help Steve with that, boss? At least look at if they'd got any further than we have before it was shelved. They might perhaps have something valuable to share.'

Ted hesitated for a moment before saying, 'Don't spend too much time on it, but do it. I don't want us to get bogged down on anything like witchcraft if it's irrelevant, but the two of you at least look for any striking similarities and keep me posted, please.'

As Ted went back to his office, Jezza sidled over to Alison and said, 'Buy you a soft drink at lunchtime as an apology for dragging you into trouble with the boss?'

Ali smiled at her as she said, 'That counts as trouble from him? I've had bosses who threw things when we stepped out of line. And I'm talking furniture, not the odd pen. But yes, why not? A swift one whilst we eat a sandwich sounds good. Thank you.'

* * *

Ted was getting the run-around and it wasn't improving his mood. He was trying to get hold of Inspector Esme Lee, at Stretford but getting nowhere fast. He'd established that she was on duty and in the building but he kept being fobbed off with excuses.

She was currently in a meeting and couldn't be disturbed. He'd just missed her because she'd gone straight from one meeting into another without seeing the message to call him.

He could hardly go steaming off to Stretford to confront her. He had far too much work to do and the last thing he wanted to do was to antagonise her. He sensed that she could be a helpful ally if he could present her with the information he now had about her rape case victim's husband, and the redacted files on him.

It wasn't evidence. Far from it. Hearsay, at best so far. But it was something on which, had he been leading the investigation, he would want further information. Even if only to rule out any hint of anything.

And having been told of her strict stance on no special treatment for any suspect, especially not for a serving officer, he felt sure she might perhaps be of the same opinion.

He finally got the call he'd been waiting for.

'DCI Darling? DI Lee, sir. I hear you've been trying to contact me. If it's to discuss the rape allegation against your officer, let me repeat what I said before, for the avoidance of doubt. I'm not prepared to discuss any aspect of that ongoing investigation with you.'

'You made your views quite clear when we met, inspector. I agree with your stance on no special treatment for police officers in such a serious case. I'm just calling to check that your policy extends to the other police officer in the case.'

He could tell by the sudden pause that he'd managed to catch her flat-footed on that. Whoever had taken statements from Eric Leader, the husband, had clearly accepted 'government employee' as his correct job title without digging any further.

'Other police officer?' she queried.

'The husband. Eric Leader. He's a serving officer. A DC.'

Ted could almost hear her puzzled frown, the next brief silence was so palpable. She recovered her stride quickly enough as she replied, 'He's down as a government employee. And if he's in the force, why has no one recognised him? Why didn't he say so?

'Can I also ask, sir, how you came by this information? This is our case, you and your team aren't supposed to have any involvement at all, for obvious reasons. So how reliable is your source? Is it simply someone trying to turn the focus away from Brown by pointing the finger elsewhere?'

'I don't know about you, DI Lee, but I dislike coincidences. They make me uneasy. Especially when they're like the one behind this.

'I have a new officer on my team. DC Alison O'Malley. She used to go out with Eric Leader. He told her he was in the force …'

DI Lee was about to interrupt him but Ted carried on determinedly.

'Not in the same force as all of us. She said he worked away frequently and was always very secretive about his whereabouts, and his role. That would explain why none of the people they occasionally socialised with together seemed to know him.

'DC O'Malley was intrigued about him so she tried doing a few searches. She found one mention of his name on one police file – as an officer, not a suspect or witness – but the whole file was so heavily redacted it told her nothing.

'She asked him about it, and about his background but he laughed it off. The next time she searched, even that one file had disappeared.'

There was a thoughtful silence at the other end of the

phone. Ted left it a moment, allowing the inspector to digest what he'd told her before he went on.

'I'm not at all telling your how to run your case, inspector, but I suspect you and I might possibly be on the same page when it comes to treating everyone as an equal. Not showing any bias towards anyone for whatever reason, no matter what their profession might be. No funny handshakes, for instance. Which is why I'm passing the information on to you, in good faith.

There was another even longer pause, at the end of which she spoke, in a considerably more respectful tone than previously.

'Thank you, sir. I appreciate the information.'

* * *

Jezza paused in her vehicle on the station car park at the end of the day, to make a phone call. She'd been hanging round shortly before to catch a word with Maurice when he came in for the second time that day. The team had worked out an unofficial rota between them for doing that, so everyone got their turn but there was never more than one of them at a time, which would look too suspicious.

As ever when she saw her friend, she'd wanted to throw her arms round him and give him the biggest hug possible. She knew she couldn't. They would both break down if she did and that was the last thing he needed right now. She'd had to content herself with a quick peck on his cheek, then had dived into the nearest toilets to burst into tears to deal with the resulting disaster to her make-up.

'Hi Megan, it's Jezza.'

She'd phoned Maurice's live-in partner, the mother of his

twin boys. She imagined Maurice would have gone straight home after reporting, so she asked, 'Is it difficult for you to talk at the moment?'

'No, not at all, he's taken the twins out in their push chair for a bit of fresh air. He looks like he needed a bit of time with them, and I'm always glad of a little break, if I'm honest.'

'Look, this is going to sound completely mad and I'm probably going to get myself sacked, and possibly charged. But I can't sit on my hands while this happens to my best friend. Whatever the risks to me. And all we need is reasonable doubt.

'So will you at least listen and then tell me honestly what you think?'

Chapter Twenty-one

Ted didn't get home until shortly before Trev returned from his evening class. There'd been so much to sort out ready for the following day's operation to try finally to get their hands on the mysterious Tonton.

Ted was beginning to think the group they were looking at must have done other, similar crimes before if they were still going ahead with their next gathering within the same division, when news of what had happened at the previous one had been all over the press and media. Particularly as they still had one of their members in custody, the husband of the dead woman and father of the twins, and all those who had been present had been interviewed at length before being bailed.

It seemed more and more as if those involved didn't acknowledge that what had happened was a crime and a serious one, at that.

The two locations for the previous gathering and the one the next day were about as far apart as it was possible to be within the same division, but they still came under the same jurisdiction. Whether or not it was ignorance or arrogance on the part of the group to stay in the same area, it might just be the bit of luck the team needed to give them a chance to wrap the case up.

'I've not been back long so supper's only been in the oven for about ten minutes or so. Sorry. It's been a bit of a long day again, and I'm afraid it's likely to be even later tomorrow. We might finally get to round up the killer in our triple murder.

'How did your class go? Was there any word from Anna?'

Trev kissed him on the way to the fridge in search of wine.

'I had a text, and it's made me more concerned and suspicious, rather than less.'

Once he'd filled his glass and taken a sip, he got his phone out, pulled up the text and read it aloud.

'I am sorry I won't be able to come to the class this evening. I am not very well, nothing serious, but I hope to see you again next week. Anna.'

'Not how she'd write it?' Ted asked him.

'Not at all. She could have had help with the translation, of course. Or it could be someone else writing it for her which probably suggests it is something serious.'

'Maybe she used an online translator? Would that give the same result? I know they're often unreliable.'

'It could do, but I can't see her using one. I've talked about them to the class and warned how unreliable they can be, so not to use them for any work they want to hand in because they have a habit of totally changing the meaning of things.'

'Do you think she's staying away because she somehow knows you would have heard about what happened and she's worried about what you might think?' Ted suggested.

'It's possible, although not much detail has been released, has it? She doesn't know I have any connection to the police. I've told the group I'm married, because we were doing that vocabulary, but not that you're a police officer. Nor that I'm gay. That's too much personal detail. In the same way I'm always telling them they don't have to give genuine personal information about themselves if it makes them uncomfortable in any way.'

'Because it might be relevant, what did she say about her domestic life? Did she say she was married, and did she mention what work her husband did?'

'She said she was married and her husband does work for the government. He has to travel a lot. I remember her saying that.

'Ted, I'm really worried about her. This message makes me think whatever coercive behaviour she's been experiencing in the past has escalated dramatically since she tried to get help. After all, she must really have been raped and assaulted by someone if she'd been examined at the rape centre. She surely couldn't have faked that.

'I know as well as you do that Maurice wouldn't have laid a finger on her, but clearly someone did. So was that her husband, or someone else entirely? And if it was her husband, does that mean she's cut off at home at the mercy of someone who could do something like that to her and then set up a perfectly innocent man to take the blame?'

* * *

'We're not likely to get another opportunity if anything goes wrong this evening,' Ted warned the team at morning briefing. 'So we need to be spot on from the start. Absolutely nothing left to chance.

'We've been lucky in one way to be getting this opportunity. You've all done very well, especially you, Steve, getting us this far. But it really is incredible that the group aren't covering their tracks anything like enough to stop us getting to them. So let's not blow this one chance by getting complacent and overlooking anything obvious.

'Rob, you'll be in first, of course, and hopefully sending images and intel as soon as there's anything to see. I'll be here in the station coordinating from what you send, so I need updating all the time, from everyone, please.

'Mike, all warrants sorted and issued?'

'All done, boss. Everything as it should be.'

Mike Hallam was a true details man and an excellent DS. Nothing was ever left to chance on his watch.

'Thanks, Mike. And you've got enough vehicles sorted to cover any eventuality of a getaway?'

'Sorted, boss.'

'And who's on foot, in case anyone tries to leg it via the gardens?'

'Ali and me, boss,' Jezza told him. 'We both do a bit of running anyway, so we have the gear and shouldn't look out of place.'

'I'll also be on foot but not running, unless I have to, boss,' Virgil put in. 'Think of me as the mobile roadblock. I'm not easy to get past.'

'In which case you in particular need to be careful. Stab vest on under whatever you're wearing, just in case anyone's carrying anything.

'We'll have a firearms presence as a precaution, and we also have two dogs and handlers on standby if our targets do give us the slip. They'll be waiting well away so as not to alert anyone, but ready to deploy immediately if we lose track of anyone and we suspect they may be hiding out in a nearby garden.

'We also have cars and further officers ready to attend if

necessary, and for any transfers of people if you do manage to arrest anyone. And that potentially means quite a few of them, so they'll all need processing, sorting and initial interviews.

'In other words, warn your nearest and dearest it's likely to be a late night for all of us.

'Stay safe, everyone, and let's get them.'

Ted's desk phone was ringing when he got back to his office.

'Sir, I have a Chief Superintendent Marston on the line, asking if you're free to speak to him.'

Ted tried not to groan out loud. His most recent dealings with the man had resulted in a sort of amnesty, at least, rather than their previous mutual dislike. Even at his best, though, Ted found Marston to be officious and pompous. Not really what he needed, today of all days. But he clearly couldn't put him off forever. He asked for him to be put through then began with, 'Good morning, sir.'

'Good morning, chief inspector. You probably weren't expecting my call, but it was the ACC himself who suggested I should contact you directly and soonish to set the wheels in motion as soon as possible.

'He filled me in on your excellent point about poor recruitment standards in some areas. He wants a detailed report on everything which is currently damaging our reputation with the public, and our proposals on what we can do to improve things.

'I've been chosen to lead and you were the first officer he suggested should be brought on board. Something with which I am entirely in agreement.'

By now Ted was ready to bang his head on the desk in frustration. He had more than enough on his plate. This was the last thing he needed right now to pile on top of everything else. Particularly working with Marston who would want to know, as the saying went, the ins and outs of a duck's arse about everything.

Then he had a lightbulb moment.

'I'd be delighted, sir. Today I'm putting together an op for this evening through which we're very much hoping to arrest a triple killer, but then I'll make myself available as soon as I can.

'Sir, one of the things which is of particular concern to me is the public perception that police officers can get away with things no member of the public could.

'One of my own officers is currently facing serious allegations of sexual assault and he is certainly not getting any special treatment. Clearly we're going nowhere near his case but my team are looking into an earlier domestic abuse complaint which is connected to his case as it concerns the husband of the victim. And he is, apparently, a serving officer.

'Our problem is that the only file we know of about him is heavily redacted, and for the moment, we can get no further. We don't even know where he serves or in what branch.

'Sir, it seems possible this serving officer may, in fact, be the perpetrator in the assault my officer is accused of, and he may be using his specialist knowledge to frame my DC. I'm up against a brick wall if the system is protecting the husband because of whatever role he plays in the force.'

'I see. That is disturbing, to say the least, and I agree. Whatever the reason, we cannot allow the system to protect someone from being held accountable, even if it is necessary to release information on a strictly need-to-know basis. If that information is only available to senior ranks, I would be more than happy to read through it myself and keep you informed of any detail relevant.

'You have my email address, so please forward all the information you have. If I can't get any further than you have, then I will take it as high as necessary to get you what you need. I agree with you. We cannot allow any whiff of preferential treatment for any serving officer, wherever he serves.

'I look forward to working with you once more.'

Ted surprised himself by replying, 'As I do with you, sir,' and finding that he actually meant it.

* * *

'In position, coffee provided, eyes on the target property, all quiet at present.'

Rob was the first to report in from the comfort of Derek Lawrence's back bedroom. The man had asked if he could stay and, after checking with the boss, Rob had agreed. Lawrence was clearly observant. Rob had run a cursory background check on him and knew that what he'd said about his previous employment was true and he had an unblemished record, so he would probably be a useful second pair of eyes for the evening ahead.

Rob continued with a detailed description of the target house's layout as he filmed and sent through to Ted.

'There's a very small conservatory to the back of the house, with the doors into the living room standing open. There's only a small side door from it which leads into the garden if you turn right, or to the garage the other way. That means that if there are about twenty people expected, and if they all decide to try to leg it when we go in, that's a tight bottleneck there, whichever way they try to run.'

'Any signs of occupants, or early visitors?'

'There's a woman bustling about making preparations. Possibly IC2 or IC6, we're having a debate about it. Not that easy to tell. She's wearing some sort of long flowing robe but not anything I would immediately associate with any particular race or culture. Mr Lawrence has more experience than me with such things with his training and he agrees. It looks like any floaty hippy-type thing you might pick up on a market stall somewhere.'

Rob kept up a running commentary on each new person to appear. Some of them stayed inside the main body of the house initially so they were harder to see in any detail, but Ted was also getting information relayed to him by officers closer to the target property.

They'd counted in sixteen visitors to the house when Jezza, running laps round the two roads, spoke up.

'Possible sighting of Tonton, walking south in the direction of target property. Suspect is around a metre eighty-five or ninety, IC6, and wearing some sort of long flowing garment. I'll lose visual on him shortly if I don't stop and if I do I might alert him.'

'Anyone else close enough to confirm that he goes into the target property?' Ted asked and immediately got a response from an officer nearby, leaning into the open bonnet of a vehicle, seemingly fiddling with something in the engine compartment.

'Presumably whatever sort of event this is should get underway shortly now he's arrived. Everyone hold your places until I give the signal. Let's not blow it by showing ourselves too soon. Wait until they're all concentrating on whatever it is they do at these gatherings.'

From his vantage point, Rob could see that as soon as the man they thought was Tonton walked through into the small conservatory, the people already in there formed a tight double circle, clapping their hands and appearing to be chanting or singing something.

Tonton had moved to stand in the centre, slowly rotating on the spot, smiling beatifically at all those present.

Ted waited until Rob reported that the man had stopped turning and everyone was standing in expectant silence before he gave the order for all units to go in as planned.

The Firearms officers appeared first, as if from nowhere. Ted had taken a calculated risk of not wanting to break the door down until they had to in case they had got this whole thing horribly wrong. As SIO on the case he always had to be mindful of the potential for further harsh criticism of police tactics if this turned out to be nothing more than an innocent and peaceful prayer meeting.

An officer from Uniform, wielding nothing more threatening than a warrant, but flanked by the shooters and wearing a protective vest, rang the bell first.

From Rob's running commentary being relayed, everyone knew that it was the presumed lady of the house on her way to open up, and there was no sign of anything untoward.

As soon as she did open the door, she was pushed carefully aside and restrained whilst every available officer was streaming through the hallway and heading towards the rear room.

'Tonton's on the move,' Rob warned them. 'Moving fast, running down the garden to the fence at the end.'

There was a pause, then his voice went up in volume.

'Shit! There's a ladder there, in the long grass. He's chucked it up and is going up it like a monkey. He's over it and running fast. Heading into the next door garden to where I am. There's a side passage from there out into the road. I'm going down to try to follow the same route and intercept him.'

It was Virgil's voice they heard next.

'I'm already outside, waiting to greet him with open arms.'

'Be careful, both of you!' Ted barked at them.

Both still had communication open so all those listening could hear what was going on, listening whilst hardly breathing for any signs all was not well with either officer. It was not that long since Rob had been stabbed trying to apprehend a suspect.

There was a collective sigh of relief when Rob reported that all was well, they had their suspect and there were no injuries.

'But boss,' Rob went on, as they could hear sounds of Virgil taking the man to the nearest vehicle which had come screeching up to collect the suspect. 'This is the man we suspect of strangling a woman to death with his bare hands.

'Except he only has one, boss. He has like a withered arm that doesn't seem to move much independently and it ends in a sort of stump, with no hand. So how can he have strangled anybody?'

Chapter Twenty-two

With so many suspects rounded up and arrested, they would have to be dispersed round several stations for processing. It could end in chaos if the whole thing was not carefully managed.

Ted wanted the main suspect, Tonton, held and interviewed at Stockport, where he could keep a watching brief. He was keen to see the man at close quarters to form his own opinion of him.

He also wanted the woman in whose house the arrests had been made to be kept at Stockport for now. Without knowing how it was determined who would host each meeting, it might somehow suggest some seniority in the hierarchy of the group.

But before anyone began questioning Tonton, Ted needed to make a phone call.

'Bizzie? It's Ted. Sorry to interrupt your evening but I need to check something with you, if I may, please.'

'No problem at all, Edwin. Douglas and I were just watching a perfectly frightful crime drama on television where the pathologist is gadding about doing the work of an entire police team and the CSIs as well. And of course, doing it far better than anyone, with never a hair out of place. So whatever you want to ask me may come as a blessed relief.'

Ted had to laugh. He could imagine the drama she was talking about. He suspected the air might have been turning a bit blue, knowing how much Bizzie hated inaccuracy.

'We've finally arrested the person we were considering as our prime suspect for the triple killing. The one who disappeared from the scene and we haven't been able to track down until now. But it's presented us with an unexpected problem.

'It seems as if they would have been incapable of killing the mother, because you mentioned powerful hands doing the strangling, and our suspect only has one.'

'Then I can tell you categorically that he did not kill the mother. The marks left on the body showed clear imprints of two hands, with definite impressions of two thumbs. Unless this is someone with some highly developed bionic arm which can reproduce that effect, and shed skin cells, your suspect can't have strangled our victim.

'He could quite easily have killed the twins, though, despite his disability. They were full term and both weighed in at just under two and a half kilos, so would have been easy to lift with one hand.'

'It couldn't have been quick, though, doing them one by one,' Ted responded. 'Which opens up the possibility of serious charges against everyone in the room at that time. The killing of the first twin could have been a complete surprise to them all. One they weren't quick enough to prevent. But to stand there and watch as the second baby was murdered in the same way, seemingly without doing anything to prevent it, at least suggests complicity.'

'But as you now at least have your prime suspect in custody, if we can get his DNA analysed as a priority, we will be able to tell you with scientific certainty, not the guesswork you know I detest, exactly what this person's role in all three killings was.

'If you can wait until Monday for further results, and if you have no objection, I can give you a lot more detail on timings, feasibility and so on. Especially as to how easy the killings would have been with one hand. I have my eager young things then, as you know, and this is precisely the sort of case to fire their interest and keep them focused.'

'Confidentiality issues, though, Bizzie, although I appreciate the offer,' Ted told her. 'Especially with a case as sensitive as this one, for so many reasons.'

Bizzie's voice was patience personified as she replied, 'Edwin, let me remind you of something. My little cherubs would literally and without hesitation sell their mothers into slavery to keep their place in my elite inner circle. I would trust them with the most sensitive of state secrets.

'Something as interesting as this would have them widdling with excitement so they would sign a confidentiality agreement in their own blood, if I asked them to.

'I will get my glamorous assistant, James, to have scale models procured, of the correct size and weight. Then the young things can run through any and every permutation of what could have happened, with exact timings.

'It would give you vital detail in building your case, and I would, as ever, ensure that it would be admissible in court. It goes without saying that I would be happy to be called as an expert witness to testify to the results, if needed.'

Ted smiled to himself. He instinctively pitied any defence counsel unwise enough to go up against the professor and challenge any of her findings. She was offering him a valuable service and, with her assurances, he was not about to turn it down.

'Thank you, Bizzie. Those timings may be critical to the

prosecution case in terms of who we charge and with what. If all those present simply stood passively by and watched all three murders committed one after the other, that opens up the way for possible joint enterprise charges against most of them, in addition to the main murder charges against our two prime suspects – the husband, and the mysterious Tonton.

'We both know how tricky such cases can be, so any and all information gratefully accepted.'

'Email me all the detail you have on your prime suspect. Anything of relevance. Height, weight, age, build, which is the functioning hand, and so on. Literally anything. We'll filter out what we don't need and we can then, at least, give you scientific facts with which to boggle the defence's brains. And don't forget to send any new DNA you obtain, as a priority.

'I have to confess I am already eagerly anticipating a glorious courtroom duel, preferably with some young barrister with ideas above their station and little knowledge of science. It's been too long since I last indulged in such larks.'

Despite the seriousness of the case and the prospect of a long night to come overseeing processing and possibly charging all those who had been arrested, Ted couldn't help but smile at Bizzie's enthusiasm.

He'd no time to phone Trev to let him know it was likely to be late – very late – before he could get away but he did at least send him a brief text to explain. Then he went to find the custody sergeant in his own nick, certain he would be firmly off his Christmas card list for this year, at least, having landed him with the unenviable task of processing so many suspects, and finding room at other stations for any who couldn't be accommodated there, at short notice.

Above all, Ted wanted Tonton kept at Stockport for as long as possible, and he wanted to watch any and all interviews with him. He was convinced the man was the key to most of this, but he needed to be there to observe his body language as he was interviewed, to get a feel for what sort of a person he was.

He'd selected Rob O'Connell to carry out the initial interview with the man. Rob was thorough, unlikely to miss much, and not one to bend any rules which could jeopardise anything which was said.

Even so, Ted wanted to watch the interview from start to finish, with the ability to talk to Rob at any moment. At present, the man was told only that he was being interviewed in connection with a serious crime. He'd been offered the opportunity to have a solicitor present.

Ted had avoided any preconceptions about their suspect. IC6 on appearance, he turned out to speak faultless English, with no hint of any accent. Well-spoken, clearly an educated man. Close to, he looked taller than the estimate they had. He also looked totally unconcerned by anything which had happened to him so far, and had rejected the offer of legal representation.

He looked calm and serene, mildly curious, if anything. Certainly not someone anticipating a murder charge.

Rob began by asking him for his name and address.

'You may call me Tonton. Everyone does. I no longer use any given name. I do not have a permanent address. I am fortunate enough to enjoy the hospitality of so many of my friends that I find it unnecessary.'

'I really do need your full name, as it appears on any official document, such as your birth certificate, passport, driving licence, or anything like that, sir.'

Rob's voice stayed polite but firm.

'I don't drive. Once again, I am most fortunate to have kind friends who transport me wherever I need to go.'

'A date and place of birth then, at least, sir, please.'

The man smiled radiantly at Rob as he said, 'I can see that we move in different circles, sergeant. You did say sergeant, didn't you? Please excuse me if I have that wrong.

'Any and all such mundane details from the time before I found the light are of no relevance to me. I exist in the present. In the here and now. With no connection to, nor interest in, the past.'

Rob was trying his best not to show his rising frustration, especially knowing the boss would be watching and listening to everything.

'Sir, we need to question you regarding an incident of two weeks ago, in which a woman and two newborn baby twins were killed. Deliberately killed, from all the signs. We have witness statements which suggest you may have been at the gathering where these killings took place.'

Again, the almost patronising smile. Rob could see where the 'uncle' nickname might come from. It was the smile a doting uncle might bestow on a nephew who was trying hard but failing to come up to the mark in something.

'Please excuse me for picking you up on your English, officer, but two twins might imply four babies in total. Twins implies two of something, so are you telling me that four newborn babies have been killed? That is appalling, as would be the death of any precious newborn.'

'Keep calm, Rob. He's playing with you, but you're doing well. Stay polite and keep at it,' Ted told him quietly through the earpiece.

'Thank you for the correction. I phrased it badly. Twins. Two babies. Killed immediately they were born. Their mother was also killed. Strangled to death.

'Were you present on that occasion?'

'I was not,' the man told him, without a flicker. 'Mercifully, by the sound of it.'

'Yet we've been told that you were present. Can you explain that? There's also CCTV which appears to show you walking very near to that scene of crime. If you maintain you were not at that location, can you tell me where you were at the time, and if there is anyone who can provide you with an alibi?'

'Since you have not yet told me the specific date and time, nor the location of where I was meant to be, I can't, of course, give you an alibi. All I can do is to repeat that I was not present anywhere where any such killings took place. And I do walk. A lot. I find it good for the mind and body. I can't always tell you where I've walked on any particular day.'

The man leaned back in his seat, smiling again, and used his one functioning arm to lift up the other one and hold it across his body. He was wearing what appeared to be a short, black sports sock over the stump at the end of it.

Ted, still watching from the next room, saw the gesture as the man emphasising his disability, without saying anything. His body language was as good as saying, "I'm not exactly equipped for killing anyone by strangulation."

He told Rob, 'Leave that for now, Rob. Ask him about the gatherings. What they're all about.'

When Rob had paused, the man's eyes went straight to the one-sided glass on the wall, clearly knowing or guessing they were being watched.

'Further instructions?' he asked, his tone one of mild amusement, nothing more. He was certainly showing no signs of being concerned.

'Coming to the event you attended this evening. The one at which you were arrested. As soon as our officers were given entry to the premises, you ran into the garden and used a ladder to attempt to make a getaway. Why was that?'

'I have lived in many places where, when police officers, especially armed ones, turn up uninvited, it's usually best to make oneself scarce as quickly as possible. Which is what I did.'

'And what exactly are these gatherings? They seem to be held regularly. Perhaps as often as twice a week, it seems.'

There was a flicker of something in the man's expression at that. Surprise, perhaps annoyance that the police already knew that much.

'Simply good friends getting together to celebrate life and offer mutual support for the trials of its daily challenges.'

'Religious gatherings?'

That made the man laugh. Seemingly genuinely.

'Religion is the sigh of the oppressed creature, the heart of a heartless world, and the soul of soulless conditions. It is the opium of the people.

'That is, of course, a slightly more accurate than usual translation of what Marx had to say about it, and I heartily agree with his sentiment.

'Not religious gatherings at all, in any sense of the phrase. We are far more mutually supportive than many mainstream religions appear to be.'

'And are you the leader of the group?'

'We have no leader. As I said, we are mutually

supportive. No one of us is any more important than any other.'

'Is there any particular significance to you and your beliefs, or those of the group, concerning the birth of twins?'

'You seem to have something of a fixation on twins, sergeant. I don't. I know of no particular significance or superstition about them, although I imagine, inevitably, there must be cultures in which they are not favourably looked on. After all, the earth's population is getting dangerously out of control. I can imagine in places of extreme poverty, the birth of more than one child at a time would hardly be looked upon as a blessing.'

It wasn't what he'd discussed with the boss but on a whim, Rob asked him, 'Have you ever been to Billinge, sir?'

The man looked at him in surprise.

'Billinge? I don't even know where that might be. Assuming you are referring to a place and not, perhaps, to some strange pastime I'm not aware of. Is "to billinge" a verb infinitive? Like to fish, or to skate perhaps?'

'He's playing with you now, Rob,' Ted told him. 'Let's see how funny he finds a night in our luxury accommodation. We have the grounds, since he's refused to answer questions and to identify himself and we're close to placing him at the scene of the crime.

'Make sure you advise him of all his rights then ask the custody sergeant to find him a nice little room for tonight, and we'll start out fresh in the morning.'

Ted did a quick tour of all the other suspects who had been brought in, advising, in most cases, on bail with strict reporting conditions. Then he did the same by phone with the other stations who'd taken the overflow.

He didn't want to be seen to be keeping people in

custody, even overnight, without a shred of any evidence against them.

One thing that he did want done before anyone knocked off for the night, was to identify and question anyone who had previously been spoken to who had mentioned 'Tonton' in their initial statement. He wanted to find out how many other births of anyone in their circle he had attended, and what, if anything, he had ever said to anyone concerning multiple births.

It was long past midnight by the time he got home. Trev had clearly been intending to wait up for him but had fallen asleep on the sofa with all the cats, the TV remote still in one hand, a mercifully empty wine glass lying on its side on the carpet.

Ted sat down quietly next to him and leaned over to kiss his cheek.

Trev opened his eyes, yawned and stretched, movements as feline as any of his companions.

'Hey, you. I waited up to see if you needed food, but I seem to have dozed off. I can put something together very quickly if you need to eat.'

'Thanks, but I've gone beyond eating. I had something earlier on, but I can't remember what.'

'Did you catch the bad guys?'

'I hope so. We've certainly arrested someone who is quite possibly one of the most chilling killers I've come across, if he is guilty, as we think. We're used to people denying charges we put to them, but I honestly think we're going to have trouble convincing this one that what he did, if it was him, is actually wrong in the eyes of the law, not to mention those of any right-thinking member of society.'

Chapter Twenty-three

Friday morning briefing began with Rob O'Connell's detailed summary of his initial interview with Tonton, who was so far refusing to give any other name than that, nor an address.

'He has also refused, so far, to provide fingerprints or DNA and we didn't push it last night. He declined legal representation so it was decided that a peaceful night in a station cell might give him the time to decide to be sensible.'

'Steve, first priority for you today please is to run his details through the system again, but with mention of that withered arm and lack of a functioning hand on that side. That's bound to be a distinctive feature, so if he's on record anywhere, you should hopefully find a mention,' Ted told him.

'On it, sir.'

'Boss, has Tonton given us his bizarre motive for the killings in what he said to Rob?' Jezza asked. 'Is his philosophy some sort of totally warped idea about population control for the greater good of the planet? Two baby girls and a woman killed on our patch, but in the case near Billinge, only the little girl died. The twin boy was left unharmed. So the child-bearing sex are killed, but not the male who could potentially make far more offspring. Is it worth pursuing that line with him during questioning?'

'Would he answer that, though,' Ali countered. 'If he

won't even give his name and address, is he likely to open up about motives? He's not even admitted being present at the scene, so surely he's not going to start claiming any knowledge of what happened, or why?'

'Could all this be extreme misogyny?' Mike Hallam put in. 'After all, we have four dead females across the two cases. Of the people we've interviewed so far, there are certainly more men than women, so is that significant?'

'What about the Merseyside case? The one near Billinge? Have we had the file on that yet and have we cross-checked names against our own case?'

'We have, boss, and I'm working my way through it,' Mike replied. 'I think it would be useful if we could somehow find out what the actual beliefs and ideals of these people are. Surely there must be more to it than wanting to kill females. If that's what they're all about, and why are there still women at the gatherings? And are they involved in the killings?'

Jezza at least managed not to sigh as she replied, 'Coercive control, sarge. We all know that women in coercive or abusive partnerships will often do anything at all their partner tells them to. Including lying and making up rape allegations against a decent man.'

'DC Vine,' Ted cut in quietly, 'completely the wrong time and place for such remarks. Stick to the case in hand, please.'

A flush of barely contained anger appeared across Jezza's cheeks at the words but she wisely said no more. For now.

'But your point is a good one, Jezza,' Ted went on. 'If he carries on refusing to provide his prints and DNA, we need to find a recordable offence we can realistically charge him with then compel him to do so.

'Favourite would be somehow to get at least one person,

preferably more, to tell us that he was actually present at the scene of either or both killings but ran off before the police or anyone else arrived. Mike, that's one for you. You're good at details like that.

'But picking up on Jezza's point, in case there is a whiff of misogyny about all of this, let's concentrate on the women first, and Jezza, you and Ali start on interviewing them. They might just relate to other females.'

'We'll probably need a load of interpreters again, boss, like we did with the first lot of interviews,' Mike cautioned. 'We had a lot of non-English speakers.'

'Sarge, sorry, but do we know that for a fact?' Ali asked him. 'Or is that simply a delaying tactic to slow the process down? Perhaps to protect the main man? To give him time to get clear, and then blame confusion for anything they did happen to say? The old "lost in translation" line.

'After all, this whole line about different dialects and so on. Could it be simply a smokescreen? I imagine most of us can make sense of most British accents, and even dialect words, in context. So surely it should be straightforward?

'We need to know what the language of these gatherings is. If there are really all these regional variations, there must be a common tongue when they all get together. Might that be English? And in which case are they deliberately misleading us to waste time? After all, we know now that Tonton himself speaks excellent English.'

'Another very good point. Thank you, Ali.'

'Boss, I could probably get a quick answer to that from young Ethan, the first person to mention this character to us,' Rob suggested. 'I have the details of his school, so I could phone and say I need to speak to him. He'd love that, a police officer calling him. But I agree. It is something we need to look about.

'Tonton's English is flawless, and as we can't seem to find any ethnic commonality between the different attendees, there's at least a strong possibility that English is used as the common language. Except for his nickname, of course, for some reason.'

'Right, everyone, target for today. Let's focus all our efforts on Tonton for now and see what, if anything, we can get any of the witnesses to say about him.

'I can't believe that amongst all the people we've talked to so far there isn't someone who's horrified by what has happened, seemingly not for the first time, and doesn't want to do something to put a stop to it all.'

* * *

'I'm getting worried about Anna,' she told her husband as she put a large breakfast on the table in front of him.

She never really knew what time of day he would suddenly appear home from work and which meal he would be wanting, although he always seemed to come back with a ravening appetite.

This time she hadn't seen him for a few days and he'd arrived back looking tired, in need of a shower and a change of clothes. She'd sent him upstairs to sort himself out whilst she got out the big frying pan and started pulling bacon, eggs and tomatoes out of the fridge, then taking a loaf out of the bread bin.

He came back down smelling a good deal better, his hair still damp. She had a large mug of strong builder's tea ready for him and plonked it down within reach while she made her comment.

'Anna? Eric's wife? I didn't know you had much to do with her.'

'I didn't. Not before that night out. You wouldn't have noticed – typical bloke, although you're supposed to be observant – but on the way home in the car she was as white as a sheet and shaking like a leaf. And after seeing how Eric kicked off in the restaurant, I could imagine why. She looked absolutely petrified. So I put my number into her mobile and told her if ever she needed any help at all, she could call me. Any time.'

'But you don't know it was Eric she was scared of.'

He was dipping the first piece of bread into his runny egg yolk now, covered in tomato ketchup, and shoving it in his mouth like a man who hadn't eaten for days. Which he probably was.

'She always seems to be a bit like a timid little mouse. But then it must be hard for her, not speaking much English. Eric lets her go to evening classes to help her, but he says she's not making much progress. He reckons she's not the sharpest knife in the drawer.

'Quite the looker though, eh? And makes the most of it. That little black dress look was stunning. No wonder there was testosterone in the air and a bit of caveman thumping going on.'

She'd taken his side plate to add more bread. She slammed it down next to him and raised her voice as she replied.

'Sometimes I wonder why I married you in the first place, let alone stayed with you! That is such a blokey thing to say. That's not a dress a woman like Anna would choose for herself. No way. That's a husband, dressing his trophy wife. It's no wonder it finished with fists, but none of that was

Anna's doing. I could tell that a mile off. And she was genuinely frightened of what was in store for her when she got home.

'And what's this "lets her go to evening classes" rubbish? Why should she need his permission to go anywhere? She's his wife, not his prisoner. Or is she?'

'So if you're worried, have you tried calling her?'

'Of course I have, but it won't connect. Nothing.'

He was still shovelling in food like there was no tomorrow. He finished his current mouthful before replying.

'Sorry, love, bloody stupid comments. I've not slept nor eaten much for two days and nights. I've been focussed on the job so I'm not thinking straight. D'you want me to give Eric a call to find out if Anna's ill, or something? Or maybe her mobile's out of order or she's lost it.'

She'd just refreshed his mug and that, too, got banged onto the table so part of the contents sloshed out.

'No! Don't say anything to him. If he is knocking her about or something like that and he finds out she's tried to signal to me for help, he could do anything. Seriously assault her. Kill her, even. You hear of it happening all the time.'

The tea was still so hot he slurped it noisily, then put it back down carefully.

'I was just trying to be helpful, love. I don't know what you want me to do, if you don't want me speaking to Eric. I mean, that's normal enough, for anyone in the team. I'll often say something like, "All right, Fred, how's the lady wife?". It wouldn't sound out of place.'

'Well, that's because you fancy Fred's wife. I can see that, and so can anyone near you. Your tongue is practically hanging out whenever we go out in a group. And she is someone who dresses like she does for the effect. Her and her silicone tits and eyelashes like tarantulas.'

He nearly choked on his latest swallow of tea at that.

'Ooohh, bitchy,' he said with a smile. 'I didn't know they were falsies, so you've effectively put me off her.'

'But Anna isn't like that. She's like a shrinking violet and I tell you, she's scared shitless of Eric. You must have his full address, to contact him. That was another clue that things might not be as they should, the fact that we had to pick them up and drop them off at the end of the road, not at the house.'

'You know most of us on the team can be a bit twitchy about anyone knowing where they live. That's why we only ever meet up on neutral ground.'

'But given my concerns, surely you can give it to me and I'll try going round there to ask her in person if she's all right. If she's not, she might really welcome a friendly face she can talk to.'

'No, don't do that,' he said, slightly too quickly and with a sharper tone than she expected.

'I mean, I can't just go giving out any of the lads' private addresses without asking them first. It wouldn't be right, and I wouldn't like it if anyone did that with mine.

'Look, when I've finished filling up with this, I need to go and crash out for a good few hours, at least. Make sure the kids don't slam the doors when they get back from school, or they may get shouted at.

'When I've woken up and feel a bit more human, I'll think of what's best to do, without blundering in. Maybe we could arrange to meet Eric and Anna in a pub somewhere. Or even have them round here for a meal, perhaps. I don't mind Eric knowing my address.

'Just let me get some sleep, love, then I'll think of the

best way to deal with this without going steaming in like a bulldozer on people's private lives.'

* * *

'Hello, Maurice, how's it going, with your spot of bother? Are you bearing up?'

Maurice looked surprised as famously grumpy and solitary ex-sergeant Bill Baxter, on the front desk, greeted him as he turned up for the second time that day to answer to his bail. He was under the strictest possible reporting conditions, given all the circumstances of his alleged offence.

Bill wasn't known for being friendly and outgoing. He was polite and competent at dealing with members of the public, but small talk didn't feature amongst his attributes. But Bill's lodger, DC Steve Ellis, had given him strict instructions to keep Maurice talking for about ten minutes, if he could.

Steve was a good lad. Scarily intelligent with a computer or anything to do with one, but a decent lad who behaved himself and was good company for Bill.

'It's not easy, sarge,' Maurice told him as he stopped at the desk. Like everyone else in the station, he always gave Bill the courtesy of using his former rank.

'I'm a bit lost, to be honest. I've never had to deal with anything like this before. It's killing me; the whole thing. I just want it all to be over.'

'I don't envy you, and I can't imagine what it must be like for you. The worry of it all.'

He could at least say that part with sincerity. He couldn't begin to think what it must be like. He'd never had a sniff of

240

anything in his long career, which had brought him his Long Service and Good Conduct medal, plus a Chief Constable's commendation for bravery.

Nor could he believe a word of the allegations against Maurice. The man was many things. A plodder, a bit of a skiver, but he couldn't believe for a moment that he could be violent.

Bill realised his conversation skills were so rusty he had no idea what else to say. But that young DC Vine, the feisty one, who more than one bloke was a bit wary of, had been clear in her brief to him, emphasising what Steve had said. He had to keep Maurice chatting for at least ten minutes, when Steve would come downstairs to relieve him of the task.

Maurice looked on the point of leaving so, rather in desperation, Bill asked him, 'How's that nice lass of yours bearing up to it all. Maggie, is it? And what about your twins? Both boys, I heard.'

Maurice's worried expression disappeared in an instant at that.

'Megan, sarge. And the twins are fine. Owain and Killian. Getting really big and bonny. They're going to break a few hearts when they get a bit older, for sure. Although I'll bring them up the right way. Always to respect women ...'

His voice broke at that point and his face began to crumple so in sheer desperation, Bill asked him, 'Have you got any photos? I've never seen the little lads.'

Bill had never been so relieved to see young Jezza when she came down and took over talking to Maurice. The two of them went to sit on the nearest chairs, heads close together, chatting away like the good friends they were.

They must have been there for twenty minutes when

young Steve came down and changed places with Jezza. Whatever game the two of them were playing, they were being thorough about it.

Upstairs in his office, Ted was stuffing things into his briefcase, determined to get home at a decent time, for once, knowing there was every likelihood he would be at least be on call throughout the weekend, if not working.

Mike Hallam had worked his magic somehow. Ted had decided it might be a case where it was best not to ask. They now had Tonton's fingerprints, a DNA sample had been taken, and he was currently remanded in police custody. They'd need to wait for DNA results, and it could be a long wait, but Steve had already run his prints through the system, so far with no results.

Ted had almost reached the door, briefcase in hand, when his desk phone started ringing. For a brief instant, he considered ignoring it. It would be a futile gesture, though. If it was important, the caller would next try his mobile phone, then probably send someone round to the house if it was work-related and urgent enough.

He picked it up warily, then got a full volume blast down his ear from a very irate-sounding Kevin Turner.

'Bloody hell, Ted. Has sodding Maurice Brown got a death wish, the daft bugger? We got a phone call to say he was hanging round in the street outside the rape victim's house, gawking at it. I couldn't ignore that. It breaches his bail conditions, so I had to send a car round to pick him up and bring him in to chuck him in a cell.

'He'll lose his bail now. I'll have to get him remanded in custody.'

Chapter Twenty-four

Jezza was the only person still in the main office when Ted left his to go downstairs to find out more about what was going on with Maurice.

He felt angry and puzzled in equal measure. He couldn't imagine what had possessed Maurice to do something so stupid, but nor could he immediately think of any valid reason he might have to be anywhere within a mile of the house. It was part of his bail conditions to stay away and he would know all too well how serious the consequences would be if he didn't.

'Everything all right, boss?' Jezza asked him as she saw the expression on his face.

He hesitated for a moment, but knew that if he didn't tell her, the jungle drums would spread the word in no time. Better to give her the official version from the outset and take the opportunity to remind her about keeping her distance. Now more than ever, with the daft stunt Maurice had pulled.

'I've just heard Maurice has been arrested, for hanging round outside the house where his alleged victim lives. He's being brought here for now, as this is where he answers to his bail, the terms of which he now seems to have broken and trampled all over.'

Jezza stared at him, wide-eyed.

'Maurice did that? What on earth was he thinking of, the

243

total idiot. When did he do it?'

'Today. Late afternoon. When he should have been here in the station, surrendering to his bail. He's only just been picked up as it wasn't considered a priority call and there was a delay getting officers to attend.'

Now Jezza was frowning as she said, 'But boss, Maurice did come in to report this afternoon. I saw him myself. He was having a chat with Sergeant Baxter on the desk. He can't have been in two places at the same time.'

Ted looked at her, long and hard. She stared back at him, blue eyes never flickering for an instant. He hoped she would never lie to his face, but with her drama training, it was never easy to read her.

'Jezza, please tell me this isn't something you've set up somehow, in a misguided attempt to get the charges against Maurice dropped. I know he's your friend and you want to help him …'

'Of course I want to help him, because I know he's innocent. But I'm not stupid. I'm not about to risk making a bad situation any worse than it already is. And how could I make him appear in two places at the same time?

'If you're going downstairs to find out what's going on, can I come with you, boss? As long as I promise to behave and not to say anything.'

Again Ted considered her at length before replying.

'Not one word. You can come with me if you stay quiet and only respond to anything I might ask you. Are we clear on that?'

'Perfectly, boss. Like I said, I don't want to do anything to rock the boat.'

As the two of them went downstairs to find out where Maurice was, they ran into a harassed-looking Kevin Turner, muttering to himself under his breath as he headed towards the interview rooms.

'We've stuck him in an interview room for now, Ted. I don't know what the hell I'm supposed to do with him next. It can't be any of us who know him well who deal with him, and the super's not here for me to ask.

'I was hoping to ship him over to Stretford to let Esme Lee sort him, but I can't spare anyone to ferry him there and she says they're stretched too thin to deal with a bail breach at the moment. Certainly not having to collect the miscreant.

'We're stretched even thinner. I've had to beg and borrow extra bodies from other places, so I thought I'd try to find someone who doesn't know him to process him, at least. The bloody stupid idiot. I thought even he would have more sense than to pull a stunt like this.'

'Who called it in?' Ted asked him.

'That was strange in itself. An anonymous male caller. Didn't say who they were. Just that there was someone suspicious hanging about and staring at a house, which turned out to be the one where the alleged rape took place. I would have thought that if the husband had called it in, he would have said who he was, surely.'

'A helpful neighbour reporting someone acting suspiciously in the street?' Ted suggested. 'Evidence that all the Neighbourhood Watch campaigns do some good, at least?

'So where is Maurice now?'

Kevin gave him the interview room number but said firmly, 'But you aren't going anywhere near him, Ted. Not on my watch. Nor you either, Jezza. I want this done by the book every inch of the way. No preferential treatment at all.'

'We can at least have a look at him through the glass

though, to check you've not got him in thumbscrews or anything,' Ted told him with a grin.

'Look, but no more. I'm going to find someone to process him. I hope you, and he, realise this daft stunt could cost him his liberty.'

As ever, Ted held open the door for Jezza to go first into the room adjacent to the one where Maurice was currently sitting, waiting to find out his fate.

He wasn't showing any sign of anxiety. Simply sitting calmly, looking around him with apparent interest, leaning slightly forward in his chair, his forearms resting on the table in front of him. He was not so much as drumming his fingers whilst he waited.

'Er, Houston, we have a problem,' Jezza said straight away, in a tone heavy with irony. 'Boss, that isn't Maurice.'

Ted looked at her in surprise.

'What d'you mean, it's not Maurice?'

'Like I've said before, boss, I know Maurice better than anyone. Look at this bloke's hands. He has a good half of a little finger missing. Maurice doesn't. You must have noticed that, boss. You're observant. You'd have seen it if he did.

'That's not Maurice.'

* * *

Alison O'Malley thought she'd try one more interview before she called it a day. Some of those who'd been brought in after Wednesday's operation had been bailed. Those who weren't considered an immediate flight risk, including those who were not known to have been at the scene of the triple murders.

She was on her way to see one younger woman who fell into that category and who, from initial questioning, did at least speak some English, so she may not need an interpreter.

She'd checked first with Mike Hallam about going there alone. They'd both agreed it seemed low risk, at least on paper, but had discussed all likely eventualities of things going wrong and how to manage the situation if they did. The information they had so far suggested that the young woman lived by herself.

The address turned out to be a pleasant enough ground floor flat in a converted large house. The young woman answered the door on the first ring of the bell. Ali wasn't sure what she'd been expecting, having only seen the members of the group dressed in their various long garments for the gathering, but now the woman was wearing loose jogging bottoms and an oversized T-shirt with a heartbeat logo on it.

Ali presented her ID and introduced herself.

'I wondered if I could ask you some more questions about the event you attended on Wednesday evening, after which you were taken to the police station for initial questioning. Is this a convenient time for you? And I understand you speak English well, is that right? And may I record our conversation, please?'

'I was born here, so yes, I can speak English, and I know you will need to record my answers. Please come in.'

She led the way into a cosy living room and invited Ali to take a seat, sitting down opposite her. From first impressions, which she knew were never reliable, she couldn't reconcile the young woman in her homely surroundings with someone who could be involved with a group which possibly advocated the killing of babies for whatever reason.

'And am I also right in thinking you didn't attend the meeting a couple of weeks earlier at which there were three fatalities.'

'That was a Welcoming, not open to everyone, so I didn't, no. I heard about it, of course, but I wasn't there, so I don't know anything about what happened there. Only hearsay, which I imagine is of no use to you.'

'Having heard about it, can I ask you why you decided to go back to another get-together? Did you not find the news disturbing?'

The young woman smoothed down her T-shirt and folded her hands in her lap.

'I couldn't believe what I was hearing. I wanted to go and find out for myself. Find answers about what had really gone on. It sounded so out of character for the people I know. I've been going to the Circles for quite some time now ...'

Ali interrupted her to query, 'Circles? Is that what these get-togethers are correctly called? We didn't have that information. And what is the basis of the Circles? Are they religious, or cultural in some way?'

'Circles, for our regular meetings, Welcomings for when there's a birth. And no, nothing like that. We're all from different backgrounds. Very diverse. Some from different religions, some from none at all. What we all have in common is a love of the planet, the Mother Earth, and a desire to help and cherish her.'

'But how do killings fit in with that philosophy?' Ali was genuinely puzzled by what she was hearing. 'You did hear about the deaths before you went back to the Circle, didn't you?'

The woman looked more evasive now. Again, she made the gesture of smoothing her T-shirt then refolding her hands.

'I didn't know. Not for sure. I'd heard talk. I needed to hear for myself first-hand what had happened and why.

'Can you tell me what happens at these Circles? What do you do? Who speaks? What sort of things do you discuss? I believe you have a leader of some sort, known as Tonton?'

'We talk. We debate. We discuss. Tonton isn't a leader as such. We don't have one. He is someone of wisdom and knowledge and we respect that.

'One of the things he is passionate about is the drastic overpopulation of the Mother Earth, and what we should be doing to alleviate the problems that causes.'

The hand movement again. And then Ali understood.

'You're pregnant yourself, aren't you? Perhaps even with twins? So you wanted to know what sort of danger you were putting yourself and your unborn baby or babies in by continuing to associate with anyone in these Circles?'

'I am pregnant, yes. I'm not sure yet if it's twins but I instinctively feel it might be, for no logical reason. I'm not even sure at the moment what to do if I find out that it is.'

* * *

Kevin Turner came to find Ted, swearing under his breath once more, and looking even more stressed than he had before.

'I can't get hold of a neutral officer for hours yet, and Stretford definitely can't help. Looks like I'm going to have to get him banged up in a cell for now and I don't like doing that. Not for Maurice, the silly sod, even though he's brought all this on himself.'

'You won't, you know, Kev ...'

Stressed as he was, Kevin was on a short fuse. Short enough not to mind what he was saying in front of DC Vine, as he usually would.

'No special treatment for anyone, not even a copper, on my watch,' he snapped.

'Except that isn't Maurice.'

'What d'you mean, it's not Maurice? Of course it bloody is. Look at him.'

'Did your arresting officers check his ID before they brought him in?'

'Don't try shifting the blame to my officers because one of yours did something bloody silly. Of course they didn't, they know him well enough by sight.'

'Except it really isn't him. DC Vine pointed out he has half a finger missing, and Maurice doesn't. Maurice is a twin. An identical twin. So we're assuming this is his brother ...' Ted stopped and looked towards Jezza, realising he couldn't recall the man's name.

'Malcolm, boss,' she supplied helpfully. 'I didn't think they were in touch at all but he must have heard what had happened and come over to lend his support.'

Ted and Kevin were both looking at her hard, now, suspicious looks on their faces.

'And this coincidence had nothing to do with you, I suppose?' Kevin asked her.

Ted was going to save his questions for her until they were alone. And he was going to want some honest answers.

'Nothing at all, sir,' Jezza assured him, with a perfectly straight face which convinced neither of them. 'I know Maurice doesn't even speak to his brother – hasn't done for years – so I certainly wouldn't know how to get in touch with him.'

Kevin looked once more to Ted as he asked, 'You're the ranking officer, so how do we dig ourselves out of this mess without a wrongful arrest complaint?'

'I'll go and talk to him. Hopefully smooth things over. Offer him an apology but without an admission of anything wrong on our part. Apart from anything else, I would be interested in how he heard about the case, if he and Maurice weren't on speaking terms.

'DC Vine, you and I will talk more once I've sorted this out.'

He was looking directly at Jezza as he said that. She was simply smiling sweetly back at him.

The man he now knew to be Malcolm Brown looked up as Ted entered the room and sat down opposite him, but with nothing more than curiosity on his face.

Close to, the facial likeness to Maurice was incredible. Without the evidence of the damaged finger, he would have been convinced it was him.

'Mr Brown, I'm Detective Chief Inspector Darling, in charge of Serious Crime. If it's all right with you, I'd like to go over a few details with you, and to record all that is said. Do you have any objection?'

'None at all. Happy to help the police, always.'

Even the voice was like Maurice's. Maurice had never lost his Geordie accent, but it was a bit less pronounced than his brother's.

'Can you give me your name, address and date of birth, please?'

'Malcolm Brown. My brother Maurice is an officer here at Stockport. My twin.'

Then he gave an address on Tyneside and a date of birth which Ted knew matched that of Maurice.

'I understand that you were arrested earlier by officers who thought you were your brother. Is that correct? And did you tell them you weren't?'

'They didn't ask me. They just assumed.'

'I apologise for their error, Mr Brown. Do you mind me asking why you were outside the address where you were arrested? You're not, of course, obliged to answer any of my questions, although it would be helpful for me to have some background details for investigations into what went wrong on this occasion.'

'I heard our Maurice was in a spot of bother, for something he probably didn't do. I thought I'd come over to show a bit of support. We've not always got along, but for something like this, family's family, isn't it? And I thought I'd start with having a little look round where this crime is supposed to have happened, to see if I could spot anything.'

'You're not, perhaps, a police officer yourself are you?'

The man laughed at the suggestion.

'Not likely. Not brave enough for that. Not like our Maurice, getting stabbed in the line of duty, and all that. Because I did hear about that, of course, on the grapevine. No, I'm a teacher. English. And drama. So I'm interested in scene-setting, that sort of thing.'

Ted looked directly at the glass as he posed his next question. Asking it of Malcolm Brown, but making sure Jezza knew it involved her.

'And would you mind telling me how you heard about DC Brown's predicament? It was my understanding that you were not in contact with one another.'

'Haven't spoken for ages,' he said cheerfully. 'We fell out when we were lads when he slammed a door shut on my hand and they couldn't save my finger. Then he pinched my girlfriend, Barbara, off me and married her. We've barely spoken since. Siblings can be like that. Even identical twins. Perhaps we're too alike. But I still hear from Barbara on occasion. She told me when he got stabbed. And wor kid's lady friend keeps in touch. Megan. Lovely person. Keeps us up to date about the bairns. Sends photos of the new twins, especially to my missus.

'And of course, once I heard wor Maurice was in a load of bother, I had to come and see if there was anything I could do to help. I thought this was a good opportunity to bury the hatchet and get back in touch.

'So now you know I've not committed any crime, I'll go round to his place to say hello, if that's all right? I can't wait to see the look on his face when he sees me. Assuming I am free to go now you know it was me outside that house, not Maurice.'

'You can indeed, Mr Brown, and thank you for your cooperation.'

Ted went back into the adjoining room where Kevin and Jezza were both still waiting.

'Nice one, Ted. Very well handled. That politics degree still comes in useful. Right, I'll now go and kick the backsides of my officers who failed to check ID before dragging him in here.'

As he left the room, Ted looked at Jezza and said, 'DC Vine, I think you and I need to have a talk.'

Chapter Twenty-five

Trev took one look at Ted when he finally got home from work and risked a humorous remark, hoping it wouldn't lead to another flare-up. In a decent impersonation of Gene Wilder's voice as The Waco Kid in one of Ted's favourite films, the totally politically incorrect Blazing Saddles, he said, 'Oh deary-dear. Look what the cat dragged in.'

At least Ted managed a smile as he crossed the kitchen to kiss him on the cheek and greet the milling felines.

'It's definitely been one of those days. Sorry I'm not very good company at the moment. I do try to leave work stuff in the office, but it's not always easy.'

'I suppose it's really not a good time to be asking again about our trip to Germany?' Trev asked, an unusual note of hesitancy in his voice. 'Only Annie is getting so excited at the idea of her first trip abroad, I'd really like to be able to book something soon.'

Ted sighed.

'I really wish I could say go ahead and I'll definitely come with you. But I can't, I honestly can't. Maurice's case is getting more complex than ever. I had to read Jezza the riot act just now and I might still have to take it further regarding her totally inappropriate behaviour. Even if she was doing it trying to help a close friend.'

He'd had to remind Jezza, in the strongest terms, that instead of making things easier for Maurice, she had potentially made an already bad situation much worse. On arrest he would have been cautioned, including the words: 'But, it may harm your defence if you do not mention when questioned something which you later rely on in court,' and so far, Maurice hadn't been able to mention any such thing as his twin brother because he was apparently totally unaware of Jezza's scheme.

Knowing Jezza, he was prepared to accept she'd been trying to help. But her interference risked turning into a disaster. It had also lost her Ted's confidence in her. He couldn't now be sure when she was telling him the truth, or when she was lying, even if she was doing so with the best of intentions.

'I think it would be worse for you, and for mam, if I said I'd come with you then had to back out at the last minute. So you two book, and I promise, if I can come, I will.'

'But what about the pussies? We'll need to book someone for them and the sitters might not be happy if we booked then had to cancel them at the last minute because you suddenly found you couldn't come.'

'Book someone anyway,' Ted told him. 'If I can't come it's likely to mean I'm working such long hours that they'd appreciate having someone around to look after them properly, and it would take the pressure off me.

'I don't think any of the sitters we've used before would be worried if they knew they might sometimes find me snoring away on the sofa. So please, book. Cat-sitter and flights. On my card. It would make me feel better for neglecting you as much as I am currently.

'Talking of Maurice's case, I don't know if or when you might see Anna back in your class but do please keep a professional distance. For your own safety, as much as

anything. Don't give her any hint you know anything about
her assault, or anything else. That could get me into a lot of
trouble, for one thing.

'And be very careful, if she does come back, to keep an
eye out for her husband either dropping her off or collecting
her. I know you can look after yourself in most situations,
but my instincts are telling me he might be someone very
dangerous. Someone who might possibly carry a weapon. So
watch yourself.

* * *

DS Harry Carver's wife hadn't been married to an
undercover copper as long as she had without picking up a
few hints along the way. And despite what he'd said about
Eric Leader's wife, Anna, she put more faith in her own
female intuition than she did in his blokey team-bonding
attitude.

She didn't know exactly where they lived but when
they'd chauffeured them for the infamous night out, when
Harry had stopped at the end of the road both times, she'd
watched the direction the couple had walked in, both times
on the same side of the road. It wasn't a long one, not all that
many houses, so she could do worse than walk up and down
it a couple of times to see if she could spot Anna anywhere
about. Or even a neighbour in a garden who might be able to
help her.

Of course, if Eric Leader was as paranoid about
protecting his personal life as Harry was, they might live
somewhere else entirely and have walked some distance for
their lift. Val Carver instinctively didn't think so. She'd
noticed how intensely uncomfortable Anna had looked in

that slutty little black dress. She wouldn't have wanted to parade very far, dressed like that. She probably wouldn't have been able to even if she had, with the teetering heels she'd been wearing.

She'd looked like a street girl. A man's fantasy of a woman. Something was badly wrong in that relationship, Val was sure, and she wanted to try to find out what.

She walked up and down the road a couple of times, to see what she could see which might give her a clue. From her own experience, she knew Eric Leader would have plenty of security cameras round his house. She knew, too, that some of them were bound to have live feed to the man's phone. She was hoping he might possibly have it switched off if he was on duty and not wanting anything to betray his presence.

She was taking a big risk if it wasn't muted and she knew it. But she was genuinely worried about Anna. She'd been prepared not to hear anything from her. The fact that her own attempts to call her had led nowhere made her want to find out at first hand why that was.

Luck was on her side. She was on her second stroll down one side of the road when she saw an elderly woman struggling with two carrier bags stuffed full of newspapers, heading towards her recycling bin which stood outside the gate awaiting collection.

'Hello, can I give you a hand with those?' Val called out over the garden gate, which was standing ajar.

'Oh, thank you, love, that would be very kind. I've hurt my wrist somehow and these bags seem to get heavier.'

Val walked up the drive and took both bags from the woman. They were heavy. No wonder she'd been struggling, even without a bad wrist.

The woman was short, slim, immaculately dressed, hair perfectly styled, full make-up on. She could have been going out to lunch at the best restaurant rather than trying to carry out her recycling.

'I keep saying I'm going to stop taking so many newspapers, but I do like to keep up with current affairs. Then there's my crosswords, and the sudoku. It's all supposed to keep your brain active, although I sometimes wonder if I've left that too late.

'It's really so very kind of you. The neighbours don't seem to be all that helpful round here. They tend to keep to themselves. I hardly ever find anyone to talk to, even, never mind to help me with little things like this.'

Val emptied the bags into the bin then asked if there was anything else she could help with.

'That's so kind of you, but those were the last bags. Would you like a cup of coffee, if you've time?'

'I'm so sorry but I'm a bit pressed just now. I came to see someone I know through work, but I've stupidly forgotten what number she lives at. I wonder if you might perhaps know her. Her name is Anna, and she's a young Polish lady.'

'I don't really know anyone, not to talk to.'

There was such a note of sadness in her voice that Val wished she could spare the time to talk to her. But she was too worried about Anna.

'I'll give you my phone number and if you ever need any help with things like carrying the recycling, please do give me a call. Have you got your mobile phone on you? I can put my number straight into it.

'I don't have one of those, dear. I don't even know how to use one. I just have an ordinary telephone, in the house.'

Val reached in her bag for the little pocket diary she still carried, despite all the modern technology on her own phone. She sometimes found it quicker to jot important events down that way.

'My name's Val. Val Carver. And this is my number. Do please feel free to call me. I mean it. I have teenagers at home who could easily cycle over and do something like this for you, and I like them to do things like that, instead of finding mischief to get up to.'

'That's so kind of you, dear. It would be such a help. And my name is Hilary. Hilary Connolly. Oh, and there is a young lady I sometimes see. Always on a Tuesday evening. I see her walking up to the bus stop. I haven't seen her this week though. She seems shy, but very polite and she always says good evening if she sees me. She has a foreign accent of some sort. She lives at that house, over there.'

Val Carver was no fool. She knew meddling in domestic abuse was potentially dangerous. Especially where someone like Eric Leader was concerned. She'd known him a good while but had never taken to him. There was a dark side to his nature that had always troubled her.

She knew the pressures of the job. The terrible strain the team members were often under and how difficult some of them found it to switch off. She also knew well enough that Eric Leader was her husband's second in command. His right-hand man. In other words, when Harry was sleeping, Eric was on duty and holding the reins.

Another thing she knew, through Harry and their own set-up at home, was that because of who they were and what they did, team members would have the latest hi-tech security devices on their homes. Spy cameras and doorbell cameras which could instantly send images of anyone at the property to the owners' phones.

There would be no letterbox to peer through, either. Nothing which could allow someone to post anything at all into the house. At best there would be a small, locked box as far from the house as it was possible to get.

Val had no idea what she was going to do, but she had no intention of leaving until she'd seen for herself what state Anna was in. If she was even inside the property and Val could find some way to see her.

* * *

Ted was just about to tuck into a delicious syrup sponge pudding when he was interrupted by his mobile phone.

'Ted, don't you dare. If it's urgent, they'll call you back. Eat your pudding first, at least,' Trev told him.

'You know I can't. Hopefully it will be something and nothing and I can eat first before I have to deal with whatever it is.'

He answered guardedly and heard a familiar voice.

'Chief Superintendent Marston here. I'm sorry to interrupt you at home, but I thought I should inform you as soon as I could.'

Ted mouthed a 'sorry' to Trev and headed towards the door to the garden. If the chief super was calling him at home in the evening, there would be a valid reason for it.

'No problem, sir.'

'I have reasonably good news for you although not, I fear, quite as good as you would have wished. Not for want of trying on my part, I can assure you, and this is most definitely a case of being thankful for what we have got.

'The good news is that all hint of any charges against your DC Maurice Brown are to be dropped with immediate effect. Each and every mention of this unfortunate case will mysteriously disappear off all systems everywhere without trace.

'The less good news is that, of course, he will never be officially cleared of the allegations so for some, there may always be a lingering doubt about what really happened.'

'Sir, that's not acceptable ...' Ted cut in, determined to fight Maurice's corner for him to the bitter end.

'Acceptable or not, chief inspector, that is the only offer which is on the table, and it is a one-time offer. A take it or leave it one. Allow me to explain.

'You told me you were concerned that your officer was being set up in order to protect another officer. One serving, perhaps, in some little-known branch who might consider themselves to be untouchable.

'I promised to get to the bottom of it and to go as far as was necessary to show that we, at least, investigate everyone equally, regardless of what their profession is. And that includes investigating our own, when necessary.

'I said I would go as high as it took to get the information I needed. Even I had no idea how high that would be. All of this is, of course, totally off the record. You and I never had this conversation.

'All that will happen now is that the charges will be dropped, and this whole incident will never be mentioned again. And yes, that does mean that a rogue officer will continue serving and will be protected from any fall-out. But his card will be firmly marked. He will never get away with anything in the future. Not so much as a parking ticket. But that is all we can achieve.'

'Sir, that's wrong on so many levels. None of us should be above the law. None, in whatever role.'

Marston said only two words. The name of a unit. The one in which the husband of the rape victim served. It sent a chill through Ted. He understood instantly why he had no hope of taking this any further. Not as long as the man was serving and doing his current job.

'I am sorry I have not been able to do more for you,' Marston continued. 'I wish I could, but my card is also now marked from on high, so I am powerless to do more. From the very top, too.

'Your officer is being informed as soon as possible. He may well already know. He too will have been sworn to secrecy and strongly reminded of the consequences of speaking of this sorry affair ever again to anyone.

'When I spoke to your very charming partner previously to ask about doing a small sketch for you as a token of my gratitude to you for how you dealt with my own difficulties that time, he told me that as well as your love for cats you were also a fan of country music. It may surprise you that I am, too. I particularly like the voice of Kenny Rogers.

'I'm sure you at least know his wonderful interpretation of Don Schlitz's lyrics to The Gambler. I would advise you simply to heed the advice of the opening lines of the refrain.

"You got to know when to hold them

Know when to fold them

Know when to walk away

And know when to run."

'This is most definitely the time to fold and run, chief inspector.

Chapter Twenty-six

Val Carver spent some time looking at the house where Eric and Anna lived. Once she saw all the security devices in places, she knew that Hilary Connolly had been talking about the right young woman. No other house in sight looked to be as well protected.

However she approached the place, more than one camera was going to pick her up immediately. If Eric Leader could use his phone, he would see her. He could be working anywhere within a forty-mile radius or more. The best she could hope for, if he had his phone on, was that he was as far away as possible, and there were endless roadworks to slow his journey.

She wasn't going to make the basic mistake of touching the doorbell and triggering its CCTV. She began by rapping on the door with her knuckles, saying, as loudly as she could, 'Anna? It's Val Carver. Are you in there? Anna?'

Total silence. Not even the sound of any movement from inside.

Val wasn't about to try creeping round the outside of the house trying to find somewhere to get a look inside. She wouldn't put it past Eric Leader to have rigged up some sort of nasty surprise booby trap for anyone stupid enough to try to get into his property. At the very least there would be something, somewhere to trigger an alert at the nearest police station. Just as there was on her own house. Knowing the sort of thing Harry and Eric got up to, she was normally glad of it.

She knocked again then spoke, putting her mouth as close to the door as she could and raising her voice.

'Anna? Anna! It's Val Carver. Are you in there? Anna? I'm not going to go away until I find out if you're all right.'

She waited a moment, not knowing if what she'd taken for a small sound from inside was simply wishful thinking on her part.

'Anna? If I don't get some sign from you that everything's all right, I'm going to call the police. Tell them I think you may be seriously injured and ask them to break in.'

The silence continued. Seconds? Minutes? Val had lost all track of time, but she became convinced there was someone on the other side of that door, listening to every word she said.

She had one more try.

'Anna, please. I only want to help you.'

She heard a fumbling sound then the clack of a bolt being pulled back. Then more clicks and rattles until finally one swollen and bloodshot eye, bruised black and blue all round, tear-filled and showing terror, peered at her through the crack.

'Oh, Anna, love, what has the bastard done to you this time?' Val asked her quietly as she saw the young woman's face disappear and heard her slide to the floor, making it impossible for her to push the door any further. Certainly without risking any more harm to someone she could clearly see already needed medical attention.

Without hesitating, she took out her phone and dialled 999. All she hoped was that the emergency services would arrive before Eric Leader did.

* * *

The first thing Ted did after the phone call from Marston, before he told Trev the good news, was to phone Maurice. His voice sounded dejected, lacking in any hope, so Ted was pleased he could at least provide some, although not yet as much as he would have liked.

'Yes, boss?'

'Maurice, I have good news for you, which I'm guessing has not yet reached you. All charges against you are being dropped, with immediate effect.'

There was a stunned silence at the other end of the line.

'I would have preferred to be able to say you were being officially cleared, but it doesn't amount quite to that. That's complicated, for all sorts of reasons. But it's over for you. All trace of any arrest or charges or anything will simply disappear, and that's as much as I'm at liberty to tell you.'

When Maurice found his voice, there was a catch in it as he asked, 'Does that mean I can come back to work, boss? To the team?'

'It does, Maurice, but I want you to take the weekend off first. I know you didn't commit any assault of any kind, but you did make some serious procedural errors in how you acted. You're going to need a return-to-work interview on Monday morning where we'll go over such things, and I may decide to refer you for further training. But you can come back and welcome. Just promise me you'll never act like such a total plonker again.'

Trev saw the relieved smile on Ted's face as he came back in from the garden and paused in his meal preparations to plant a kiss on his cheek.

'I'm guessing that whatever it was is good news and I'm so pleased for you. It's about time you had something to smile about. Am I allowed to know what it was or is it classified?'

'Strictly speaking, it is, but I'll at least tell you that the call was to tell me Maurice is off the hook. He can come back to work on Monday. All charges dropped.'

Trev put down the cooking utensils he was wielding and wrapped Ted in a hug.

'Oh, Ted, that's wonderful news! I know you're fond of Maurice. I am too. The way he came with me that night to find you told me all I need to know about him. I really am pleased for you, and for him, of course.

'Are you ready to eat now? The food's ready whenever you are.'

Ted hesitated, then said, 'Actually, can you give me another five minutes? There's another call I really should make, as a courtesy. And also to assure someone that this is the right decision and I've not been getting rules bent because Maurice is one of my team.'

He dialled Inspector Esme Lee's direct line, which he'd asked for and been given the last time they spoke, in case of any developments.

'DCI Darling, Inspector Lee. I have just this minute heard from Chief Superintendent Marston that all charges against Maurice Brown are being dropped immediately. I thought I'd inform you myself, as soon as I heard, as a courtesy.'

He could almost hear her start to bristle as she began, 'Sir, I hoped you were being honest with me when you said there would be no bias. This all sounds a bit too convenient ...'

'Oh, there is certainly bias behind this decision, and

someone is being protected, but it definitely isn't DC Brown.'

He repeated the same two-word unit name to her as Marston had recounted to him and heard her sharp intake of breath. The implication behind those little words tended to have that effect.

'Mr Marston took this as high as he could go. High enough at least to discover what we're up against. Officially, it's case closed. Unofficially, I have a feeling you and I might be on the same page in thinking that despite protection from on high, there might possibly be more to be done to right a wrong. But for now, I think we watch and wait.'

'I'm not a very patient person, sir, I should warn you.'

'Sometimes, inspector, it's better to wait quietly in the wings, watching for the right opportunity. That's certainly what we need to do for now.'

'We, sir?' she asked him.

'We, definitely, inspector. You and I certainly seem to be singing from the same hymn sheet on this one. To misquote Orwell slightly, all of us are equal and none is more equal than others.'

* * *

All that Val Carver could do as she crouched outside the front door was to squeeze one arm through the narrow gap and, as gently as she could, stroke whatever bit of Anna Wójcik's battered body she could reach, all the time speaking as calmly and reassuringly as she could.

'Don't worry about anything, Anna, love. There's an ambulance on its way and I've stressed that it's urgent. The police will attend, too. That's routine for a serious assault.'

Anna tried to speak at that but she was too weak to produce more than a barely audible croak.

'No police. Please, no.'

'Sweetie, yes. You need help. Seriously. If Eric's done this to you ...'

Somehow Anna found the strength to raise her voice.

'Not Eric, no, he not do this.'

'Oh, love, there's no point defending him. I saw how afraid you were on that night out. I know it's him, and it's time for it to stop. He needs help, as much as anything. Any man who can to this to a woman, especially his wife, is seriously sick. He needs help, not just punishment. He's not right.

'And if he can't control himself any better than this, he's in completely the wrong job. If he can blow up this easily, he risks the safety of the whole team. Harry will throw him out, as soon as he hears about this. And he will.'

Val could hear Anna repeating 'No, no, no,' over and over, in a tone of anguish. Then, to her surprise she felt the door slowly inch towards closing as Anna somehow summoned up the strength from somewhere to start pushing against it.

'Oh, no you don't, lady,' she told her firmly. 'This has been going on long enough and this time he's gone way too far. Whether you want help or not, I'm not letting him get away with this,' and she started to shove back, hard.

She could see through the gap that the floor covering was ceramic tiles, and the only door mat was outside on the step where she was. The smooth surface would make it easier for her to move Anna. Weak as she was, she hadn't the strength to resist as, slowly, her battered body was pushed, firmly but gently and the door began to open wider.

It was more difficult than Val had thought as she was trying so hard not to hurt Anna any further. She couldn't remember ever having been more pleased to hear an ambulance siren give a short blast of caution as it turned into the road and came to a halt outside the front gates.

* * *

The team had split the weekend between them; half in on Saturday, half on Sunday. They needed to keep cracking on with the triple murder case. The media were already starting to snipe about the lack of even any news of a suspect, let alone the suggestion of arrests which might go somewhere.

Ted was in first and was pleased that both Jezza and Steve were on duty. They were the ones he wanted to be among the first to hear the good news about Maurice, being the closest to him of any of the team.

He would certainly need to speak to Jezza again to inform her of what he'd decided to do about her actions. He strongly suspected that Steve had been in on her plan, too, so he would be another one who would need reminding of his boundaries.

Jezza was the first to show her feelings once Ted told them the news. She let out a 'Yes!' of triumph and gave an air punch.

'Maurice will come back to the team on Monday. I have warned him I will be referring him for retraining on correct procedure, but I think that can wait until we at least wrap up the triple murder. We need all hands on deck for that one.

'Mike, where are we up to with it? Any new developments?'

Alison O'Malley spoke before Mike could.

'Sarge, sorry to interrupt, but I've not had time to update you on my last interview yesterday. There is just a chance that the young woman I spoke to at length might be a willing and cooperative witness about the group in general, although she wasn't present for the killing.

'One incidental useful thing which she told me was that they call their gatherings Circles, and when there are numbers of them present at a birth, that's called a Welcoming.'

'Welcoming? That is so sick,' Jezza cut in. 'You mean like "hello, baby, welcome to the world, but because you're a girl, we're going to bash your brains in"?'

Ted was glaring at her now.

'Totally unacceptable, DC Vine. Anywhere, and certainly out of order in a briefing.'

His tone was unusually sharp so Jezza had the sense to at least look contrite and she said, 'Sorry, boss. Bad taste. I'm just gobsmacked by everything to do with these people.'

'Will this young woman testify on the record about them?' Ted asked Ali. 'And will she say anything of use to us? After all, it's just hearsay if she wasn't present at the murder scene.'

'I think she will, boss, and I think she would make a powerful witness. She's found out that she's pregnant. She's worried it might be with twins, as they run in the family, so she wanted to find out what the position was. If the triple killing was one rogue member of the Circles who lost it for some reason and went on a killing spree, or if it was incited by something in their beliefs.

'She also told me that Tonton is always saying that to protect the Mother Earth the population has to be drastically reduced, by whatever means available.'

'It's tenuous, but it's the best we have so far, so run with that for now, please.'

Ted made to go towards his office but paused to say, 'DC Vine, another word, please.'

* * *

'This is Anna Wójcik. She appears to have been seriously assaulted. I'm a friend, Val Carver. I'm the one who called you. I came round and found her like this. She didn't want to let me in but I managed to push her out of the way as carefully as I could to check on her. I think it's possible she might have been assaulted by her husband, so I've also asked for the police to attend in case it's a serious domestic abuse case. Oh, and she's Polish; her English isn't very good.'

The ambulance crew, one male, one female, were inside the house now so Val stepped out of their way to allow them space to make their initial assessments.

'Hello, Anna, is it? I'm Lucy and this is my colleague, Cliff. Is it all right if I examine you, please? And can you tell me what happened?'

Close to, Val could see the terrible damage inflicted on Anna. Now she could see all of her face, she saw that both eyes were swollen almost shut and her lips were split in several places. When she tried to move them she could also see that her front teeth were broken.

'I raped. Saturday. Report at centre, Manchester.'

Her voice was so weak now as to be hard to hear.

'Saturday?' Lucy queried. 'You mean today?'

She was clearly wondering, as was Val, what the woman was doing lying here on the floor in such a state if she'd been seen at the sexual assault centre earlier that day.

'Before,' Anna said. 'Saturday before.'

The three of them exchanged glances. The injuries they were confronted with were not remotely from a week ago. The split lips were still bleeding, every time Anna tried to speak, for one thing.

There was another brief siren blast as a police car pulled up behind the ambulance. Another vehicle Val was heartily thankful to see. Two officers got out, another male and female team, and started walking towards the house.

Before they reached it, another car came screeching round the corner on two wheels and stopped as close to the house as it could get. The driver's door was flung open and a man jumped out, running up the drive, a police badge in one hand, a gun in the other.

The female police officer's hand went straight to her radio until she saw the man's gun lock onto her as he shouted, 'Police! Protected witness. Get out of here, now, all of you.'

'Eric?' Val Carver asked, astonished at the sight of Anna's husband, Eric Leader. 'What are you talking about?'

'All of you. Get lost. I've got this. You don't know what you're meddling in. No funny business, just go. I am authorised to shoot if necessary.'

'You know this man?' the female officer asked Val Carver.

'Yes. My husband's his DS. It's … complicated. But he probably is authorised to shoot.'

'Right, everyone back out into the road, now, while we radio for further instruction. I can't make any decision until we know what we're dealing with here.'

Val couldn't bear to see the expression on Anna's face. All hope drained away in an instant, replaced only by pure terror. She'd no idea what to do, but perhaps if they all pulled back, Eric might calm down a bit. She could also try phoning Harry, her husband. It wouldn't take him long to get round here, if she could wake him, and he might be able to make sense of what was going on.

They all pulled back, slowly, keeping their eyes fixed on the scene just inside the open door as they did so.

They heard the door slam shut.

Then they heard a single gunshot.

Chapter Twenty-seven

'Ted? Roly. Duty inspector, and why does it always happen to me?'

Ted had just finished telling Jezza her fortune in no uncertain terms when his phone rang as she was closing the door behind her. Quietly. She was subdued, for once. Ted wished he could believe she wouldn't do the same thing again in the future. Her fierce loyalty to those she was close to was at the same time one of her best qualities, and one which could interfere with her judgement.

'What's the problem?'

'We have an armed siege situation. One shot fired, no information on casualties. There's an ambulance and one area car there already. They'd been called to a reported serious assault. Then the husband of the alleged victim turned up, flashing a warrant card and a gun, shut himself in the house and there was a shot. It's all gone quiet so we don't know who the victim is, if there is one. It could have been a warning.

'I've called for Firearms back-up, of course, but there's a delay and they can't yet tell me how long. I checked with Her Majesty and she said to call you, as you're firearms trained, at least. She's on her way in to oversee but in the meantime, can you help?'

'I can certainly go and try to stop anyone doing anything stupid, hopefully. We'll need a trained negotiator, though, by the sounds of it. Any further info? And what's the address?'

'Well, that's where it gets really strange. It's the home of that woman who made the claim about Maurice raping her.'

Ted was already on his feet and heading for the door. He'd need to take his service vehicle so he'd at least have blues if he needed to get through rubberneckers coming to find out what was going on. They seemed to have radar for any such incident and to flock to the scene, making the job of the emergency services that much harder.

Ted asked Roly to wait a moment while he told Mike Hallam where he was going and what for, then listened again, carrying on out of the door and down the stairs as Roly told him, 'There's a female witness who says she knows the gunman, he's a police officer, and she describes him as appearing to be dangerously unstable. Her husband is his sergeant. She's trying to get hold of him to attend but he's just come off a long shift and might be asleep with his phone turned off.'

Ted was in his car now, pulling out of the station car park, keeping his phone on speaker in case of updates. He was hoping for light traffic. The last thing he needed was to get stuck in any snarl-ups.

'Is it worth sending a car round for the sergeant? To wake him up and get him there as soon as possible.'

'In an ideal world, yes. Meanwhile, on Planet Earth, so many reasons why I can't. First off, I haven't a spare unit to send. I've already sent a second one to the house, to keep people away, for one thing. But most of all, his wife says it would be unwise. She hinted that waking him up suddenly might provoke an unwanted action. She won't say what unit they're from, not over the phone to me, at least, but she's dropped plenty of hints that they play by big boys' rules and it might end very badly.'

'If they're on our patch, they play by our rules. I don't care who they are …' Ted started, but Roly cut across him.

'The Ice Queen said you'd say that so she told me to tell you that you are to take no action without first checking with her. She's Gold Command on this one. She wants you at the scene specifically to stop anyone getting themselves shot. And that, of course, includes you.'

* * *

'Let me at least go nearer to try to find out what's happened,' Val Carver was telling the police officers. 'Whether that was just a warning shot or if one of them is now seriously injured, or worse. Eric's not going to shoot me, if he's still alive in there. He won't dare shoot his sergeant's wife. He knows Harry would kill him if he did.'

'Nobody's going anywhere near that house for now.'

The female police officer, who'd given her name as Rigby, seemed to be the more senior of the two. She was certainly the one making all the decisions, including calling for urgent back-up, and firearms officers. And she was definitely not going to be ordered about by a civilian claiming to be married to a police officer.

'If that gunshot wasn't fatal, there could be someone inside there bleeding out who could be saved by some swift first aid,' Val Carver told her.

'And if the person with the gun is as dangerous as you keep telling us, you can't possibly know what he would or wouldn't do in a situation like this. Assuming he's the one still alive.

'At the moment I'm in charge here, until anyone more

senior turns up. So you either need to stay back and do as I tell you or I'll have to arrest you for obstruction, for starters, handcuff you and lock you away safely in the back of the car. Your choice.'

'You really have no idea who you're up against. Who Eric is and what he does. Is there a senior officer on the way? I need to talk to someone more senior who will understand the risks. We need my husband here. If Eric is still capable of listening to anyone, he'll listen to Harry. He can always calm him down.'

PC Rigby was certainly sharp. She pounced on the words straight away.

'Does that mean this man in there is prone to violent outbursts if he often needs calming down? What else can you tell us which we need to know in the circumstances?'

'That's the problem, right there. A lot of what I know about Eric Leader, because my husband is in the same unit, is on a strictly need-to-know basis. I'm happy to tell a senior officer everything I know. I will say that Eric has a short fuse so he needs careful handling. But I'm more concerned about that shot and the prospect of someone possibly bleeding out.

'I'll keep trying my husband. He'll know what to do. But you need to let Control know this is a critical incident.'

* * *

A second area car was now on scene and its officers were closing off the road to non-essential traffic, trying to persuade people milling round hoping to catch a glimpse of some action to turn off their phones and get out from under their feet.

It was the sort of quiet residential area which wasn't used

to seeing such activity. By the time Ted arrived, shortly after them, he wasn't surprised to see the dogged local newspaper reporter, Penny Hunter, was already there and had managed to get herself inside the cordon so she could see and hear all that was going on.

As soon as she saw Ted arrive she trotted up to him, recording device in hand, and started her questions.

'Can you tell me what's going on, chief inspector? People are talking about gunshots coming from that house. Have there been any injuries? Is that why the ambulance is there? Any fatalities?'

Ted was busy putting on his body armour. He was still issued with it because he was on occasion, such as the present incident, called in to such situations in an advisory role, and he was known for getting in where the action was.

'Penny, as you can see, I've just arrived here myself and I'm not gifted with second sight. I wish I was, it would make my job a lot easier. You need to be right back behind the cordon, please. All I can tell you for now is that as soon as I know anything which can be released, I'll make sure you're briefed. For now, please withdraw. I don't have an officer to spare to escort you but I'll find one if I have to.'

He waited until he saw she was well out of earshot before he went over to where the two officers from the first area car on site were waiting for instructions. The ambulance crew had taken refuge in their vehicle until they got the all-clear to go in to see to any casualties. The officers were with a woman in civilian clothes who Ted took to be the sergeant's wife he'd heard about.

It was the woman who accosted him first, before either of the officers could get a word in.

'Are you the SIO on this?' she asked him. She knew the

jargon, at least.

'My husband is a sergeant in the same unit as the man in the house, Eric Leader. I can't tell you what unit they're with but …'

'I know that information already, Mrs …?'

'Carver. Val Carver. Then you'll know how potentially dangerous Eric is. I've been trying to phone my husband to come but he's just come off a long shift and probably has his phone off. He might be able to talk Eric down.'

'How far away do you live?' Ted asked her.

'About fifteen minutes, if traffic isn't too bad.'

'Right, probably the best thing you can do for now is go home and get your husband. It sounds as if he would indeed be helpful. PC Rigby, can you arrange for the second car to take Mrs Carver to get the sergeant, please? That should help with any traffic issues.'

'But I wanted to be here to make sure Anna is all right, and to help her …'

'Mrs Carver, we have an ambulance and crew on site. I'm sure they'll be more than capable of doing that. Please, go and get your husband. It sounds as if he could be useful to us.'

As the two officers moved away with Mrs Carver, Ted turned to the other PC present.

'Right, PC Blake. Any sound or signs of movement from the house since the gunshot?'

'Nothing, sir. We didn't try going any nearer, pending further instruction, although we were anxious about the fate of the woman inside.'

'You did absolutely the right thing. It would have been dangerous and reckless to attempt anything. So from now on, it's going to be a case of do as I say, not as I do.

'Do you, by any chance, have a loud hailer in the vehicle? I can at least try to open discussions while we wait for Firearms to show up, and a proper negotiator to attend.'

'We do, sir.'

PC Blake went to get it from the car to hand to Ted, by which time PC Rigby had returned from delivering Val Carver to the other team for transporting.

'At least they have nice solid brick gateposts,' Ted said as he went to stand behind one, giving it a pat as he said, 'I do like a convenient gatepost.'

He raised the loud hailer and spoke through it, as quietly and calmly as ever.

'Constable Leader? Eric? This is DCI Darling, from Stockport. If you can hear me, can you give me a sign, please?'

Nothing.

Not a sound nor a movement.

At least there was no more gunfire.

He tried again.

'Anna? Anna Wójcik? Can you hear me?'

'Should we try to move closer, sir? PC Blake asked. 'If he's not replying or shooting further, could we at least try to see if the woman could be rescued.'

'No, PC Blake, we shouldn't. Knowing what I know about this officer, if he's alive and unharmed, that's exactly the move he will be expecting us to make. And the consequences for any of us would be disastrous if we tried.

'All we can do for now is wait for Firearms to arrive then do exactly as their Tactical Commander tells us to.'

'But sir, what if his wife is in there seriously injured and bleeding, like Mrs Carver suggested? We can't leave her to die without trying to help her.'

Ted turned to look at him. Young, keen, had clearly either not read or had forgotten the bit in the training manual which said do as instructed by the senior office in charge. In other words, when they say jump, ask only how high.

Ted was a lot kinder than some senior officers would be in such a tense situation, having their instructions challenged. He asked only, 'PC Blake, how many potential fatalities do you want to be responsible for today?'

* * *

Jezza knew she had a long way to go to get back into the boss's good books. And that was where she preferred to be. He was the best senior officer she had ever served under, and she'd joined his team after a string of disasters and clashes with previous ones she'd worked with.

He'd been the first who had even tried to find out why she was struggling so much with work when she clearly had the ability to do the job well. Once he'd found out about her problems with her younger brother, Tommy, and had got others on the team, notably Maurice and Steve, to rally round to help and support her, he'd seen a transformation in her.

Maurice's kindness to her, and to Tommy, was the reason she'd gone so far out on a limb to try to help him in the face of the false allegations against him. But now it was time to show the boss she could equally well use her skills to get them further forward with the triple murder.

They still had Tonton and the husband of the dead woman, father of the twins, remanded in custody with no possibility of bail for the moment. But apart from the one young woman Ali had spoken too, they had little in the way of anything much to explain what sort of a hold Tonton had over the others that would allow him to do such appalling things with impunity.

She'd read right through Ali's notes, and been impressed with how she'd handled a difficult interview with the witness. She couldn't comprehend a young pregnant woman sitting there calmly taking about Circles and Welcomings without seemingly turning a hair at what appeared to be behind the group: the dark and deadly philosophy of an extreme form of population control.

She'd also got hold of the case notes from Merseyside for their similar, though less drastic, case – the suspicious death of one of a set of twins at a Welcoming on their patch, near to Billinge.

She made a call, hoping that the DC whose notes she'd read, might also be working a Saturday. She was, and Jezza was lucky enough to be put straight through to her.

'Hi, is that DC Amanda Howden? I'm DC Jezza Vine from GMP, based at Stockport. We're both working on cases involving the same happy band of pilgrims who seem to think killing twins is the answer to the earth's current populations problems. I wondered if you had time for us to pool ideas and information and see if we can't both advance our cases in some way?'

* * *

'DC Leader? I really do need to know what the situation is in there, please. We understand that your wife might be seriously injured and in need of medical attention. There's an ambulance crew waiting ready to assist, but you'll understand, of course, why I can't allow them to proceed after hearing gunfire.

'Can you at least tell me if your wife is alive, and would you consider letting her come out to the ambulance, if you don't want anyone to come in.

'Firearms officers are on their way. You're an experienced officer, in a specialist unit. You know what will happen next. You must understand that the likely outcome for you is not good, and it gets worse the longer you try to resist.

'At least let Anna go, if she is able. Such a gesture on your part now can only count in your favour.

'Your sergeant is on his way here, too. I'm sure he's going to tell you exactly the same as I have. You're not doing yourself any favours in refusing your wife medical assistance.'

Ted wasn't sure if he was saying the right things or possibly making the situation worse. He didn't want to wait for the negotiator to arrive before at least trying something. From what Val Carver had reported, Anna Wójcik was in a bad way and needed help.

Still nothing. Not a sound. No reaction.

Then he heard a rattling noise from inside. A scrabbling movement. Someone trying to open the door. Ted signalled quickly for everyone nearby to take whatever cover they could find. He had no idea of who might be about to come through that front door, and whether or not they would be carrying a firearm which they would be prepared to use.

The battered and bloodied form of Anna Wójcik staggered through the now open doorway, barely able to stay upright. She only made it as far as the mat on the doorstep before she collapsed to her knees, holding up her open hands to show they were empty, sobbing uncontrollably.

Ted could see the prone form of Eric Leader lying on the

hall floor behind her. From the size of the gaping hole in the side of his head, Ted knew he no longer presented any danger to anyone.

Chapter Twenty-eight

Anna Wójcik was now safe. Badly injured, with a partially collapsed lung, probably caused by a savage kick which had broken more than one rib, but alive.

One of the ambulance crew had formally checked Eric Leader for any signs of life and found none, as expected, so had turned his attention back to Anna, who would need to be stabilised before transfer to hospital.

Now Ted would have to open an enquiry into a possible murder. The gun which had killed Leader, his own service-issue handgun at quick first glance, had been found on the floor between Leader's body and where his wife had been lying, judging by the blood there.

He knew, because of what had happened with Maurice, that the man had cameras which would send automatically to his phone if someone approached the house.

If Leader had seen that happening with Val Carver, he would know he risked being found out for what he had done to Anna, and seemingly not for the first time. That was probably what sent him rushing back to the house to find the police already there. That must have shocked him into taking what seemed to be the only remaining way out – shooting himself.

All Ted's instincts were telling him that Leader had snapped, for reasons he didn't yet know. Lost control completely and beaten up his wife more badly than ever, before going to work, not suspecting for a moment that Val Carver would decide to visit his home.

But there was at least a possibility that the fatal shot, far from being the straightforward suicide it appeared to be on the surface, had in fact been made by Leader's wife, Anna. And whether that had been a deliberate act or an accidental discharge during a struggle would have to be determined.

As a first basic precaution, he asked the ambulance crew to put bags over Anna's hands, to preserve any trace of gunshot residue. He could tell by the looks they both threw at him what they thought of that idea when they had enough to do to stabilise her, but it was standard procedure.

Next he asked PC Rigby if she could clear the scene of onlookers, then cordon the site off to preserve any evidence, whilst he got on the phone to the Ice Queen, to report further on the situation.

'I'm hoping it was a straightforward suicide by Leader, ma'am, which is what my instinct is telling me, but there is that small degree of ambiguity, so I'm proceeding with caution.'

'How likely is it, if she was as badly injured as you describe, that she could somehow have wrestled the gun away from a trained officer?'

'Slight in the extreme, I would say,' Ted told her. 'But I can't dismiss the possibility out of hand. After all, she did somehow find the strength to get up to open the door and let us in.'

'You do right to consider any and all scenarios. Any such death needs in-depth investigation, of course. You'll let the coroner's office know?'

'I will, ma'am, and I'll also let the professor know in person. She'll no doubt want to come out to the scene herself as soon as possible, to ensure nothing is missed from the start. And I'd really welcome her input.

'We're getting a cordon up and trying to keep everyone away but I'm going to need more officers from Uniform to help with that. There's quite a crowd forming already.

'I'll also get some of the team out to start checking door-to door-for any witnesses. Someone is bound to have heard or seen something.'

'And I assume our friends from the press and media are already starting to arrive?'

'Penny Hunter was here when I arrived, so no doubt she's earned a nice little bonus tipping off the nationals.'

The superintendent didn't quite sigh but her pause spoke volumes. Any case like this was bound to put them under the spotlight. The press seemed to love the sort of 'cop gone bad' story which was becoming worryingly more frequent.

'I know you'll run this by the book, as always, but I'll come over at some point. A gesture of solidarity, not in any way a reflection on your ability. I hope you know that.

'I'm struggling to understand at the moment how someone like this man Leader was still serving in a unit like that, and able to carry a firearm at all times.'

Ted wasn't surprised she was across all the details of the case straight away. There was very little going on in the division of which she was not aware.

'Ma'am, I've come across officers doing roles like his before, especially on some of Mr Green's more extreme courses. You probably have yourself, on some of his firearms update training. Some of them are on a knife edge at the best of times. It takes a certain mindset to kill anyone, even under orders. And I'm not making excuses for him. Simply stating a fact. It's sometimes easier than we might think for them to tip over to the wrong side.'

Ted was speaking from personal experience. He'd once had to shoot an armed hostage-taker dead, in his Firearms days. He'd attended the mandatory counselling afterwards. He liked to think it hadn't affected him, but he knew that wasn't strictly true. He sometimes still had bad dreams about it, when under stress. He was glad he'd never had to do it again.

'I don't want to pile any more pressure onto what is already a difficult case. But we both know the police service as a whole has never been under more scrutiny, nor come in for more criticism, than it is currently receiving. The public are, quite rightly, going to want to know how this man was still serving and how no one had picked up on his state of mind,' the superintendent went on.

'I know you raised the possibility of a review of selection processes in an attempt to improve our reputation. In light of this case, that is something which needs to happen, and soon. Along with measures for better continued assessment of serving officers. Because we cannot, of course, even attempt to hide that fact that this man was one of our own.

'I'm confident that you will wrap this case up with your usual swift efficiency. Then we need to look long and hard at improved procedures going forward. I look forward to your proposals as soon as possible.'

Ted was left looking at his phone as she rang off, muttering to himself, 'The impossible I do today. Miracles take a little longer.'

* * *

'Sarge, I've been speaking to a DC from Merseyside

about their similar case of a baby being killed at one of these so-called Welcoming ceremonies,' Jezza told Mike Hallam after she'd finished her call with DC Amanda Howden.

'Lots of potential crossover between our cases. We both thought it might be valuable if we met up in the flesh to share notes and ideas with a view to finding the breakthrough we both need. Her DS is happy to action a meeting today, as she's working on that file anyway. So would you be willing to do the same?'

'Is this not something you could do by phone? Now there's been this other killing on our patch, I'm going to need every officer available.'

'Half an hour each way if we meet roughly in the middle, at Birchwood services. So less than three hours, tops. And we both think it might be easier to do in the flesh.'

'You can't be discussing a case that sensitive in a service station café, Jezza. So many details we don't want to leak out into the public domain to make the job even more complicated than it already is.'

Jezza didn't quite do a sigh and an eye roll, although it took all her willpower not to.

'We were thinking more of sitting in one car to discuss the case, sarge. Go in and grab a coffee to take away, probably use the loos but then sit in the car to discuss.'

'And what if one of the cars gets broken into and the files are taken?'

'You have the suspicious mind only a copper would have, sarge. But all right, we'll take turns to buy the coffee and use the loo, then one of us can always watch the cars. Because we can't just dump our triple murder for this shooting, surely, and this is as close to a sniff of a new lead as I've found so far.'

Mike Hallam thought for a bit. He knew the boss was going to be asking for more officers for this fatal shooting he was attending, but Jezza was right. They couldn't even think of dropping their existing case, still with too little progress, in favour of the newer one.

'All right. Three hours at the most, and make sure I can contact you whenever I need to. And don't spend too much of the time on your witchcraft theory, either. Let's stick to some hard and provable facts that might advance both our cases.'

'Not so much as a hex or a hocus, never mind a pocus,' she told him glibly, as she went off to get her things together.

Mike smiled to himself and shook his head. Jezza Vine was certainly one of a kind, but she was a good officer, with excellent instincts. He'd risk letting her run free, within the time constraints, on this one. They had precious little else concrete to go on, after all.

* * *

Ted went himself to greet Professor Bizzie Nelson when she arrived at the scene in her old and mud-splattered Volvo. He'd told officers at the end of the road who were keeping away unwanted attention to allow her straight through the tape.

He always felt relief once she took control. Quirky, beyond eccentric, but one of the best there was in her profession. He knew she would miss nothing, no matter how seemingly insignificant. And this one was going to be difficult enough without any slip-ups.

Crime Scene Investigators had also arrived and were setting up. Cat-fancier Doug, who had given young Adam to

Ted, would be manager once more. Something else which was reassuring Ted. At least he wouldn't have to worry about anything being missed, or mistakes being made with labelling anything found and seized at the scene. Not with Doug in charge.

Ted was now in full coveralls so he could show the professor to the scene, using the stepping plates Doug had already ensured were put in place. Ted still sometimes had difficulty reconciling the brilliant, professional woman of science with the closet pot-smoking disreputable hippy he knew Bizzie to be in her private life.

'Tim's been and certified death of the male victim,' Ted told her to begin with.

Bizzie gave him one of her special looks as she said, 'Thank you, but with a clear gunshot wound like that, situated as it is, it would be a medical miracle if he were to be still alive.

'Have his hands been swabbed for gunshot residue?'

Doug was working away, within earshot, so he answered, 'One of the first things we did, professor.'

'And what of the other person present on the scene at the time of death?'

'She's been taken to hospital with at least one broken rib and a collapsed lung, as well as other serious injuries consistent with a savage and sustained physical assault. We had her hands bagged and I'll get them swabbed as soon as we're allowed access to her.'

'Height, weight and build?' Bizzie asked him, still looking at the deceased from every angle.

Ted told her, so she replied, 'So you have been wondering if it would have been at all possible for the assault victim somehow to have rallied herself, after such injuries as you describe, to wrestle the gun away from a clearly physically very fit man of this size and turn it on him to inflict the fatal wound. To which I would have to reply, scientifically speaking, that that would be about as probable as me winning the next Miss World competition.'

* * *

Rumour had it that one copper could always recognise another, without any need to see ID. Jezza remained sceptical, knowing how often her drama training had allowed her to pass herself off as anything but the serving officer she was.

She and Amanda Howden had exchanged car numbers and arranged a quiet area of the parking in which to meet. Even without checking the plates of the car nor running through the description she'd been given, she knew immediately that the long, lithe figure leaning nonchalantly against a vehicle, was the officer she'd come to meet.

Amanda Howden was taller than average, hair done in cornrows, definitely dressed for comfort and freedom of movement. She was wearing a pair of trainers which Jezza knew came with an eye-watering price tag. She had a feeling that any villain deciding to run when approached by this officer would find themselves overtaken over a very short distance.

'Amanda? I'm Jezza Vine.'

She gave her a discreet flash of her ID, just to make sure, although she was pretty certain there wouldn't be two people matching the description lurking about the service station car park on a damp and dismal Saturday.

'Hi, Jezza. How do you want to play this? Might be a bit

public in there to talk shop,' Amanda said, indicating the coffee shop with a lift of her chin.

Jezza smiled at that.

'My DS was flapping like a budgie at the mere idea. I told him one of us would probably go and get the coffees while the other guarded the cars.'

'Sounds sensible, although I don't drink coffee, and I have mineral water in the car. Plenty to share, unless you're in need of a caffeine hit?'

In the end they opted to sit in Amanda Howden's service vehicle to exchange information. But before she started she said, 'I have an update first, though. I spoke to one of our witnesses again earlier today. One who speaks reasonable English so we don't need an interpreter. Just a bit of patience and initiative.

'She'd heard of your case, although she wasn't there. But nothing like the full details of it. She was shocked rigid by what I told her.

'When I interviewed her previously she kept saying she believed the baby in our case had been stillborn. She swore she didn't see anyone do anything to it. But she was horrified at the full details of your case and I could hear the doubt creeping into her voice. To the extent that she's agreed to talk to both of us. As soon as we can get there. And the good news is she lives not all that far away. We could be there in under half an hour.'

'And she will definitely talk? Only this is likely to tip my sarge over the edge if I tell him I'm going to be longer than I thought. And I'll have to do that rather than disappear for longer than planned. There was an ongoing armed hostage situation when I left so it's all hands on deck.

'My DCI went to attend but they're likely to need more

officers depending on how it plays out. That's why the DS wasn't keen on me coming over here at all and put a curfew on it.'

'Oh yes, you've got the famous Karate Kid for a boss, haven't you?'

Jezza smiled at that.

'Top tip: if ever you meet him, never let him hear you calling him that. And believe me, he's got the hearing of a greater wax moth.'

Amanda frowned as she asked, 'Do they have good hearing? Can moths even hear? I thought bats were the best. Anyway, on the basis you're bound to be able to persuade your sarge this is a good idea, we can both go in my car, if you bring your stuff with you. I need to come back in this direction afterwards so I can easily drop you off here.

'Then you can spend some of the journey time telling me why you know so much about the hearing levels of various animals.'

Chapter Twenty-nine

'What I'm still struggling with is why the flock, or whatever they call themselves, keep going along with this bloke Tonton when some of them have seen at first hand what he is. What he's capable of,' Jezza told Amanda as they headed off to speak to their potential witness.

'My colleague, Ali, interviewed a young woman who's pregnant, possibly with twins, and she went back to one of the Circles after hearing what happened at the Welcoming in our area. She wasn't actually there at the time of that one, but she must have heard the details. We tried to keep a tight lid on it but there was still a fair bit in the press, and not all of it speculation, about what happened.'

'In a bizarre sort of way, I agree with the sentiment that the earth's population needs to decrease – drastically – if there's to be any hope of survival,' Amanda replied. 'But I'd draw the line well short of any mass euthanasia, especially of babies, as a way to bring it down to manageable levels.

'I'd start by making it easier for elderly people to decide for themselves when to bring their own life to an end.'

Then she laughed as she threw a quick sideways glance at Jezza.

'Sorry, that sounds as if you're sharing a car with a total psychopath. I've never wanted children. I do a lot of competitive sports, around work time. County level, inter-force stuff. That sort of thing. Too selfish to give all that up to bring up kids. And my gran, who I love literally to the moon and back, is dying, slowly and horribly, from a disease with no cure. All she wants to do now is die. She can't make that happen herself, and no one can do it for her, or even help her to do it, the way the law stands.'

She laughed again as she said, 'We should get back to the case before I implicate myself and you feel obliged to arrest me for intent.

'So now you have Tonton in custody, d'you think you can make a case against him for all three of your killings? Or at least one of them, to get him put away for a nice long stretch?'

'Well, clearly we can't even charge him for the mother's death by strangulation. Not now we've seen his arm. We could never make a case that would even get past CPS, let alone stand up in court. Any jury would only have to look at his arm to kick the case right out.'

Amanda glanced at her again, for slightly longer, until an angry horn blast from behind her jerked her back to putting her full concentration into her driving.

'What about his arm? Am I missing something?'

'We only found out when we arrested him. One arm is completely withered and non-functioning and there's no formed hand at the end of it. No digits at all, certainly not a thumb, and the PM report specifically mentions two opposing thumb prints on the neck of the mother in our case, who died from strangulation.

'You must have been informed. We circulated the new intel as soon as we had it, certainly to your unit, as you'd had the similar case.'

Amanda made a snorting sound of disgust.

'Bloody typical. You get The Karate Kid. We get Mr

Pissquick. He wouldn't dream of doing anything as obvious as sharing updates with us poor footsoldiers. Too busy sloping off round to the pub when he thinks he can get away with it. And he does, most of the time. When he does condescend to roll back in, he goes off on one that we're not reaching arrest and conviction targets.

'He probably did his usual trick of burying your update in his non-existent filing system where important information goes to die. We all swear he's only still in post because he either has friends in high places, or he knows where the bodies are buried, so they're all just counting the days to his retirement.'

'Well, we're pretty certain we can rule Tonton out as the actual killer of the mother in our case, because of the arm, although the boss is keen on pushing for joint enterprise charges so he could still go down for it, if we can get a conviction. But with your open verdict and possible stillbirth, you're a bit stuck to get him easily on that, and it would clearly help both of us to get as much as we can. Unless this person we're going to see really would consider at least telling us everything she saw and heard.

'I know my boss has mentioned the idea of trying to get a second post-mortem done on the baby in your case – the supposed stillbirth – by a Home Office pathologist, with the possibility, even if faint, that it could have been a cleverly disguised murder. He'll be working with one of the best there is at this crime scene he's at now. Professor Nelson. If he has the opportunity, I'm sure he'll sound her out about the possibility of her doing a follow-up PM.

'I know the body's not yet been released for burial because of the inconclusive findings, so the professor might well leap in. She never misses a trick. If anyone can find evidence of a crime in such a death, she can.'

* * *

'Do we have anyone who can confirm for me that the deceased is, in fact, right-handed, chief inspector?' Professor Nelson asked Ted, formally, in front of others, as she continued to make her initial observations of the scene and of the body of Eric Leader. 'And can anyone tell me the same for the woman? Both pieces of information are vital to finding out exactly what has happened here, pending what the gunshot residue shows.'

'The deceased is a police officer. His sergeant's wife is outside. She's the one who sounded the alarm. She was worried when she couldn't get hold of the deceased's wife so she came round to find out if anything was wrong. That was shortly before he arrived home brandishing a gun and shut himself in the house with his wife.'

'Why was he carrying a firearm? Do we know?'

'We do. Routine for anyone doing what he does. Did,' Ted told her, then mentioned once again the two words to identify which unit Leader had been serving in. He knew Bizzie would understand the significance.

She did.

She said no more than a loaded 'Aaaahhh.'

Ted went outside to see if Val Carver was back on site having returned with Leader's sergeant. He'd be someone useful for Ted to talk to for more background on the deceased. Between the two of them, they would be bound to know whether the couple were right or left-handed.

Harry Carver had clearly had Ted pointed out to him as SIO, as he headed straight towards him, his wife not far behind, and held up his ID.

'DCI Darling? Sergeant Carver. If you need a formal ID on the deceased, I could do that for you. Eric and Anna had no family that I'm aware of.'

'That would be helpful, sergeant. First of all, can you tell me, please if Leader was right or left-handed? And the same for Anna Wójcik, if possible.'

'Right-handed, Eric, certainly. I'm not sure about Anna.'

He turned to his wife as he asked, 'Do you know, love?'

'Also right-handed. I saw her make a note of a new word once. She really has been trying to improve her English. That's why she's been going to evening classes,' Val Carver replied. 'I was surprised Eric let her. He was always obsessively jealous about her. That's why he started the punch-up last time …'

She stopped abruptly as she saw the warning look from her husband and the slight shake of the head. Ted didn't miss it, either. He'd have a word with the sergeant when they were alone to remind him that as SIO he needed any and all background on the deceased, not the edited version.

'Right, thank you both. Sergeant Carver, it would be helpful if you could come with me now to do that ID.'

As they walked together the short distance to the house, Ted told him, 'No matter what unit you're from, this is now a murder investigation and I'm the SIO. I need all available information, and it's up to me to determine which is relevant to the case or otherwise.

'I have the necessary security clearance, if you want to check, but for now, I want straight answers to any and all questions I pose. Are we clear on that, sergeant?'

'Clear enough for now. But there may well be occasions when I need to seek higher authority to respond. I'm sure you'll understand.'

Ted had peeled off his protective clothing before going out into the road and had had it bagged and labelled. He and the sergeant were issued with new sets then went inside together, where Ted introduced Carver to Professor Nelson, who barely glanced at him.

'Both of them were right-handed, I now have it on good authority, professor,' he told her.

'And I can confirm that the body is that of Eric Leader, one of my team.'

Carver turned back to Ted to ask, 'Can I stay?'

It was the professor who answered him, her tone sharp.

'No, you may not. I do not allow spectators on my crime scenes. You were allowed in specifically to make the ID, which you have now done. So, thank you, and goodbye.'

Carver didn't say a word in reply but his expression was enough. He simply turned on his heel and left the house.

There was no one else in earshot so the professor addressed Ted by his full name, known to few.

'You are the exception, Edwin, but I do find that sometimes, if you give a particular type of man a gun and some sort of open sesame badge to wave at lesser mortals, they assume it gives then super-powers. Divine rights over said lesser beings.

'Those were the distinct vibes I was getting from that officer. I felt it opportune to remind him that, even in his particular unit, a sergeant most definitely does not outrank a Home Office pathologist.'

Ted wisely said nothing to that, instead asking, 'How does knowing what was the predominant arm for each of them advance us?' although, firearms trained himself, he suspected he knew the answer and it might be good news, in a sense.

'I'm discounting any likelihood of this woman attempting any such shot as that which killed the deceased with her non-dominant hand. Assuming she knew anything about firing a weapon at all and was in any condition to make an attempt.

'Given the build and skills of the deceased, she would have needed absolutely all the odds possible in her favour to get a gun anywhere near him. Let alone for point-blank range, which was the case in this instance.

'Her being right-handed would mean the fatal wound would be to his left temple.

'All of this, of course, is subject to gunshot residue testing, to determine which of them fired the weapon, but as you can see, the shot which killed him was to his right temple. Exactly where it would be for a self-inflicted wound fired by a right-handed person.

'And speaking of hands and their use, it is woefully remiss of me that I have not yet sent you the results of my little experiments for your other case. The tests done by my students, involving swinging babies against walls and manually strangling people. Or rather simulating the actions using appropriate dummies. Including the feasibility of doing any of that with one hand, yet leaving two thumbprints. As was the case for the strangulation.

'In brief, the former was disconcertingly simple. The latter, to leave the marks I found post-mortem, as impossible as I had imagined. And believe me, my little cherubs were most inventive in the things they came up with and tried.

'There is still a very slim chance that once we finally get back all of the DNA and blood sample results we may have something, at least, with which to tie in your one-armed suspect to all three killings, but I certainly wouldn't count on it

'In summary, your disabled suspect could easily have murdered one or both babies, but could not remotely have strangled their mother. That would most definitely have required two hands and two fully-functioning thumbs. That is, of course, not sufficient to clear him. Blood and DNA might show he used his valid arm to help the husband with the task, or to encourage him.

'An unforgivable oversight on my part not to have sent those before now, for which my profuse apologies. I will rectify that as soon as I return from here to my lair.'

* * *

'I've been going over and over in my mind what I saw with my own eyes and what details my imagination might have added, based on me thinking I saw something. If any of that makes any sense?'

Jezza and Amanda were sitting in a bright, neat and clean kitchen, drinking water, in Amanda's case and masala chai for Jezza, listening to the young woman they had come to interview. The one person who had been present for the supposed stillbirth who had agreed to talk to them.

She'd been interviewed previously and had little to say. It wasn't until news broke of the triple killing in the Stockport area that she had voluntarily come forward to say she wanted to talk to someone about her concerns.

'I first got interested in these people because they did seem to have some sound and sensible ideas about what could be done to help the Mother Earth as she's going through a crisis far too many people don't seem to be aware of.

'And that's a major part of the problem. "Far too many people". A problem people are unwilling to talk about. These people were talking about it. Not anything as severe as the Chinese one child laws were, but certainly encouraging more people to at least consider limiting family sizes.'

Although there was a slight accent there, the young woman's English was excellent. Jezza suspected that if she'd been one of those requiring an interpreter previously, it could have been simply a move on her part to give her more thinking time about how she phrased things.

She was being careful now. Pausing often to take a sip of chai. Weighing everything she said before she spoke.

'I was intrigued about these so-called Welcomings, so I thought I'd go and see for myself rather than judging something on the basis of hearsay. So I went.

'It felt strange and intrusive to be present at something so intimate when I wasn't connected to the family. I didn't know the woman was expecting twins, but she was very big. She's someone from the Circles who speaks hardly any English and we don't have a language in common so I'd never spoken to her.

'Tonton was there. I mean right there. Up close and personal, and as far as I know, he has no medical training. He supervised the father cutting the cord for the first twin and they seemed to do that properly.'

Jezza cut in, 'Do you know what his profession is? Tonton, that is?'

'I don't. None of us do. There's a bit of an air of mystery about him, although he does seem to know a lot about climate science, ecology, that sort of thing.

'The first baby to be born was the boy and he made a

noisy entrance into the world so there was certainly nothing wrong with him. Tonton picked him up – I think you probably know he only has one working arm – and held him up for all to see. Bringing him round to everyone, showing him off, so we could all say hello. That felt nice and, yes, very welcoming.

'That was very strange because Tonton was behaving almost as if he was the proud father, rather than letting the poor husband have a hold of his own first-born baby.

'No one was taking any notice at all of the poor mother. I think I was the only one to even look at her, wondering how she must be feeling to see everyone else cooing over her son and she hadn't even got to hold him yet.

'That's when I noticed she was starting to look distressed. She was looking like she had for the first birth but nothing was happening. I thought she probably needed some proper assistance, in case there was another baby. I've never been at a birth before so I didn't know what should happen, but it didn't look right to me.

'I told Tonton so he gave the baby to the father and went back to the mother. Of course everyone's eyes were fixed on the new baby and no one was so much as looking at the mother, even me, for a while, although she was starting to sound distressed.'

'How long was it before anyone did take notice?' Jezza asked her. 'Did no one, at any point, suggest calling for urgent medical help?'

'I was the first one to turn round, I'm pretty sure. By then the baby was out but lying perfectly still. No sound, no sign of life. I went back to the bed and told Tonton we should really call 999 straight away as the mother clearly needed medical attention, and someone on the phone could at least tell us what to do to try to revive the baby.

'He looked at me with such a strange expression. I'd never noticed before how cold his eyes could be. He said "There is no point. The Mother Earth has rejected this little one. She has no need of another female to increase her population, so she has simply let her go."

'I've no idea if my witness account would be of any use at all to you in bringing a case against Tonton. But I really believe someone needs to try. I've no idea how you would go about proving it, but I really believe he was somehow responsible for the death of that little baby girl.'

Chapter Thirty

Jezza had muted any incoming calls whilst she used her phone to record what their potential witness had to tell them. Except they could now drop the 'potential' label with a sigh of relief. Once she'd started talking, the young woman had been hard to stop. She was quite determined that she would testify in court, even though it potentially put her in a bad light for having been present at the fatal Welcoming, and not having spoken up sooner about everything she'd seen.

Once she was back in her own car, about to head east to Stockport, Jezza had a quick check to see what calls she had missed. They mostly turned out to have been from DS Mike Hallam. The first had a brief message reminding her she should be on her way back. The last, which was terse in tone, told her in no uncertain terms, that she was to get herself back or call with a plausible reason as to why not.

She used her phone on hands free to phone him back as she drove.

'Sorry, sarge, it took longer than anticipated, but I hope you'll be happy with the results. We now have an eyewitness to the supposed stillborn baby near Billinge, and we didn't even need to bewitch the woman to get it.'

She could never resist an ironic comment, even when the DS was sounding as fraught as he was.

'Get back here asap and write up your notes and let's see how useful it's likely to be to us. Because we really are up against it with officer numbers. But it does sound like it might be helpful, a least. The boss is still out but he phoned me to say he's spoken to Professor Nelson about the possibility of a repeat post-mortem, so make sure you copy her in on your notes. And liaise with Ali, about her witness. If her woman knows there's someone else prepared to testify, it might just push her into doing the same thing.

'It would be a big tick on the books for us if we can pull enough together on this to get it to trial at least.'

* * *

Now that all risk of shooting was gone, with the death of Eric Leader and the firearm safely seized, made safe and on its way for forensic examination, Ted was back in his own office to write up his notes of all that had occurred.

He'd first been to update Superintendent Caldwell who was anxious, as he would have expected, to know if there was anything they could or should have done to prevent such a tragedy on their patch.

'Did we back away too easily, once we knew who this Eric Leader was? It was presumably him who assaulted his wife a second time and left her in such a bad state. Was that preventable?'

'I don't see how, ma'am,' Ted told her. 'We did at least try to help her in the first place, which ended so badly for Maurice. Leader's own sergeant's wife said Leader was increasingly unstable and called him obsessively jealous about Anna. I would say if anyone made an error of judgement about his state of mind, it was Carver or whoever he answers to.'

'Speaking of DC Brown, whilst I am delighted he has

been cleared of any suspicion of assault, he did, after all, display a serious lack of judgement in the way he behaved. How are you planning on dealing with him? And also with DC Vine. Loyalty to a colleague is an admiral quality, but not when it spills over into something as serious as what she appears to have done.'

Again, Ted wasn't at all surprised she was up to speed on everything, not just the edited highlights. She was like that. It's why she was so good at her job.

'For a start I'll stick Maurice on collating. That should keep him safely chained to his desk for long enough to remind him of the error of his ways.

'I've already had strong words with Jezza. I'll arrange some retraining for both of them, once we're at least nearing completion on both our cases.'

He hadn't planned on mentioning it but on a sudden whim he said, 'Once we are at that stage, ma'am, I was thinking of taking some leave. DI Smith has invited Trev and myself to visit him in Germany, at his grandmother's house, and take my mother with us. She's never been abroad.'

The Ice Queen did no more than arch one regal eyebrow, although it was so rare for either of them to bring up personal stuff in the workplace.

'I didn't realise you were that close to DI Smith.'

'I'm not, really. But there's no doubt he potentially saved my life, and for some strange reason, Trev gets on with him like a house on fire, so he's really keen.'

'Then of course you must go. I think I've said before, we are all entitled to some time away from the job, for our own welfare. It would seem, on the face of it, that Eric Leader provides an object lesson in that to us all.

'There will need to be an enquiry into what went wrong

there, of course. Why no one spotted the man spiralling out of control and allowed it to get as far as it did.'

'It's something, no doubt, which Mr Marston will be keen to follow up on when we meet next to discuss how recruitment and continuous assessment issues aren't helping with the public's currently low opinion of us.'

'Ah, yes. Mr Marston,' she said, the ghost of a smile hovering round her lips. 'I'm so glad the two of you seem at least to get along. He's known for being somewhat …'

'Pedantic, ma'am?' Ted suggested.

The half smile widened slightly at that.

'Punctilious?'

The smile was rapidly becoming a grin. Something Ted so seldom saw her do in the workplace.

'Fastidious? Fussy? Finicky?'

She was definitely chuckling to herself as Ted left the office to head upstairs to catch up with Mike Hallam, update him on the fatal shooting and find out about any developments on the Tonton case.

Mike was in grumbling mode about Jezza, despite the excellent new lead she'd brought back, which finally took them forward in the case.

'She's good, boss, there's no denying that, but she's always off ploughing her own furrow and I don't know where she is or what she's actually doing half the time. And that stunt she pulled with Maurice's twin. I know she was trying to help but that was a very risky gamble to take. What if Eric Leader had come out of the house with his service weapon at the sight of who he thought was Maurice? He could have been killed.'

'Remember when she first joined the team, Mike? I asked you to let her run free of the pack for a time? It worked out well doing that. She's a cracking officer, if a bit unorthodox. I'll talk to her. Remind her of her boundaries. Send her on some retraining courses she will absolutely hate but should remind her of where the line is before she crosses it again.

'Are you happy enough to leave her to me to sort out? I'll also deal with Maurice's return-to-work interview on Monday morning, and sort some update training courses for him too.

'Does that suit you? Oh, and I'm also planning a spot of leave as soon as all that's been sorted. I think we're all probably in need of a break with everything that's been going on.'

* * *

It was earlier than he feared when Ted managed to get home. He'd armed himself with a decent bottle of wine for Trev, aware how much he'd been having to neglect him with the intensity of all that had been going on at work.

He found him in the back garden, sitting on one of the steamer chairs, the nervous little black cat, Barcelona, on his knees, purring for once, as he tried gently to tease something sticky out of her coat with a fine comb.

'I've no idea where Barcie's been or what she's been doing but this is revolting. It's like chewing gum or something.'

He looked up then and spotted the wine.

'Hmmm, don't tell me. Home unexpectedly early, bearing gifts of fine wine. So that was you, then, at the armed siege I heard about on the radio? Were you actually going to tell me at some point?'

'I didn't want to worry you,' Ted said evasively. 'It was

all safe and routine for me. Danger level low.'

'But low isn't zero. We've talked about this before, Ted. Honesty, in a relationship. It's so much more than not telling lies. I'd always prefer to know what you're up to, rather than getting a knock on the door with someone bringing me some posthumous bravery award for you.'

'Sorry, you're right. But it was honestly fine,' he sat down in the second steamer chair, his space immediately invaded by some of the other cats, led by young Adam.

'I'll tell you, but it's not for public discussion, please. Anna Wójcik's husband assaulted her again, badly, but then shot himself at the scene.'

'Oh no, that's awful! Poor Anna, she's already been through so much. Is she going to be all right? Do you think it would be all right if I went to see her in hospital?'

'I'd let the dust settle a bit first, but I promise to let you know as soon as I hear anything about her.'

'This has all been such a dirty business for you. And for poor Maurice. How's he doing?'

Ted sighed as he said, 'I am going to have to read him the riot act in a big way when he comes back on Monday morning. The big soft beggar, he put himself in so much danger, doing what he did.'

'That's because he's such a lovely man. Please don't trample all over that streak of kindness in him. It's such a rare quality, especially these days.'

'But you know the rules of any kind of aid as well as I do – never put yourself in danger, or you're no use to anyone.'

'Yes, says the man with the big knife scar up his arm and on his leg from where he forgot to practise what he preaches.'

Ted laughed guiltily.

'All right, you got me on that one, so I'll bear that in mind when I talk to Maurice. But we made some progress on the triple murder today, so I've told the Ice Queen I'm going to take some leave. If you still want to do this mad trip to see Oscar and his granny, go ahead and arrange it, in, say about three weeks, and I'll do my very best to be free to come with you.'

Trev unceremoniously plonked Barcelona back on the ground, got up and leaned over to throw his arms round Ted's neck.

'Really? That's fantastic. Thank you. Annie is going to love every minute of it. Just please try not to let us down at the last minute.'

* * *

When Maurice Brown walked into the office on Monday morning, on time, but still the last one to arrive, he received a standing ovation from his colleagues which saw tears start to his eyes.

Jezza Vine leapt up, ran to him and flung her arms round him.

'It's so good to have you back, you big soft idiot. Promise me you'll never put yourself in danger like that again.'

Maurice hugged her back as he said, 'No danger of that, bonny lass. I've never been so scared before, about anything.'

Ted and Mike Hallam had both come out of their offices to see what the noise was about. Mike did no more than nod to him, but Ted, his voice ominously quiet, told him, 'Welcome back, Maurice. You and I will have a few words after briefing.'

'Yes, boss.'

Ted summarised for all present what had happened in the armed hostage situation on Saturday, telling them, 'Professor Nelson is satisfied that Eric Leader shot himself, after another savage assault on his wife, Anna Wójcik, who is still in hospital but her condition is now stable and no longer giving cause for concern.'

'I still can hardly believe any of this about Eric, boss,' Ali O'Malley told him. 'I knew his job was definitely not softly-softly, but I honestly never saw a violent side to his nature, all the time I was with him. Something must have tipped him over the edge. It's a shame no one noticed before it came to this.

'What will happen to Anna now? Have you heard?'

'Not much, only that she and Leader were officially married, so her status to stay in the country should be secure. She'll get her police widow's pension, at least, but I've no idea what she intends to do. She'll need to stay in the country for now as she'll be called to testify at the inquest, of course, which is likely to be difficult for her.

'Luckily the sergeant's wife, Val Carver, seems to be keeping an eye on her welfare.'

'Pity no one thought to do that before, when he'd clearly been beating seven bells out of her, and trying to frame Maurice for sexually assaulting her,' Jezza put in, looking defiantly at the boss as she did so.

'I intend to deal with that issue, DC Vine, rest assured. I'll be meeting soon with Chief Superintendent Marston to discuss issues such as recruiting methods, and ongoing monitoring of all serving officers, especially those in particular units, with regard to mental health concerns.

'For now, we have a triple murder to wrap up and thanks

to some good work by yourself, Jezza, and you, Ali, we have finally got two witnesses prepared to testify about Tonton's involvement. This will involve working with Merseyside initially as there's crossover.

'Professor Nelson has agreed to carry out a second post-mortem on the baby from the Billinge case. If there is anything to find, she will find it.

'Maurice, you're in charge of collating. I want the file which goes to CPS to be the tightest ever. I don't just want it to pass the threshold, I want it to go way beyond. Nothing at all left to chance.

'I want this Tonton put away, for as long as possible, where he can't start up any of his tricks again.

'Thank you, everyone.

'Maurice? That word.'

* * *

Once he'd firmly told Maurice his fortune, emphasising that it really was his last informal warning, Ted wrote up a report about Eric Leader, highlighting possible failings in the system which had allowed a man so clearly dangerously on the edge to carry on serving, and carrying a concealed firearm. He then sent it through to Chief Superintendent Marston.

He wasn't surprised when the man called him back before too long. Just long enough to have read through the report.

'Chief Superintendent Marston, chief inspector,' the man began when he was put through. As formal, verging on the pompous, as ever.

'Thank you for the excellent report. Meticulously

detailed, as ever. Now, can we compare diaries for when we can meet to discuss where we are going next with our joint report of recruiting and retention measures?'

He mentioned a forthcoming date at which Ted silently groaned.

'I had actually just put in for leave then, sir. I could change it, though, if that's your only availability,' he said hesitantly.

'Not at all, you are entitled some time away. I hope it's to somewhere nice?'

To his own surprise, Ted found himself replying, 'I've been invited to Germany by DI Oscar Smith, from the Met, with whom I've worked on a couple of occasions. We're going to stay with his grandmother.'

'Well, that all sounds far too nice to miss, so how would the following week work for you?'

Ted was smiling his satisfaction as Marston ended his call, a new date found, and the holiday safely intact.

He was starting on his next round of paperwork when his mobile rang. A masked number. He considered ignoring it. He had an ominous premonition that it was not going to be something he wanted to hear.

Eventually he answered it, tentatively.

'Green here. Change of plan.'

The voice of his special skills instructor. As usual without preamble.

The man said nothing more than a date, time and grid reference, different to the ones he'd previously given Ted, as well as mentioning the names of Oscar Smith and Jock McLintock, before ringing off.

The new date should have been the last weekend of his Germany trip with Trev and his mother, to visit Oscar's grandmother. He'd visualised some final sightseeing, probably some shopping for Trev's sake, then a few leisurely meals out to sample the local food.

Instead, he was checking out the grid reference, although it was already familiar to him. Crib Goch. The most difficult ascent of Yr Wyddfa – Mount Snowdon – the notorious mountain in North Wales.

He kept himself fairly fit, but it was still going to stretch him. Jock had looked fitter, at least, when he'd seen him last, and looked as if he stayed that way. He dreaded to think how Oscar Smith was going to cope with anything that challenging, based on his form when Ted had last seen him.

As if on cue, his phone rang again. Oscar Smith calling him.

'Who the fuck is this man Green? Did you give him my number? And why does he think he can order me around? What rank was he?'

'WO1,' Ted told him. 'No, I didn't give him your number. I didn't need to. He has his own methods of intelligence gathering. And if I were you, I wouldn't start off on the wrong side of him by trying to pull rank on him. Number one, it won't work and number two you'll only make him angry. Believe me, you don't want to see Mr Green when he's angry.'

'I can't just drop everything at the bidding of some bloke I don't even know and go pissing about playing at Boy Scouts up some hill in Wales. And anyway, you and I will be in Germany that weekend.'

'A couple more bits of advice for you, Oscar, which you can take or leave, as you choose.

'Believe it or not, this is actually something of an honour. He must see some potential of some sort in you to include you on one of his extra special courses.

'So my advice to you would be to spend every moment between now and the date he's given you to get yourself as fit as you possibly can for what's likely to be the toughest training session you've ever done, even in your Army days.

'And no, you and I won't be in Germany because we will be flying back early, leaving Trev and my mother with your grandma. Because believe me, the only possible answer when you get a summons like this is "Yes, Mr Green".'

About the author

L M Krier is the pen-name of former journalist (court reporter) and freelance copywriter, Lesley Tither, who also writes travel memoirs under the name Tottie Limejuice. Lesley also worked as a case tracker for the Crown Prosecution Service. Now retired, she lives in Central France and enjoys walking her dogs and going camping.

Contact details

If you would like to get in touch, please do so at:

https://www.teddarlingcrimeseries.uk/

tottielimejuice@gmail.com

facebook.com/LMKrier

facebook.com/groups/1450797141836111/

twitter.com/tottielimejuice

For a lighter look at Ted and Trev, why not join the fun in the We Love Ted Darling group? on Facebook. FREE 'Ted Darling is billirant' badge for each member.

Acknowledgements

I would just like to thank the people who have helped me bring Ted Darling to life.

Alpha and Beta readers: Jill Pennington, Kate Pill, Karen Corcoran, Bren Kübler, Alan Wood, Paul Kemp, Eileen Payne, Valérie Goutte, Margaret Johnson.

Police consultants – The Three Karens.

Finally a very special thanks to all Ted's loyal friends in the We Love Ted Darling Facebook group. Always so supportive and full of great ideas to be incorporated into the next Ted book. FREE 'Ted Darling is billirant' badge for all members.

Discover the Ted Darling

Crime Series

If you've enjoyed meeting Ted Darling you may like to discover the other books in the series. All books are available as e-books and in paperback format. The First Time Ever is also now available as an audiobook, brilliantly read by Christopher Corcoran. Watch out for audiobook versions of other books in the series, coming soon, as well as further books in the series:

The First Time Ever
Baby's Got Blue Eyes
Two Little Boys
When I'm Old and Grey
Shut Up and Drive
Only the Lonely
Wild Thing
Walk On By
Preacher Man
Cry for the Bad Man
Every Game You Play
Where the Girls Are
Down Down Down
The Cuckoo is a Pretty Bird
Dirty Old Town
The End of the Line
It's Oh So Quiet
A Woman's Heart
No Way to Say Goodbye

The First Time Ever is also available translated into French by Jean Sauvanet, under the title of 'Darling.'

Printed in Great Britain
by Amazon

28541887R00182